Honoring Juanita

Honoring Juanita

by
Hans Ostrom

Congruent Angle Press

Cover Photo: Image∗After, used with permission
Author Photo: Ross Mulhausen
Book Design: Robert A. Beezer
Production Editor: Robert A. Beezer

First edition: 2010

ISBN: 978-0-9844175-06

Author's Note, Acknowledgements, and Dedication

A woman known now as Juanita was hanged during the Gold Rush at a mining camp in the canyon of the North Yuba River. Few facts about incidents leading to her hanging have survived, so any telling of Juanita's tale, including the present one, must be a form of fiction and may be a source of disagreement. So it goes with the histories of California. As for the rest of the novel: it is fiction, too. Resemblances to actual persons or places are apparitional.

First, I must express sincere but inadequate thanks to Rob Beezer, whose cheerful but indefatigable determination and rare expertise were the driving forces behind publication of this book. I'm grateful to Bryan Smith for his generosity and expertise as well. My colleagues Beverly Conner, Denise Despres, William Haltom, and Ann Putnam have been constant colleagues, their own work sources of inspiration. To Jackie and Spencer: At least a thousand thanks for more than a thousand reasons.

I dedicate this book to my brothers, Ike and Sven, who know the place and many of its tales.

One

Water races precipitously through narrow, chuted canyons cut in that stone massif, the Sierra Nevada, what John Muir called the Range of Light. The water's gravity-mad to get to the Central Valley, to find its level there where the sea, before time began, covered land we've covered with our ocean of concrete, asphalt, steel, plastic, and wood.

I'd chained myself to a rock in the middle of a river in those mountains.

The river's sounds surrounded me, coming at me directly but also bouncing off blue canyon-walls. It was a constant cacophony, but if you had the time to listen, and I did, you could pick out innumerable particular sounds: trickle, gurgle, surge, splash; a kind of permanent river-sigh; almost-hidden sounds of individual whirlpools and of rapids falling off into pools.

I was perched on a boulder, mid-stream, thousands of feet and hundreds of miles above the great Valley. I watched that morning's water race over blue bedrock, plunge into foamy shaded pools, sprint again over boulders of diorite and granite. This was the one river I would know well in my life. With my body, I'd staked my claim to it.

As a trout would do, I faced upstream. The right side of the canyon remained as it had always been; where there weren't sheer bluffs, thick patches of live-oak and manzanita brush took over, and then came noble stands of tall conifers, all the way up to the ridge, at least a thousand feet more of elevation above the canyon. It was cold where I was, the sun just rimming the eastern ridge, the canyon in the shadow of the ridge. The canyon was lit but not yet heated.

Its left side had been clear-cut. A makeshift, zig-zag construction road had been carved into the slope to connect the blue state highway with the beige construction site.

The dam-site lay five miles northeast and up the canyon from Tamarack, a miniature town of 200 in the Sierra Nevada. In this, the globalized 21st century, it is hard to imagine how a town, a mere microsettlement like Tamarack, could be less consequential, and yet global venture-capitalists, California state authorities, and county officials had set in motion processes by which men, women, equipment, reinforced concrete, and an electricity-generating plant would block a river to use the water gravity had been pulling for millennia. Tamarack couldn't rely even on its obscurity anymore. How very odd. The wee town has GPS coordinates like every other point on the Googled globe, and it has the makings of energy in a world of energy-junkies.

Yes, a loosely organized "we" had tried to stop the dam. No, it doesn't make sense to dam up a nearly pristine alpine river of the Sierra Nevada. Yes, there's enough water in a small river—if you dam it—to run turbines. Yes, countless times people have asked me, "Can they do that? Don't they have to file an environmental impact report?" Yes, they have to file an environmental impact report, after which, if the votes, deals, and money go their way, they can indeed "do that." I wonder how many times in history and in how many languages someone has asked, and not rhetorically, "Hey, can they do that?" Yes, they can.

In this case, the doing involved dump-trucks, earth-movers, pick-ups, trailers, temporary toilets and sheds, generators, compressors, stacks of pipe and drilling equipment, hoses, rolled up fencing, steel re-bar, conical piles of gravel, a crane, an aluminum house-trailer that served as an office: a landscape I was familiar with; it was the landscape of my father's work. The moment of nostalgia was expected. It passed.

I'd parked the car a half-mile south, dropped down to the river, and picked my way along the bank until I got to the site. As I was making my way, the melody and some of the words of the folksong, "She'll Be Coming 'Round the Mountain," cycled themselves round and round my brain, simply because, as I'd passed by the bathroom that morning when my husband shaved, he'd been whistling the tune. It's not a bad tune, and the lyrics have always amused and intrigued me. Who is "she"? Which mountain? From where and to where is she coming around the mountain (when she comes)? Why is she driving six white horses—and by herself, apparently? Nonetheless, any song stuck in your head early in the morning annoys.

When I made my way down to the river, there lay Bar Rock in the middle of it, looking like the back of a beast.

In quirky corridors of the Sierra—of all mountain ranges, is my guess—some rocks have names, I mean besides "rock." I'd reasoned that if I did decide to chain myself to a rock, why not make it a locally famous one? Less fancifully, more tactically, I knew that Bar Rock had become the X that marked the spot of the dam-to-be. The construction company, Reicher, had strung thick cables across the river just upstream from the rock, ten/twelve feet above the water but sagging in the middle. Engineers and workers could wheel out there on a little cart.

Bar Rock was Bar Rock because, in the 1930s, someone had staked a claim there—during the Great Depression, when scratching for gold seemed as good a way to make a living, or at least to stay busy, as any, and better than most. A now-nameless person had drilled the rock and pounded in a long steel bar. Who knows why? Frustration maybe. The bar had a looped end. It looked like a needle Gulliver might have left behind in Lilliput.

I'd made it there by seven a.m. I'd gotten up before my husband, Mr. Bluestone, one of my names for him. Others include Lloyd, Sheriff, and just Bluestone, depending on my mood and his.

I'd showered, dressed, eaten. He showered and shaved—that's when I walked past the bathroom—and came out in his uniform—tan shirt, green trousers, badge. Mountain sheriff.

We did the kitchen dance of the long-married—eating standing up, getting vitamins, rinsing dishes. My bowels were in a nervous riot. Sitting at the table, Lloyd and I mumbled words about nothing; the nearby river mumbled, too. My green flannel shirt itched me. Bluestone itched me. Life, Juanita, my big ideas—everything itched, and nothing scratched. Bluestone got ready to leave and tried to help me out of my chair so he could hug me, but I refused: I don't know why. Or I guess I do: Angry at myself, I got mulish. Also his aftershave was too thick.

He leaned down and kissed me—a big Bluestone kiss, wet and sweet. He said, "Careful. All those rocks are slippery of a morning."

"Of a morning." Bluestone's language is stitched together like a quilt made of phrases other people discard. It's because he listens hard to everybody and gets a piece of their language in his head.

He got his gun and holster and a clipboard full of notes. In the 21st century, a rural county sheriff is a bureaucrat who dresses like a gunslinger. As he walked, the leather of his boots moaned. He went out and started the Sheriff's Department Ford Bronco and backed it out into the road. I listened to him ease it down the hill into the middle of Claytonville.

To this day, I wish we'd talked out what I was about to do. But I had a vague, confused idea about protecting him from consequences, and I was so unsure about what I was doing that I didn't want to talk about it. I just needed to put my head down and get it done. It was, it would be, a futile, embarrassing protest, so I treated it the way an adolescent treats a chore.

Out in the woodshed, I took the lock and light chain Bluestone had shown me. Looking at them—the lock locked to the chain, the key snug in the lock—I knew I was going to go through with it. A nice term, "to go through," as if a person compressed the flow of life, channeled the flow through a turbine to make power, or at least to create the illusion of power.

In the blue Toyota, powered with what was fast becoming old fash-ioned gasoline, I seemed to float the twelve miles up the gray-blue, hair-pin-curved highway into heavier timber: the terrain surrounding Tamarack, all national forest, although when a forest becomes "na-tional," I think it is close to ceasing to be a forest, but that is a recurring argument belonging to my marriage, not to this story. I shot through that little town, parked a mile this side of the construction site, got out, made my way down into the canyon, didn't slip or mis-step once.

Getting only my shoes and the hems of my blue-jeans wet, I fol-lowed the pattern of rocks out to Bar Rock, climbed up it, sat. The canyon was dim and cold.

Clammy, the canyon didn't seem worth saving. And Old Juanita seemed purely my own invention. I was lethargic and thoughtless, drained of impulse and will. The air coming off the water numbed my knuckles. A fat fatigue squatted on me like a hibernating bear ine-briated with system-shut-down. I felt weak and nonsensical. I figured I wasn't the first protester to feel this way. I knew my feelings, if in a roundabout way, added up to a loss of nerve.

I tried to open the lock. The key turned; actually it squirmed, but nothing happened. Nothing. The lock was frozen.

"Shit!" I yelled. The river consumed my expression of anger. Some-times the canyon takes what you say, amplifies it, and bounces it around. Sometimes it just swallows it, and you may as well have said nothing. The laugh I then laughed tasted like burnt popcorn. Why hadn't I sprayed the goddamned lock with WD-40 in the shop? What a moron.

I picked up the lock and chain, ready to toss them to the river, but mottled sunlight creeping over water settled me. I looked up at the sagging red-brown cables. Something made me turn my head toward the bank. A man was there.

A dark-skinned man. In khaki clothes and a powder-blue hard hat. His back was to me. He was in that unmistakable stance of male urina-tion: the hands down there, held reverently; the head looking around; steam coming up from cool soil and rocks. When men pee outdoors, they act like they just lied to their grandmothers.

My padlock didn't work, I was watching a man urinate beside the dumb, unconscious river, and the cold boulder named Bar Rock made my ass itch. This was protest?

I looked upstream and pretended not to notice him. In peripheral vision I saw him futzing around with something near where the cables were attached to a big pine tree that had escaped the clear-cut. That had been allowed to escape the clear-cut.

Then I looked over there, and he finally saw me, turning square to me and folding his arms, his look severe. I held my gaze—a you-got-a-problem-with-me-sitting-on-this-boulder?-gaze.

He climbed into the metal cart attached at the top to the cables. Here he came.

It seemed a terribly long interval for him and me, two strangers, to wait to meet, especially when the meeting was to take place in the middle of an obscure river and a muddled political era. I'm always envious of playwrights in such moments of human clumsiness; they can make art of it all. How can a wood-carver like me reveal such a forlorn predicament?

Then there he was. — Crouched in the cart a few feet from me. His scowl bunched itself up around his nose. "Black" is such an inaccurate word for his skin color, which was many colors of tan and a hint of something not unlike a greatly muted purple. His skin was shiny from all his activity. Mine must have been too, more from anxiety than activity. He wore the powder-blue hard-hat tipped back. His middle was thick but not flabby.

I couldn't tell from his look whether he was angry, embarrassed, or confused. He didn't say a word but tossed me a lightweight rope. I caught it.

He said, "Tie it to the bar."

I did so, clumsily, like a child being observed too closely by a grownup.

Using the rope, he inched himself closer to Bar Rock, stepped down, and snugged up the rope so the car would stay close and stay put. The river seemed to get louder around us. We were both embarrassed. He didn't like towering over me and tried to scrunch down.

I thought, in a flash, of some the histories that had brought us both to Bar Rock.... The mixed-up blood, accidents of survival, evils imposed, graces interjected—the Africa, the Atlantic, the Europe, the cotton, gold, and petroleum, the Spain and Mexico and California of it all—and there the mere two of us were, Of a Morning.

"What are you doing here? This is—we're building a dam," he said, yelling not out of anger but just to get his voice over the sound of the North Meredith. His voice was deep and succulent, with just a hint of rasp—a juicy cactus of speech. He glanced at the chain and lock lying in my lap.

I started to tell him my tale—I can't remember the words. My voice got small, the river swallowed it, and he bellowed:

"I can't hear you, ma'am!" He leaned closer, smelled of cinnamon.

I leaned toward him and put a hand on his shoulder for balance. This mortified him. His posture stiffened. I spoke up. I talked into his right ear, the way I used to talk to our son Gabriel when he was two years old.

I got it all said: the evil, not to mention unnecessary, dam; the protest; the padlock having frozen shut. I didn't think it was the right moment to bring in the obscure stuff about Juanita.

His face was placid.

Then he laughed, the scowl getting busier with humor, the whole face rushing to meet at his nose, the eyes closing in an expression of large joy.

Since he was treating it as comedy, I felt like saying, "And what's more—I'm the sheriff's wife!"

"I'm Mary Bluestone," I said, offering my hand.

"Rupert Williams," he said. "I run the driller. S'posed to drill this sumbitch today and blast it. And here you are." His face got serious again.

I said I knew: the schedule of blasting was in the weekly newspaper.

He scowled again. Said, "Why can't you people just stay out the way? Goddamnit!"

I liked how he dropped the "of." "Out the way." It was the kind of phrase Bluestone would pick up and add to his speech-quilt. Maybe these two would meet one day. Maybe today, within hours. Perhaps Bluestone would ask Williams questions in an official capacity.

I shrugged. What did Rupert Williams mean by "you people"? I considered my hopeless gesture—made even more hopeless by a frozen padlock—as entirely my own. How was he grouping me? "Mexicans"? Women? Environmentalists—still sometimes referred to as "hippies" in these parts? Tree-sitters who became rock sitters? Yokels?

He struggled into the cart, signaled me to undo the rope, worked his way back to the riverbank. I was about to ask him what he was going to do but thought better of it.

The whole crew would be there soon. What if Lloyd merely cited me? We hadn't talked about that. It would be a mean trick, especially when he knew how desperately I'd like to get back to carving wood. The worst trick is the trick that gets you where your temptations live. I thought of crawling off the rock then and there, slithering back to the Toyota, slipping out of my so-called principles and leaving them like snakeskin.

Rupert Williams came squeaking back on his cart. We did the rope trick again. He stepped down onto Bar Rock.

He carried a can of spray-lubricant, with a tiny red straw attached for precise delivery.

I watched as he sprayed the key-hole, worked the key, sprayed some more, worked the key. The mist of the oil substance flared out over the river, and for a second a miniature petroleum-mist rainbow materialized. He knocked the lock on Bar Rock.

The lock sprang free. He took a red handkerchief from his back pocket and wiped it.

"There you are," he said, loud and flat. "I don't know what the hell you're trying to do, but go on and do it."

He glanced furtively back at the work site, then at me. "Just don't tell anybody I had anything to do with this. Right?"

I nodded.

"Right?" he repeated.

"Right. I promise." I may have raised my right hand, my left hand on Bar Rock, its own kind of sacred text. Why had he helped me? I knew I'd need to ask him later. For the moment, I leapt to the sentimental conclusion that someone in his family had been in civil-rights protests, back in the day.

After I promised, he nodded, got back on his cart. I released the rope, and before he'd gotten back to the bank, I'd padlocked myself to the steel bar, looping and re-looping the chain around me so that they'd have to cut the lock or the chain to get me off.

I threw the key into the river. It was gone more quickly than breath. It would get wedged in bedrock somewhere, and the river would eat it, saucing it with rust, although it might end up in a placer miner's pan some day, glinting like mica, inducing the miner to wonder, "How the heck...?"

I relaxed my shoulders and tried to ignore my need to pee. I glanced back over at Rupert Williams, who walked back up the switch-backed road to the highway, kicking rocks with his steel-toed boots.

Sunlight crept up Bar Rock toward my legs. I had the sensation of falling through time, straight down through Everything That Ever Happened. Even though I was sitting down, I felt as if I'd lost my balance.

Then came the sound of vehicles. Dust rose into June sunlight radiating above the highway. Men in hardhats started walking toward the river, pointing at me, putting their hands on their hips, tilting their hats back, offering opinions to each other the way men do.

I assumed they were saying lots of ugly things. I saw Rupert Williams hang his head and fold his arms.

I didn't feel like I was falling through time anymore. Instead, my butt itched from sitting on clammy Bar Rock.

Then I watched another man come down the zig-zag road, a thin, purposeful man. A Boss Man. He stopped. Someone said something to him, gesturing toward me. He stared. He sought out Rupert Williams. He wouldn't turn squarely toward Rupert, but stood at an arrogant angle. White man/black man? Worker/foreman? Or maybe just two people who weren't cut out to be friends. Hard to tell. He looked at me again, this man, and stormed down the hill to the river and leapt in the cart.

I coughed, and I spit into the river.

Two

I'd been watching a trout work its way diagonally across the river; it managed the current with small fin-adjustments. It seemed more liquid than the water in which it lived. You might not guess it, based on my impulsive "defense" of the river, but I'm not really the outdoorsy type, let alone a nature freak. I live in the Sierra Nevada because several accidents of fate and character collided, or, put less melodramatically, coincided.

Over the years, I've become addicted to fresh, thin mountain air, I love looking at mountains, and I lost my virginity—also my autonomy—beside a mountain stream. The virginity/autonomy thing was one of the more consequential accidents of fated character. But I'm one of those people who believe the best way to show respect for the wilderness is to let it continue to be the wilderness. I don't need to hike in it, scale its peaks or cliffs, ride its snow, roar into it on three-wheeled motorized buggies, photograph it, or act like I created it to know it's a good thing. If I happen to see a doe standing, as still as a tomb, in the copse of oak trees near my garden, I stand and watch her wet, black nose quiver, I look at her large, black-brown, knowledge-able eyes, I wait for her to bound away, she bounds away, tail up, and I smile. When oaks, aspens, and alders explode into reds, oranges, and yellows in October, extravagant billows of color frozen amongst the grand expanse of evergreens, I look, and I sigh, every year, year after year. And when a red snow-plant is simply there one winter morning, beneath a tree, more creature than plant, I know it's its own species of miracle, as is the whole "range of light," the Sierra Nevada, as Muir said. But these things mainly make me want to leave what is wild be, to go into my garden, our house, or my work-shed, and to tend to my business.

Nonetheless, watching that trout, I felt privileged, and I kept watch-ing. How many generations of native rainbow trout had preceded him—or her? Millions? A virtuoso, the nine-inch trout was manag-ing hundreds of cubic feet of water per second, tons of force—enough force, indeed, to light and heat thousands of homes; hence the idea for the dam. The trout was all the more exquisite for being just an ordinary trout. It wasn't Moby Dick, a symbol for something. It was completely self-contained, not straining to be something else, unlike a certain someone who'd chained herself to a rock like a cartoon version of Prometheus.

Then the man, the foreman, was on me, yelling even before he'd gotten the cart near Bar Rock. He was a sinewy, electrically charged man engorged with rage. When he stopped the cart, it swung and wobbled, so that he almost lost his balance, his hardhat going askew—all this made him more furious. He grabbed the rusted pipe railing and leaned down to scream. His rage tore through the sound of the river. It contorted his face into a tortured mask.

"You fucking bitch! I oughtta stick some dynamite up your ass!" He fired the cannon-ball word. Cunt. My husband Sheriff Bluestone trusts no man who refers to a woman as a cunt. In this instance, I side with my husband. We disagree about other things.

Bar Rock had so numbed me that this blotchy, thin man's explosion moved me physically, not emotionally, first. It buffeted me like hard wind. By the time I became insulted, sickened, he'd gone squeaking back across the North Meredith. He hadn't touched me, but I felt knocked down. I hadn't spoken, but I felt hoarse.

It all triggered memories of bosses my father had worked for. Nervous, beef-jerky men. Smokers and drinkers. The frayed human insulation between the work and the money. And there's little that's worse for a foreman than an idle crew, which is what he had on his hands now that I'd plunked myself down on Bar Rock. Up on the highway and down by the river the men had gathered—squatting, fidgeting, chewing and smoking tobacco. Wising off. It would remind Wade Landers (his name, I would learn) of everything that was wrong with his job—not enough money, not enough control, not enough time, not enough material, not enough respect from these men and women, who would respect him only as long he drove them.

Weeks if not months earlier, he'd no doubt discovered one truth of human existence in the Sierra Nevada: building anything here will be twice as hard as building it in the flatlands or even the foothills. The ground is harder, the inclines are steeper, the distance between material and site is farther, the season is shorter, the air is thinner, and technology can do only so much. To make matters unbearably worse, I'd shown up, here in the 21st century, with my anachronistic 1960s schtick—some vaguely Mexican-looking chick with a length of chain, keeping his crew from working. The minute they were idle, they were free to hate his guts.

Sunlight finally hit part of the river and caromed a glare that hurt my eyes. I had a headache, and I needed to pee. Wade Landers had his troubles, and I had mine.

It took a full forty minutes for Landers to call the Law, my husband, and for my husband the Law to show up. By then I thought my bladder had expanded to my ribs.

In the years I've been married to Bluestone, there have been maybe five or six times when I've seen him "objectively"; it's like when you know someone really well, and then you see the person walk into a room, and you don't see the one you know as the one you know. Something unfamiliar—an odd distance—gets in the way.

That's how I saw Bluestone as he strolled the dirt construction-road, dust coming up in puffs as he put down each boot. The crew, who had been milling restlessly, got real still where they squatted or stood. Landers walked up the road to meet Lloyd. They did not shake hands. I wondered what Bluestone would do if Landers started calling me a cunt. I wondered what I'd want him to do. Perhaps simply to remind the man to mind his manners.

In this objective way I was seeing Lloyd, I caught a stiffness in his posture, saw him as he must have stood before the two people who were to become his permanent foster parents at age seven-plus: braving it out.

He turned from Landers and looked out at me. I wanted to wave but didn't. A kind of panic caught me—the river roaring in my ears. My husband got out a small notebook.

For the first time since I'd been contemplating protest—I'd been contemplating it for a year—I squarely confronted the idea that I was putting myself in trouble. I realized I would be punished.

Lloyd climbed in the cart and came toward me. He kept his face, his attention, on working the cart, but even at a distance I saw the embarrassment on his face. I'd always imagined that he would take this lightly, make a joke, draw on his considerable reservoir of wry humor. Now I knew I was hurting him.

I think I croaked "hello" when the cart arrived. Otherwise we didn't talk. He'd brought a pair of red bolt-cutters with him—Landers had handed them to him. With these he snipped the chain. It had been smart of Lloyd not to bring his own. It would have demonstrated that he'd had foreknowledge. He had me hand him the chain and lock. Evidence. He handled them carefully—so as to preserve fingerprints, I assumed. How smart of Rupert Williams to have wiped the lock.

I got up in the cart with him, and we staggered above the noisy current, over the river we liked a lot. The cart swayed and swayed, and we inched toward shore. I got just a touch seasick.

The riverbank. —Where I was formally arrested. Bluestone read me my rights without so much as an ironic grin—and cuffed me. Hands in front, at least; he knew about my bad deltoid, which acts up when I carve too much, and I carve too much. Bluestone was sweating bad. He'd left his hat in the car. His dark hair and brown skin gleamed. Until then I'd forgotten that it was summer, late June—when days heat up all at once, in a rush, mid-morning. The air takes on heat in one gulp and holds onto it 'til evening when it exhales it back through the myriad canyons, the complex bronchia of the Sierra Nevada.

I walked the gauntlet of the crew, who lined both sides of the dusty, makeshift road.

Some of the faces betrayed embarrassment. A couple were mean. The kind of superior, ugly face that looks like it wants to hurt a woman. There were two women. Their faces were no more or less sympathetic. Landers' face had a crazy leer to it, a cracked triumphant smile. Big Rupert Williams crossed his arms and spat in the dust and shot me the quickest, most imperceptible wink I'd ever seen—one not even Bluestone caught.

Mostly the construction faces—leathery tan, nicked, deeply wrinkled—made me think of my father's face. How would he have reacted? He would have been almost as furious as Landers, but he wouldn't have yelled; he would have let the rage solder his arteries shut.

Even before Bluestone and I reached his squad car, diesel motors started. I fancied Bar Rock being blown to bits while it was still warm with the heat of my backside.

"So," I said to Lloyd when we got to the car, "I did it."

"You sure as hell did," he said. He opened the rear door. He wouldn't look at me.

"I really, really have to pee," I said.

"I can imagine."

"Hey, damn it, look at me. What's the matter?" I said.

"The matter? I just arrested my wife. I just listened to a man call my wife names."

"Hey, you don't know the half of it. He's a pig. Besides, you've heard people call me names. That's not what you're mad at. What are you mad at?"

"Did Landers touch you?"

"No, he didn't." That was when I first heard Landers' name. "You knew about this. We talked about it." Then I finally got it: He had never ever—not even the night before, when he was sulking—thought I'd go through it. I was so ticked off, I forgot for the moment about the epic size of my bladder.

"Well, screw it, then," I said. "I did it, okay? I'm doing it. Get used to it." Normally, we didn't fight this way, Lloyd and me. Normally, we didn't fight. In the early days of marriage we didn't have much time to do anything but sleep, and neither of us drank, so we never got the hang of daily or nightly marital warfare, which, like the United States, requires a great deal of energy.

"It's not me who has to get used to it," he said. He guided me into the backseat, making sure I tilted my head. He had eased back into flat Bluestone speech.

"What's that supposed to mean? You could take these cuffs off."

"You're under arrest," he said.

He shut the door. He got in, and I stared at his neck through the black cage. The back seat smelled like Lysol. It wasn't noon yet, and the car was sweltering. My sweaty clothes stuck to me. When the day had started, I'd never imagined I'd be that furious at my husband—my husband who agreed with me about the river, woodcarving, how to cook vegetables, and many other important topics in life.

"Stop in Tamarack," I barked at him.

"Why?"

"Because if you don't, I'll pee on your back seat."

He brayed a mocking laugh. "You wouldn't be the first."

He slammed his door and started the car, grabbing up the radio and talking into it as he eased out on the highway.

"Do you hear me?" I said. I believe there are times in every marriage when a wife looks at a husband's neck and hates it wildly because for a blind instant it contains everything piggish and obstinate about husbands—about all men, stretching back a million years. Evolution lives in those necks. I couldn't wait to get my hands out of those cuffs and grab a chisel and start in on a piece of oak and make something stiff and square and opinionated and brutish and call it "The Husband Neck" and sell it to a divorced woman in San Francisco.

As we picked up speed on the state highway, I thought of the little padlock-key—lodged, by now, downstream in bedrock; and of Rupert Williams—getting ready to drill a hole in Bar Rock, to blast the North Fork of the Meredith River into a portfolio of French investment. Indeed, the money for the dam had come from France. Go figure. On the other hand, when hasn't the economy been global? What the heck were colonialism, the slave trade, spice-hunting, and the only reason the canyon of the North Fork of the Meredith had ever been inhabited by white folk (the Gold Rush), if not global economics?

Steep red-brown embankments—exposed originally by the 49ers, who cut the trails that became roads and highways—rolled by, dotted with Indian paintbrush and other wildflowers; golden sunlight brightened immense mountainsides of evergreens; juicy yellow and green guts of summer bugs Jackson-Pollocked the windshield. Bluestone scratched his neck, and I began to realize sharply that I'd started something others would finish.

Three

Once I overheard someone say that the Bank of England never apologizes and never explains. I wonder if that was true then and, if so, whether it's still true. I wonder if, in fact, the Bank of England is still owned by England.

Anyway, I'm not the Bank of England. I'm just a person named Mary Bluestone (baptized Mary—not Maria—Herrera). I'm a daughter, a mother, a wife, and a wood-carver, and I've listed these roughly in chronological order.

I'm also an American, so naturally I have a lot of explaining to do. I'm of mixed ancestry, ethnicity, or race: choose your term, and you may choose all three or none. Myself, I prefer the phrase "of mixed results." Results of what? The past. That should about cover it.

I jumped in and started with the bit about chaining myself to a boulder that had a name. It was a straightforward way to begin and thus made sense to me, but it got me out ahead of myself as usual.

Allow me to back-fill.

My husband Bluestone's a big guy, with broad shoulders and a serene brown face. Lloyd's father was a Washo Indian, his mother white. They were killed in a car wreck in Nevada when he was six. He doesn't particularly like to speak their names. Me, I'm a foot shorter than Lloyd. I belong to a brown face, too, but it's a little lighter. A few faint freckles, too. My mother, Eileen Herrera, is white. I've mentioned my father, a construction-worker who built highways. His name was Jack Herrera. He had big hands and a stern voice. He's dead.

A couple named Kjellstrom (shell-strum) became Lloyd's permanent foster-parents. How Lloyd was transferred from one state to another and parented by the Kjellstroms without their having adopted him is quite a tale, one that Lloyd, the Kjellstroms, Lloyd's blood-relatives, and dozens of bureaucrats and a couple lawyers prefer to leave as untold as possible, so I'll oblige them, although if only the bureaucrats were asking, I'd refuse. That the extraordinary circumstances—I almost said screw-up—worked out very well for him is a miracle. What I mean to say is that the Kjellstroms loved him and did right by him

15

and that he loved them, thinks of them as his parents.

At some point before Lloyd's seventh birthday, the Kjellstroms, in any event, took him from Sagetown, Nevada, where he was staying with a family on the Washo rancheria or "reservation" to a little town called Tamarack in a little county redundantly called Tamarack on the western slope of the Sierra. What turns redundancy into farce is that the namers got "tamarack" from the name of a tree, except that the correct moniker for the tree is the Sierra Lodgepole Pine, not Tamarack. So it goes with naming, especially in California.

Incidentally, Axel and Betty are the Kjellstrom's first names. Axel is dead.

Lloyd was 17 when I met him, and I was about to turn the same age. He worked for Axel in the summers, attending tiny Claytonville High School (12 miles from Tamarack) fall through spring. Beginning when he was 15, he also handled bloodhounds for the Sheriff's Department. He can take or leave dogs as pets, but he was born with an uncanny ability to handle tracking dogs. They intuitively take to him, and he intuitively knows which dog can do what. This was all discovered by a deputy sheriff quite by accident when Lloyd and Axel rode along on a search for a missing hiker. The deputy found Lloyd's simpatico with dogs to be "spooky"; the sheriff found it to be useful.

Lloyd spent most of his days off and many evenings hiking the creek ravines, catching fish, finding arrowheads in invisible campsites of the Maidu, Nisenan, and Washo peoples, some of whom had summered in high country for innumerable generations. Some people call the Maidu the Northern Maidu, and some people call the Nisenan the Southern Maidu. The Washo people only just spilled over into what is called California now. The North Meredith Canyon seems to have been at the edge of all three peoples' territories, which were their territories for what must have seemed to them forever and up until white men rapped on history's door—then kicked it down. Once James Marshall discovered gold, many peoples would reach the end of civilization as they had known it, and many of their territories would become the "private property" or "national forest" of other people.

In that summer when Lloyd and I were both roughly 17, a large highway-construction crew came to Tamarack from Sacramento to rebuild five miles of State Highway 48 northeast of the little alpine town. The crew stayed in the (only) two small motels, makeshift boarding houses, and—in my family's case—trailer houses.

My father, Jack Herrera, drove one of the lime-green Euclids—

short-run dump-trucks the size of dinosaurs and I'm not exaggerating. My mother Eileen did her best to keep our trailer-house clean and to make friends with local families. She dressed the same in the mountains as she did in Sacramento. I still see her in those pedal-pushers, as they were called then, and sleeveless blouses, her hair, nails, and face always done up, a perspiring glass of iced tea always ready for Papa when he came home at 5:30, dinner ready before 6:30.

I first met Lloyd at a deep pool in the river where teenagers from town gathered to smoke cigarettes, drink Dr. Pepper, and swim. Girls lay on the rocks experimenting with seductiveness. Boys wore SCUBA masks and cutoff jeans and dove deep in pools to spear sucker-fish with rusty frog gigs. Simpler times. No meth, no cell-phones.

I liked to swim with the boys. From the first minute I saw Lloyd, I teased him. I was such a smart-ass, so aggressive. Hey, I was a Sacramento girl in this little cockroach town. And I was afraid of boys and more afraid of them knowing it. Lloyd was so deep within himself he scared me even worse. And he was the only boy there who was my color! He took the teasing hard. Later he said he first thought I was one of those people born to hate Indians.

I went looking for him one evening—a hot June one. A dry breeze made big cedars and pines in Tamarack crackle. I didn't tease him that night. He started smiling a little.

For several weekends running, if Lloyd was off work, we'd ditch the other kids to hike and swim by ourselves. Lloyd gave me a ring he'd found at the bottom of the river in an eddy of silt, twigs, and periwinkles.

One night I kissed him with my tongue. He smelled like soap. There was something sweet-but-metallic about the taste of his mouth. After the kiss his eyes went vacant. I had to laugh. Later he told me about how his parents had been killed. I had to frown. He explained he was part Washo. I didn't know exactly what that meant, but at least it gave a reason for his being brown like me.

The hike up Willow Creek that changed our lives: Lloyd's idea. He wanted to show me his favorite place in the mountains, to take me up where the creek flattened out, where pale-green willows and white birches flourished in a meadow.

We didn't make it as far as that magical meadow. Heat got in the way: I wasn't used to hiking—we were nearly five thousand feet up, after all. For me, a Sacramento kid, an incline was the curb you stepped up on before you ducked into a mall. My lungs ached. My feet swelled.

From far below the ravine, we heard the faint roar of the highway crew. I was sixteen. I imagined my father sweating in his dump-truck, a cloud of beige dust following him. At night his blue shirts were streaked white with salt. He got silent and mean—didn't like working away from Sacramento, but that's where the summer contracts were.

Lloyd told me to take off my shoes at a big pool and soak my feet. I did it. We sat there for a long time, such as fifteen minutes.

He said he wished we'd brought our swimming trunks. I knew what I was going to say. I was sixteen, and I felt like I was standing on the high dive at high school, looking into faraway blue water.

"Who needs a swimming suit?" I asked, real tough and calm. Jump.

So we dared each other and giggled and dared each other for a good ten minutes. We negotiated stages of stripping. If you take away the pregnancy part, it was all cute and silly. But taking "the pregnancy part" out of our lives is like taking "the gold part" out of California history.

My white panties were so bright in the sun that looking at them hurt my eyes. Lloyd's boxer shorts were tattered like the flag of a conquered fort.

When we both were naked, I looked at Lloyd. I couldn't tell whether he was elated or terror-struck, poor boy. Both I guess. For his sake, I hoped the cold water wouldn't draw up his privates. That phenomenon was all the boys talked about in swimming class.

I saw him glance at my nipples, my purplish-brown nipples on my high, hard breasts; and at my hair, down there.

He observed that I was the color of Axel's chickens' eggs. Every egg I'd ever seen was white, so I didn't know what he meant. He seemed, however, to mean it as a compliment.

We slid into the deep, flat pool. The water was even colder than the water of the North Meredith. This was Earth-water the sun hadn't heated.

We got out and lay beside each other on baking rocks. I put my hand then my head on his chest. Down there way past his chest he got real big. I wanted to giggle at it. God, I was scared. Sixteen years old and here was a penis standing straight up staring at me like a little sci-fi monster.

Lloyd took me by the hand and led me to a shelf of grass above the water's edge. I decided I would let him do "everything except."

I'll always remember glancing up at wisps of high clouds that marched across the sky, the breeze in oaks and pines, my hair falling on his eyes and chest—that chest with the big flat Kennedy-half-dollar-size aureoles.

I told him I'd slept with a boy and "knew how." It was a half truth. Kyle Donovan had gotten my top off a couple times and fingered me—the rude, insistent little sonofabitch. Kyle, that hombre, wore Hai Karate or Jade East, one of those. Aftershave that would gag a maggot. I was still a virgin, but Cindy Barnes—who'd been screwing boys non-stop since she was just barely 15—had told me about getting on top.

Cindy Barnes had also assured me how hard it was to get pregnant.

Suddenly Lloyd was in me. I was so scared and thrilled, not to mention in quite a bit of pain. I'd never done anything so dangerous, so thrilling.

My crying out scared both of us. The whole woods would hear! My father in his dump-truck would hear! Lloyd cried out a few minutes later and came and scared me even more. His moaning seemed to echo off walls of the ravine.

What have I done? I asked myself, breathing hard on his chest, Lloyd still firm inside me. Although I had goose-flesh, my body seemed as toasty inside as a space-heater. I wanted to hold him there forever. In the next instant, I wanted to run and run and run.

We were shy afterwards and agreed how fine the warm, dry cotton of our clothes felt. —How we both could eat five hamburgers. I hugged him tight and hard and said—confessed—I'd been a virgin, too.

The big pool was covered with afternoon shadows. Whenever I think of those shadows now, I feel just the strangest mixture of regret and joy. Lloyd pointed at a trout near the surface. It leapt all the way out of the water after a small, blue butterfly, fell back, and disappeared, shadow among shadows.

I told Lloyd I was pregnant on a day when thunderheads took over the sky and didn't move, didn't let loose rain. The odds were lottery-like, I reckon, but virgins do get pregnant the first time. I'm Exhibit One.

After I told Lloyd, his lips turned dry like pine needles. We shivered in gray light and walked around and around Tamarack, that broken little town surrounded by massive mountains covered with conifers. Such sustained panic I had never felt before. My stomach cramped constantly from the worry.

I'd told my mom already. We cried together. When I think back to the early days of my getting my period and imagine her soaking my blood-spotted panties in bleach, I still want to weep. One day you're telling your daughter how to handle her period, and not long after your daughter tells you she's pregnant.

She was afraid to tell my dad because she believed he'd kill Bluestone with his hands or a gun. Mom hid the gun, a pistol. Concerning the hands, she prayed a lot.

Later Lloyd told me that he spent one sleepless night planning to pack up and walk across America. It would take him a year, he figured, to reach New York City. He would handle bloodhounds for the police department there and send money to me, and then I'd take a train and bring the baby. In his plan we'd live in New York City until the baby was ten, then move back to Tamarack, at which point he fell asleep, he said, and didn't make any more plans.

Joaquin Herrera, my dad, was told.

He did not kill Lloyd or me or anyone else.

Back then my mom, Eileen Herrera, wore bright lipstick, pedal-pushers, and sleeveless white blouses. Betty Kjellstrom, Lloyd's mom, was a round woman who wore aprons over cotton dresses and took surprisingly long, bold strides, like a courageous bird. The two women arranged a meeting at the Kjellstrom's place.

It lay just west of Tamarack, set back from the highway in a grove of pines. There was a white clapboard structure, roomy like a farmhouse, and four cottages that Betty ran for tourists and (in autumn) hunters of deer and bear.

Axel Kjellstrom and Jack Herrera. Two silent, enraged, embarrassed men. They sat opposite each other at the kitchen table, which was covered with a red-checkered table cloth that bore tiny brown holes from stray ashes of Axel's pipe—ah, that old Swede, Axel, his skin almost translucent, the color of his eyes shifting between blue and gray. And daddy—his skin leathery deep summer-brown.

Axel and Jack did not drink their coffee, which steamed in morning light and cooled into dead brown pools.

Betty and Eileen walked around the kitchen or leaned on counters. I remember them folding their arms a lot. How immobile the men were! Jack finally spilled his cold coffee. With a cloth Axel pushed it around the waxed table cloth for a few moments until Betty went over and cleaned up properly.

Lloyd and I viewed our futures—our common future—from the living room. There was a braided rug and a black-and-white television set. We sat in the fabric-covered chairs from which Axel and Betty watched The News.

Talk came in short bursts. Then long stretches of silence, throat-clearing. Sometimes Betty and Eileen cried, and the men shot fierce looks their way, as if crying were distilled embarrassment, liqueur of shame. I tried to concentrate on what I saw, not what I heard—the dentist-chair tactic. So I looked at the men's hands—thick, bony, strong. Axel's were dry and cracked from stone work. My father's were brown, of course, and then browner with diesel-stains.

Out of that morning's long agony came a plan: I would return to Sacramento with Mom right away, then finish one more term of high school, probably in "continuation school," which was for "hoods" and pregnant girls and pregnant hoods.

If after the baby came Lloyd and I wanted to get married, well, then the parents would go along with it. That was the agreement. If we did marry, we'd live in Tamarack. Why? Well, Betty and Axel had those cottages, and they could give one to us. Lloyd had jobs with Axel and the sheriff's office. Income was nothing to snort at. Betty worked at home, and my mom didn't (she was a teacher's aid), so Betty could help more with the baby. This tore my mom up, of course, being away from her grand-daughter (she imagined that it would be a grand-daughter.) But Betty said, *If they get married, Eileen, you're always welcome here.* If we got married, and when I got settled, I would help Betty clean the cottages and draw a little salary, more like an allowance. My dad didn't want them to pay me—he was mortified that I was even going to live with them. But Axel insisted. "Fair's fair," he said, a saying Lloyd picked up from him. It sounds like it means a lot.

Gabriel Bluestone was born in late spring when heavy rains hit all of California hard.

The summer after Gabriel was born was the worst of our lives, of our life together. Up to that point, anyway.

For some reason Axel got angrier—couldn't forgive. I guess he'd wanted Lloyd, his adopted Indian, to go to college. He worked Lloyd ragged, demanded perfection in the stone-work. Gabriel was not an easy sleeper. We found ourselves in a stupor of half sleep, fatigue, resentment. We never made love. We spoke in grunts or gave each other orders. I cried all the time and hated these fucking mountains and the dinky dumb town that was smaller than a mall, missed my Sacramento so much. One of my breasts got infected. I felt trapped in the small cottage between the river and the Kjellstrom's large place.

In August Betty Kjellstrom intervened. She told Axel to give Lloyd a week off. She took the baby, who was weaned. She took cash from a copper canister and told me and Lloyd to go to Reno and sleep for a week. We gambled and laughed—and slept, and made love (with dedication, condoms, and spermicide), and slept some more. We went out to dinner all scrubbed, and we practiced restaurant manners in a steakhouse overlooking the Truckee River. I remember looking down at the white cotton tablecloth and, realizing that it didn't matter if I spilled something on it, I wept.

When we came back, Axel and Betty had painted our cottage inside and bought us a new television and a bigger bed. Axel's anger was all spent. He started to tease again and cooked up a big trout dinner, which still almost made me gag as if I was pregnant. But I ate it and smiled, the dead-fish-heads frowning back, so glad was I that he seemed to be accepting me. Gabriel laughed at our faces like a miracle. Finally the changes wrought by Willow Creek seemed manageable, most days.

Before the Reicher Corporation went after the North Meredith with a dam, other investors and another company built a dam on Willow Creek, so the meadow in which Gabriel was conceived is now under water, and the trees that once lived there look like enormous dead white spiky hairs.

We—a few of us in the county—tried to stop that little dam from being built—and failed. We learned a thing or two. For instance, the "environmental community" was split, at best, on the issue. A lot of environmentalists liked the idea of hydro-electricity because it wasn't nuclear energy. Other environmentalists thought Willow Creek ravine just wasn't sexy enough to defend. Provincial is provincial is provincial, I guess. Willow Creek may have fared better if it were in downtown Los Angeles, but then it would be in downtown Los Angeles, so there goes the net-gain, but I acknowledge I'm bitter. And provincial.

I don't know if it's "the ultimate irony" or not, but here's the fact: in spite of all the engineering reports, the creek really didn't have enough umph to create hydroelectricity, so most of the time, the turbines are silent. In the summer, below the dam, the creek is a sickly, algae-filled series of puddles. Yes, the water was supposed to be efficiently re-routed back into the creek so that the creek would remain healthy. No, it didn't quite work out that way, so below the dam, the temperature, velocity, and volume of water changed, and that changed just about everything.

Native trout no longer spawn there, of course. It was a bad idea all the way around, the dam. Lloyd and I took it personally because we rather liked Willow Creek and its associations. Next thing you know, the vague but vast group of persons known as "they" were plotting to dam the North Meredith. Unthinkable? Oh, sure. "Can they do that?"

And the next next-thing Lloyd knew, I'd chained myself to Bar Rock, and he had to put me in the patrol car.

Four

My protest became a many splendored thing.

Maybe the metamorphosis began as early as when Lloyd stopped in Tamarack to let me out of the car and to take off the handcuffs so I could go in a café and use the bathroom.

The northernmost point on my story's map, by the way, is where I chained myself to Bar Rock, in case your temperament runs to the topographical or you have a GPS gizmo on your dashboard.

Just southwest of there is where Willow Creek—site of virginity lost and dam imposed—joins the North Meredith River. And let me say I fully realize that the question of where creeks join rivers may not seem entirely relevant to the bulk of 21st century humans, but it's a bit of an obsession with mountain folk here and, I suspect, around the world, and maybe it will become a ubiquitous obsession if more turf globally gets parched. Creeks may take on celebrity-status. Who knows?

Then, still moving southwesterly on this imaginary map—please draw a line between Lake Tahoe and San Francisco—comes the little town of Tamarack.

Twelve miles down that line sits Claytonville—county seat, where Lloyd and I live, I was jailed, and a woman named Juanita was lynched in 1850. And no, I don't know who came up with the concept of a county being seated, just as I haven't a clue who invented standing committees, when committees do little but sit. Contrasted to lynching, this arcane bit of terminology seems trivial, and I'm sure Juanita would have agreed.

A fingertip can easily cover this terrain on a map of California. Especially with the Sierra Nevada, however, maps are deceptive. Plopped down in the High Sierra, you quickly find yourself in unbroken country, sucking on thin oxygen, stuck in brush as tall as trees, and always, seemingly, about to fall off a ledge of rock. These are middle-aged, steep mountains. I read somewhere that scientists found old raindrops, and the chemicals in the raindrops said the Sierra were 400 million years old. Where old raindrops can be found and which chemicals have so

23

much to say—that I don't know. I think the Rockies are older, the Cascades mere youths.

Anyway, those millions of years ago, what they call the Sierra Basolith got shoved up thousands of feet and then leaned West, sheer and massive. To me, the steep, narrow canyons still look like they were opened with a straight-razor yesterday, and the ridges and peaks still seem to defy erosion. Austere gray cliffs and carved spires protrude from pale green manzanita brush and great stands of pines and cedar, fir and oak. The landscape is big, brutal, and beautiful—holy and remote. Even in the 21st century, the high places of the Sierra seem to have defied pollution, the smear of industrialism. When newcomers look up into a moonless Sierra night-sky for the first time, they suck a breath in quickly and have the urge to stoop because the load of stars they've never seen before seems impossibly large and low.

I've long felt an inexplicable kinship to the little town of Tamarack, where the sheriff, my husband, let me out, like a pet, to pee. Tamarack's where Lloyd and I met, for one thing. Also, the town has a weird spirit. Lloyd has always said crimes and complaints there aren't like any others in the county. If there's a report of a UFO sighting, it will come from Tamarack. Decades-long disputes over property boundaries. Gunshots no one can account for.

Apparitions. Parked vehicles that slip out of gear at midnight and tumble toward and sometimes into the river. There's even something called the Tamarack Jazz Society, to which Lloyd belongs, and which meets in the town hall there.

So I was doubly glad when Lloyd pulled over there and let me out to use the john at the High Grade Café, an old clapboard wreck of a place that changed hands every three years and got cuter with every new owner: you know, more antiques, folksy doilies, and ornate names for hamburgers ("The Miner Forty-Niner," with a side of "Gold Rush Fries").

Lloyd got out, uncuffed me, let me out, then proceeded to suck on a matchstick petulantly. We gave each other smoky glares, didn't speak.

I got to the back of the café and into the restroom without speaking to anybody. Sitting there on the can, I heard the sound of the river through the open window. When I was washing up, I had the urge to climb through the window and escape from my husband.

When I came out, Lloyd was talking to a guy named Barker Updike, a retired Navy pilot.

Chunky; gray buzz-cut; full of himself; but cute.

"Hey, there's the Missus," Barker said.

"'Morning," I said.

Barker started to say something, but a fighter-jet fairly exploded over our heads. Its roar vibrated my ribs and rattled the antenna on Lloyd's car.

The jets come from a base in Nevada; their pilots love to use the North Meredith Canyon as a marker as they rip into the Central Valley, bank at Sacramento (or so I imagine), and scream back to the sagebrush plateau. They fly too low and too often, but that morning I was glad the jet prevented Barker Updike from getting on a conversational roll.

"There go the tax dollars," Lloyd said, "right out the ass of that jet." The roar subsided as the fighter disappeared down-canyon.

Barker stiffened. "Well, goddamnit, you never know when some asshole's going to go crazy in the Middle East again. Or South America, Lloyd. Better to have too much defense than too little. That's how I figure it."

Bluestone shrugged his disagreement. He had his hands full with me, his impulsive wife; he didn't need to be getting into national politics with a retired pilot.

"So what you folks up to?" Barker asked.

"I'm arresting my wife," Lloyd said.

Barker guffawed. While he was laughing, I got in the car and slammed the door. Lloyd got in, too, and we were about to leave Barker Updike a little forlorn and confused, the smile melting off this square face. Then I decided that if I was going to get arrested, I needed to tell people why, because that's the way protests are supposed to go, aren't they? Lloyd hadn't handcuffed me again, so I got out of the car.

"Hi, again, Barker," I said. "I wanted to let you know that I chained myself to a boulder up there at the dam-site. I'm hoping you and others will join me in protesting the dam."

Barker didn't look shocked, just befuddled, as if I'd tapped him on the forehead gently with a fly-swatter.

"Lloyd, wasn't kidding, huh? He arrested you." Barker still wasn't sure. As if on cue, Lloyd got out of the car.

"Will you join me, Barker? In protesting the dam?" I said.

"No, Mary, I don't think so. It's not that I'm for the dam...."

"Barker, you're a fly-fisherman. You love this river. They ruined Willow Creek already."

"God, I miss fishing there." I thought he was going to cry. When a fly-fisherman—or fisherperson—falls in love with a river, that's one thing. When he, she, and they fall in love with a little creek, it's hopeless. "Do you need bail-money?" he said.

"Let's go, Mary," Lloyd said. Now he was embarrassed—a man had just offered to bail his wife out of jail. I ignored Lloyd.

"No, thanks, Barker, but that's kind of you. I don't need anything. The river needs your help. It's like what they did to Juanita, back in the Gold Rush. Lynched her. No proper trial, no real due process." Now I'd totally lost Barker. To me, connecting a Gold Rush lynching of a Mexican woman to a 21st century dam was as easy as 2+2. But as I learned in my interchange with Barker, my arithmetic was to other people advanced calculus.

Lloyd looked at me the way spouses look at spouses who don't appear to realize their effect on people anymore—a look that combines longtime loyalty with mortification.

"Honey," he said, "Barker doesn't want to hear about all that."

I looked at Barker's sad, patriotic face, and in a flash I thought about what a perfect victim he was, if victim is the word. He'd risked his life for the USA, he was a conservative, religious man who believed business and corporations almost always meant well, for that is what he'd been told, and above all, he was enormously polite, even chivalrous. In his fisherman's bones, he may have hated what they were doing to the river, but his whole sense of himself necessarily opposed what I was doing.

"Mary, you got every right to do what you're doing," he said. "You and Lloyd are good people. It's just that, well, maybe we do need the electricity...." He looked down, for he wasn't even convincing himself. He looked up. "I don't get the Juanita part," he said.

"Mary," Lloyd said, "we gotta go."

"All right," I replied. To Barker I said, "It's about fairness and justice. That's all, Barker. It's about powerful people rolling over rivers like this one and people like Juanita, way back when. But I know it makes more sense to me than anyone else. Okay?"

"Okay, Mary," Barker said. He looked at Lloyd as if to say, Can't you please get her out of here?

"Take care, Barker," I said. I remembered he was a gardener, like Lloyd and me. "You going to do the elephant garlic again?"

"Absolutely. Time to order the bulbs, almost." Barker's face displayed great relief. We were back to a normal conversation, free of lynching and ruined fly-fishing waters. "I always order too much. You want some?"

"Sure."

Lloyd said goodbye to Barker. The sheriff and I got in the sheriff's car.

Lloyd started it and looked at me by using the rear-view mirror. He said, "That was quite a speech."

"It wasn't a speech."

"You really expected Barker to agree with you?"

"Shut up and drive," I said. "If you're mad at me, just say so," I told Lloyd from my back-seat perch as we slipped down the highway out of Tamarack. "Don't make snide remarks."

"I don't have anything more to say," he said.

And he didn't say anything, and I didn't, for 12 miles. It's a spectacular 12 miles—unless you've lived there for 20 years or have just been arrested or want to murder your stiff-necked husband. The highway stays married to the curves and cliffs of the river canyon. Panoramas explode out of nowhere. Stately mountains, magnificent. Huge stands of conifers line the roadway—cedar and fir and pine. Lush live-oak and manzanita upholster the mountainsides, filling in where the conifer forest stops. Tourists are always comparing the place to the Italian Alps. I'll take their word for it. I didn't really absorb any postcard beauty that day.

We pulled up to the courthouse in Claytonville, and Lloyd got me out and cuffed me again, hands in front. By the time we got up the steps, at least three people we knew saw us, smiled, stopped smiling, froze, and watched us enter the building.

Lloyd led me into the sheriff's office and took off the cuffs. A deputy was there, and a dispatcher, and they both started making jokes.

Lloyd hooked the cuffs to his belt again and turned to his staff.

"This is for real. You might as well get used to it. Mary's under arrest, and she's going to sit in jail."

That was for my benefit, of course. The faces of the deputy and the dispatcher looked tense. Those two got very busy finding something to be very busy about. I smiled wanly at them; it felt wanly anyway. The deputy then tried to slip out. Bad move.

"Finger-print her," Lloyd said.

"Yes sir," the deputy said—and the deputies almost never call Lloyd "sir."

The deputy—Mike Cussler, a young, red-headed, muscled "kid" who wore too much sweet aftershave—rolled my right fingers through the ink and onto the paper. I'd wiped off those fingers and was getting ready to give him my other hand when I did what I never ever expected to do.

I fainted. I'm not a fainter, but for the love god, I fainted.

Of course, the June day was surprisingly hot, and I'd felt a little light-headed ever since the foreman had spewed his fire-hose of hate on me. It was mostly dehydration, I figure.

My knees, two pats of butter, melted. I put a hand on the counter; now the knees evaporated altogether; things went—well, they just went.

When I came to, Mike Cussler had a finger on my neck artery, and the dispatcher, Brenda McDonald, was patting me with a wet washcloth.

I propped myself up on my elbows and saw Bluestone sitting in a chair just behind Mike, off to my left.

"You all right?" he said, still sucking on his matchstick.

"Apparently not," I said. Brenda giggled. Bluestone turned his head slowly toward her, like a big desert lizard; she stopped the giggle.

By that time, a clot of county workers had gathered outside the windowed door of the main sheriff's office. I looked at them, Mike Cussler looked at them, Brenda McDonald looked at them. Lloyd shifted his lizard gaze from Brenda to me.

One of the county workers started to ease the door open. Bluestone wheeled around in his chair and glared. The worker pulled the door shut again. Bluestone kept staring at the workers. And staring. The clot dissolved, everyone muttering and looking back over their shoulders.

I knew Lloyd was worried about me, but Cussler and Brenda didn't know this. Fine, I thought, let them think he's my hard-assed husband, why not?

"Well, get her up here in a chair." Cussler and Brenda helped me up. My head went light again but stabilized.

"Finish printing her, take her valuables, and put her in the first cell," Lloyd said. "We'll get her some county clothes later. Brenda, call the doctor over here, and then call the D.A. Mike, get her some water and something to eat."

"Her name's Mary," Brenda announced, flushing, helping me up. That caught everybody by surprise.

Cussler and I looked over at Lloyd to see how he'd handle the tepid insubordination.

He took a deep breath and slid down a little in the chair. He crossed his legs at the ankles and tipped back his sheriff's hat, which he'd put on when we'd gotten out of the car. He rested his hands on his lap.

"Yeah, I know, Brenda," Lloyd said. "We are not going to—um, veer—from what we usually do, though. By the book. Okay?"

Cussler and Brenda nodded gravely. What a word, veer. I'm not sure anyone but my husband would have used it in the situation.

Lloyd looked at me. "Okay?"

"You're the sheriff."

Within the hour, I was sitting in jail eating a hamburger and drinking a cherry coke out of a paper cup—Mike Cussler's idea of a meal. Not a bad idea, really, and after my exciting morning, I could have eaten rotten goat meet. The County had taken away my shoes, my belt, my keys and coins and all the rest. The county doctor, name of Loban, had come and taken away my temperature and heartbeat, a reading of them anyway. Loban was a sallow man with a hang-dog look. He was probably fifty. A good head of hair, except for the dandruff. He was always remarkably clean-shaven, as if he took an electric razor to his face before seeing each patient or going on a call; yes, he made house-calls, and not just to the jail. I took Loban's word that my fainting had been Nothing Serious. Loban didn't seem especially curious about why I was in jail. He was the medical man, and Lloyd was the lawman.

They'd left me my jeans (but not my belt), a T-shirt, and my underwear and socks. "County clothes"—an orange jumpsuit and cheap slippers—were on the way.

My cell—one of three—was the only one with a window. Two-by-two, barred, with a storm window in winter but not now. On my tippy-tip toes, hanging on the bars after I'd eaten half a hamburger, I could look out and see a piece of Claytonville, see the bridge over the river, the bridge between the courthouse and the middle of Claytonville. Bright June sunlight glinted off silver steel. It was probably the fifth version of the bridge from which the mob had hung Juanita in 1850. For the first time all day, I felt I'd made contact with Juanita's story, felt I'd tuned it in like a lost radio show.

It's a story I'd thought about for two decades, but it had always remained "history"—fascinating but dead, like a dried rare beetle in a bottle. As I looked at the bridge, the story took on warmth.

I sat on the hard bunk. Fatigue overtook me. I lay down and slept. Woke at what I guessed to be eight p.m. The light coming in the window was dusky, smoky orange.

A detail of the Juanita story fixed itself in my mind: She was supposed to have been pregnant. Or at least a doctor on the scene had tried to convince "the jury" she was with child. She was pregnant (let us assume), and she knifed a man who had broken down the door of her shack, and they hung her from the bridge. I was chilly, the way I sometimes am after a summer nap. I got up and tried the door to my cell to see if it really was locked: I wondered what percentage of inmates did that, and if they did it every day. The county building was quiet. Then I heard someone rustling around in the outer office. Wanted to call out but only if it was Lloyd out there, not a deputy, a dispatcher, or a janitor.

I lay down again on my bunk and covered myself with one thin blanket. Stared at the oddly shaped steel toilet with its miniature sink on top. I wondered where it had been manufactured. I saw no imprint of a corporation. My mind ran to practical things, base things: I thought of how horrifically smelly the canyon would have been during the Gold Rush, thousands of miners crowded into this narrow corridor, no plumbing, not even a hint of planning as to who should live where and why.

The next day I'd be arraigned, a word I'd never really knew the meaning of. Some day I'd look it up in a dictionary, track the etymology, report what I'd found to Lloyd, who would be interested.

Smoky orange light withdrew. Nightfall. I was a middle-aged mother and wood-carver, I was mad about a dam and obsessed with an obscure dead Mexican woman, and I was spending my first night ever in jail. Life was good.

Five

In 1850 Claytonville would have been a camp, not a town. Huts and shacks built fast. Canvas tents. Squirming chaos. A few bona fide buildings—saloon, blacksmith's, supply store. Something that would work as a whorehouse, even if it was one shack or tent. A wooden bridge across the river, probably made of peeled pine logs, spiked and lashed.

Men everywhere, few women. Squat, filthy men, bearded, stringy-haired, and stupendously unbathed, living in their clothes. The smell of Claytonville must have been overpowering. Human waste, horse manure, warm mud, sweat, rot, vomit, smoke. Water was used to sluice gravel and to drink, not to bathe in. Two or three thousand men, all scratching at the surface of the earth. Two or three thousand in a canyon-pocket that now seems just right for 600. The shelf of land on which Claytonville now sits would have been mainly one large plot of muddy slop, with sluice-boxes, ditches, potholes, shacks, campfires, and tents, all of it unplanned, ad hoc, rushed indeed, and permanently temporary. In mid-summer, much of the slop would have dried and gone to dust.

The work would not have been frenzied; the Rush was what happened before men arrived in California and took a look at steep, rocky, razored canyons of the Sierra—saw the cruel sense of humor God (or God's ambassador, geology) had when it came to the placement of gold.

And if they reached a gold camp, a sluggishness would have taken over. Digging for gold is slow, hard, menial, manual work. Shoveling, picking; hammering boards together for flumes and sluice-boxes; slogging through water, hours on end; shoving donkeys, horses, or mules around, rolling boulders, lifting, grunting; busting up knuckles and hands and arms and shins. Lifting shovels full of gravel, convinced each one holds gold. Scratching dirt out of blue bedrock-crevices. Getting lucky, maybe, and finding exposed veins of quartz, breaking up what you hoped was ore, a word that once upon a time had something to do with the word sacred. There's a joke in there somewhere, especially from God's point of view.

Sometimes I sit myself down in my mind on a bluff overlooking Claytonville and peer down on the defoliated site, 1850, horses, donkeys, simian miners, and a few wagons crawling back and forth. A muddy, makeshift, broiling place over which loomed huge mountains.

A place that for ages, forever, had seen only light Indian "traffic," a funny word to apply to people now identified as Maidu, Nisenan, and Washo, who were as easy on the land as bird-shadows, and for whom this canyon was a frontier; none of them, as far as I know, took up residence here, although there's clear evidence of hunting and gathering, of passing through on purpose. The Maidu lived north of here, the Nisenan or Southern Maidu, south and west, the Washo east, mainly in what is now Nevada, but spilling over into what we call California. I think it is amusing that even for the indigenous people, this canyon might have been considered a provincial place, at the edges of their several territories.

Colonel Robert Clayton and Mr. George Meredith led a small band of men into the canyon in the early 1840s. James Beckwourth would discover a mountain-pass northeast of the region years later, but Clayton, Meredith, and their men wandered up from the Central Valley. They weren't sure what they were looking for. Fur trade, maybe.

They bivouacked in open ground near the river, encountered Indians who knew what they were looking for: deer, squirrels, berries, acorns, and more acorns. The Indians did their level best to ignore the strangers, the way a person should avoid an animal that's frothing at the mouth and won't run away: Let the woods take care of such an aberration. Clayton and Meredith named the place Clayton's Flat, named the river the Meredith, which later became the North Meredith: Maybe that's all they sought, something to name after themselves.

A few years later, James Marshall found his golden pebbles near Sacramento. Ka-boom; cha-ching. From the Indians' point of view, of course, the discovery of gold brought a catastrophe of unimaginable proportions. It was the beginning of their apocalypse.

When Marshall discovered gold, Clayton's Flat was already known to exist, existed on a map, existed in gold country, existed in men's minds as an image of gold. It was descended upon, overwhelmed.

Where did Juanita come from, and why did she come to this place?

I've gathered just a few scraps from the Tamarack County Historical Society—newspaper articles about her lynching, mainly. Also, years ago I took a California history class offered by a community-college extension program in Claytonville; the textbook mentioned Juanita. It said her lynching was an example of California's penchant for vigilantism, so Juanita to history was only her lynching, not herself, and her lynching was an example, not really even her lynching anymore. I tried to ask the professor about Juanita herself, but I didn't know how to ask. The prof and the class made me feel as if I was a Mexican woman asking about a Mexican woman, wasting time, wanting History to be too personal. They were right, of course. One lesson of the class seemed to be that history consisted of Ideas, Patterns, Topics, and Themes in capital letters, but not people, at least not Juanita People.

"It is said" she came to Claytonville with a companion, José. Was he her husband? Hard to say; hard to say even whether the names "Juanita" and "José" are accurate. Some accounts call her Josepha—and "Juanita & José" has more the flavor of balladry than of fact.

This José was not a miner but a gambler, the articles say. Does this make Juanita a prostitute? Could be. No hint of it in the articles, but what else was she doing up there? But as far as I know, and I don't know much, camps operated on a brothel system—women, congregated—not a pimp system, not one woman working for one man. She was young, in her twenties, born either in Mexico proper or in California Territory—maybe in a valley near Monterey. If the latter was the case, she was of the Californio people, at least from our perspective. Only the people who lived back then knew what names really mattered to them, meant something.

I like Juanita because she would have looked askance at this new exploding California culture, this men-as-stampeding-farm-animals-phenomenon. She was a mix of Spanish and Indian but would have been mystified by both the shy, stunned Sierra Nevada Indians and the crazy men, most of them white, flailing at the river, ripping up the earth for gold, almost never finding enough to satisfy them, gambling and drinking away what they did find. She probably would have felt out of place no matter where she was and—my supposition—may have sensed the more deliberate, agrarian "Spanish" California getting shoved aside by these determined, insistent, aggressive, frantic Anglos—a word she wouldn't have used, I assume; she would have had her own words to express how different the Gold Rushers seemed from her.

She would've found herself in Claytonville, higher in mountains than she'd ever been before, several thousand feet, with tall peaks surrounding her; found herself making do in a shabby shack on one of the "streets"—a path of dried mud. Dust.

Dust filled the air July 4, 1850. Most miners were drinking, not working. The high hills were scrubby and parched, the sky a baked-pottery blue, the tents along the river grimy gray—color of old soiled undergarments.

Juanita and José made love that morning, according to me. She smelled José's rank odor, felt his three-day stubble on her cheek and bosom. Already the shack seemed too hot. She and José didn't exactly understand the July Fourth rigmarole. Didn't all of that happen a long time ago, thousands of miles away, and what did it have to do with California and gold? But everyone in camp had been talking about the celebration, the candidate for U.S. Senate coming all the way up and across three canyons to speak, the platform with soiled bunting, the fresh shipments of whiskey and ale, salt pork and dry white-beans, shiny new tools. California was going to have a U.S. Senator, two of them in fact, Juanita had learned, but she didn't know what she'd learned.

A band of men had gone out on the third and shot deer. The men had been roasting the deer slowly over open fires down on a claim near the river, and sometimes the smoke drifted Juanita's way. Sweet venison smoke, gamy, pungent.

Around noon, Juanita and José wandered the couple hundred yards to the center of Claytonville. Juanita would have looked, again, at the stupendous mountains enclosing the camp, and maybe, once more, she would have felt herself enclosed. Men were already drunk. The candidate for Senate—Juanita thought she heard him named as "Weller"—was on the platform. He seemed strange to her up there, huffing, puffing, yelling out his speech, getting red and sweating, wiping his brow with a blue silk kerchief, not ever really looking at anyone. His words reminded her of large summer clouds. He was speaking to the clouds. He said that God had provided the gold in these canyons. He kept using the word "providence." It was an American duty, he said, to settle the newest state in the Union, to make it the greatest state. Juanita wasn't exactly sure what a state was and how it got to be a state, let alone a great state. José had told her that California would join the United States in a couple of months. She assumed that once a territory was filled with a certain number of white men from elsewhere, it became this "state" Weller talked about.

She marveled at Weller's capacity to talk on and on, but she didn't know why he was talking to these miners, some of whom were passing out or shouting back at him or cursing at each other. She and José stayed at the edge of the crowd. That day more than ever, she was aware of being brown. The mass of miners was too packed in, too loud and smelly. Almost none in the crowd were from Mexico. Some of the miners were Mexican, and a few were Indians, but that day they hung back.

She wanted to go back to the shack, but José insisted on walking around. She held his arm. She wanted the men to know she was with him. She felt uneasy in the canyon and wished José wanted to go back to the Central Valley, or to Monterey, or even back to Mexico.

Then as now, the canyon might have seemed airless at midday, but toward evening, breezes would have begun again to move, relieve the canyon of some smoke and stench.

They returned to the shack. Out back José washed his face with water brought up from the river. He put on a cleaner shirt and his dusty coat, ate some cornbread Juanita cooked over open flame outside: They were planning to buy a cast-iron stove and a piece of chimney pipe in the Fall (if they stayed that long), have it hauled in pieces by wagon from Sacramento.

At seven o'clock José went down to the saloon. If all went well, he'd bring home a lot of gold—fine gold, almost dust, not nuggets— and coins from the poker games. They needed supplies, the sooner the better, what with the new shipment in. Juanita hoped he wouldn't get too drunk, would stop playing cards at the right time, would not get shot. Or knifed.

And what would she have done that evening, as darkness came down on the canyon between eight and nine o'clock? Here is where it seemed hardest to look through my veil of books, magazines, newspapers, radio, television, and telephone and peer into her mind. All I could imagine (sitting in jail) was a kind of lethargy on her part, a fatigue I associated not so much with my hardest-working days as with being a teenager, when my mind was overheated, torpid. I saw her in her long cotton dress, standing in back of the shack, listening to the river. And now it excited me to wonder how close her shack was to where Lloyd and I now lived, a matter of yards, perhaps; it excited me to think that the same pattern of morning and evening breezes which blew through her hair have blown through mine.

And then I had her lying down on the rickety bed, dozing, dreaming, her dreams filled with high-plateau Mexican landscapes, bright dresses, a gila-monster, and the face of an old, old woman in her village.

Juanita drifted from dozing down into a night's sleep.

The miners—footlessly drunk, some of them still not used to how quickly alcohol goes to work at elevation—began whooping and hollering. Fistfights broke out, dissolving quickly into wrestling and wallowing in dust and mud. Miners fired pistols in the air. This noise woke Juanita, who got up and found a shawl.

For five months, a big man named Cannon had lived in Claytonville. He was loud and friendly, garrulous and popular, a man's man. He left the saloon with three or four men to prowl the streets. José saw him leave, folded his poker hand (only a pair of deuces, let's guess), retired from the game, and without appearing to do so, followed the clot of drunken men. José sometimes had good instincts, I had to assume.

Cannon and his friends wandered the streets, a generous term for wide pathways; the men shouted, thumped on shacks, howled songs. José stayed a safe distance away—until they ended up at his shack, as he knew, with dreadful certainty, they would—until they started saying things like "Isn't this where the Mez-can girl lives?" as he knew they would. José made his living knowing how white miners think, when they would risk more than the cards dictated, when they would fold and bluff, when booze overtook judgment like a coyote running down a rabbit.

When Juanita heard the yelling, panic struck. Once in her village, a drunken old man had tried to rape her, throwing her to the ground, groping her. An uncle had pulled him off and beaten him, and she'd never stopped being terrified of the event—what the man did, what her uncle did to the man. The walls of the shack seemed thin, like tanned deer-hide.

Outside, José approached Cannon and his friends. He took his hat off and smiled deferentially.

"Good evening, my friends." José had to have assumed at this point that they would rob him. He was prepared to hand over the money, gladly, before they beat him.

"José!" Cannon said, too drunkenly, too falsely familiar—like a card player who doesn't want to admit he's lost too much. "Just paying our respects to your lady-friend."

"Thank you," José said. He played it like a card game. He could not overpower them, would not bluff them. He could only wait them out. He was hoping they wouldn't remember how much money or gold he'd won from each of them.

"Happy Fourth of July!" one of the men shouted at the shack. He was a stout man whose nose had been broken several times. "See, Mez-can, just paying our respects." Cannon and the others hooted. "Yes, I'd sure as hell like to respect her," one of them muttered, spitting the words out.

The accounts describe an "altercation" or an "argument" that night. In my cell, I imagined Juanita's feelings going fast from panic to anger. Maybe José's presence perturbed her; maybe she wanted him to do more. He was of necessity, she knew, a passive man. To be an aggressive

Mexican in a gold camp white men controlled meant inviting death, especially if you were a gambler, not a miner. But couldn't he do more for her? Couldn't he stand up for her the way her uncles and brothers used to do?

Or maybe José's being there emboldened her to do what she did: fling open the door of the shack and curse the men in Spanish.

The words flew out of her. The black shawl fell to the ground. The men laughed at first, the way they would laugh at a child. José's face went taut with fear. His eyes shifted from Juanita to the men and back to Juanita.

The men started yelling back. One of them shouted Whore! Cannon just smiled at her. And walked toward the shack. "José," he said, "y'all have a feisty one here."

"Get away from my house!" Juanita shouted. It was in English, which she spoke well. "Pig!" she shouted.

The word did not echo; it went into the night air like all mining-camp words. But it seemed to hang, for a heartbeat, in the air. No one moved. Cannon's face darkened. José stepped forward, his hat in his hands. He began to speak. But Cannon yelled.

"Shut up!" In a sense Cannon had sobered up, and so had the other men. In another sense, they hadn't. The sobriety was only an inch deep. José knew if Cannon gave the word, the men would descend on him and Juanita. They'd both be beaten, and Juanita would likely be raped.

Probably they both would die; it was a toss-up, he figured. It wasn't a hand he'd bet on. José prayed, something he didn't do when playing cards; in José's view of the world, a praying card-player was a bird with a broken wing. He felt like a bird now.

"And you need to shut that whore's mouth, too," Cannon said.

Juanita gasped. José slid sideways in front of Cannon, got between Cannon and Juanita. This was about the only card he felt he could play. He stepped on the black shawl.

"*Silencia*," he said to Juanita in what amounted to a stage whisper. Then to Cannon, he said,

"Please, let us not have trouble on this"—he groped for a word—"celebration day. July the Fourth. Accept our apologies, Señor Cannon."

Cannon's smile was thin and mean. He looked squarely at José, then at Juanita, then back to José. José knew the look. "Do not," the look said, "forget who's boss. Ever."

Juanita's fist seized the cloth of José's coat. José prayed she would remain silent.

"Stay the hell out of my way," Cannon said, "both of you. You goddamned little card-sharp." He spit heavily into the dirt. Some spattered José's boots. He led the men away.

José turned and gently pushed Juanita back into the shack, shutting the door. His heart in his ribcage was making a racket. They cursed each other and held each other in the light of the single wood-alcohol lamp. Now it was all in Spanish, of course. They sat down. Juanita wept, cursed more. She accused José of letting the men treat her like a tramp. José tried to explain there was no choice. She moved to the bed.

José sat slumped in a chair, ashamed and afraid but delighted to be alive. His hands shook in his lap. Sweat poured off his forehead.

Juanita lay on the bed, exhausted. She hated the way Cannon and the men had made her feel. She loathed the intrusion. She felt as if there was no dignity, no privacy, for a woman in this canyon; nowhere to go to be alone and safe. It was a mistake to have come up here to these high, cursed hills, this narrow canyon. From the bed she said, in her own language, "Please, José, please. Take me out of here. Take me to Sacramento, Monterey, away."

José didn't look at her. He said, "The Valley is so far away now." He reached for the lamp, turning down the wick. From the bed, Juanita saw that his hands still trembled. He mumbled, "There's gold to be gotten here. They dig it up and bring it to the table, get drunk, play cards." His voice trailed off. The light went out. She stared at his shape and listened to the river. She tried to muster the energy to pray, but she couldn't pray. She sank into fitful sleep.

I sat on my lumpy jail cot, all the decades later, having been arrested for locking myself to a boulder.

If only Juanita could walk out of those dull concrete blocks, I thought. She'd surely be smaller and stouter than I had imagined, of course, not as romantic as I imagined her. Her hair would be long but pinned up; it would not be clean, but it would be as clean as she could keep it. If only she would walk into the cell and tell me if I had done her justice, had felt something of what she felt, had got it even a little bit right. I was exhausted and exhilarated at the same time. Had I touched her somehow, brushed her cheek like a breeze? I doubted so.

Mercurial is the word for history. I've seen mercury outside of a thermometer only once—although word has it that I ingest mercury every time I eat a tuna salad these days. Lloyd's adoptive father, Axel, kept some; he used it to amalgamate with gold dust, which is misnamed and is really more like gold sand; the amalgamation produced a kind of cooked-up nugget of gold. He often whistled or hummed the tune of "She'll Be Coming 'Round the Mountain" when he puttered around at such tasks and hobbies.

He put a teardrop of mercury in the cauldron. I looked down at it.

He hummed the tune, stopped humming, and said, "Don' touch it. Use a stick." I attempted to prod the mercury, to control the magical but heavy, sluggish but slippery silvery droplet. Even when it didn't move, it seemed to move; it was a cool but liquid trembling metal. It was always out of reach, until Axel heated the cauldron to hell's temperature. First the heat fused mercury to gold dust, then gold dust congealed into a wad, and then the heat burned the mercury into vapor. Axel had told me to put a hand over my mouth and nose; of course he didn't have anything as elaborate as a mask.

"You don't want to inhale mercury vapors," he advised, inhaling mercury vapors. He chuckled. "How about that, Mary? Gold. That's alchemy, that is."

It didn't really look like gold. It looked like a fried lump of foodstuff. But it was gold, all right, cooked up in Axel's cauldron. Axel sang, "She'll be driving six white horses when she comes." "When she comes!" I sang, sort of. My refrain surprised and amused Axel–back then, in the history between me and my late father-and-law. Mercurial history. I'd certainly inhaled some of the vapors from her story, Juanita's. She was coming around my mountain, and she was driving six white horses.

Six

My jailer, my husband, flicked on a light in the dingy, concrete-block corridor.

He'd dragged along a brown, metal folding-chair. An orange jumpsuit was draped over one of his arms.

I sat up, and he sat down.

"Feeling better?"

"Physically, yes," I said. "What about you? Still pissed off?"

He shrugged.

He wasn't wearing his sheriff's hat. The yellow bulb highlighted his thick black hair, combed straight back.

"You were embarrassed," I said. Our eyes locked.

"A true fact," said he.

Bluestone can handle himself. I guess it's natural to think of any small-county sheriff as Andy Griffith in-character, aw-shucksing around all day and then eating homemade ice-cream on the front porch while June bugs bang into screens and corn-pone wisdom is shared. But Lloyd's seen most of what law enforcement has to "offer":

Men who shoot their wives, men who force their children to have sex with them. A man who slit his own throat—effectively. Another who hacked his dog to death with a chainsaw. A woman hiker who fell a hundred feet onto a pile of rocks. An angel-dusted teenager from LA who shot his three friends in a campsite and—literally—did not the next day remember doing so. A liquored-up teenager from Reno who went into a pine tree on a motorcycle doing 90. A famous San Francisco lawyer who, in search of Extremity, went hiking in Winter by himself. He froze to death. Lloyd hauled his stiff carcass out of the woods and made the call to the famous lawyer's widow.

He went into law enforcement without really thinking about it. Much later he ran for sheriff because the man who was sheriff, Keith Harding, abruptly resigned, Lloyd became interim sheriff, and no one else seem interested in the job. When the election came round, he just filed the papers to get his name on the ballot. The next time around, he was opposed, but he won handily without campaigning.

People in the county trust him because he does the job and long ago he found the right mask, the face with which to meet the other faces, the laconic Bluestone's unaffected affect.

When I chained myself to the rock, I shone a lamp on one of the shyer animals in the human forest. Lloyd: cornered by notoriety. Just to say No to a dam and Yes to a dead woman, I'd gone and blown his cover.

"So what have you been doing to keep yourself busy?" I said.

"Well, I went home for a bit—"

"—Any mail for me?"

"Not to speak of. I sent somebody for your car. I tried to water most of your garden."

Suddenly it was "my" garden. "Then I answered a lot of questions," he muttered, with a wry smile.

"I can imagine. The whole building wants to know what's going on."

"The whole building and the whole world, my dear."

"Right."

"No kidding. I've talked with the *Sacramento Bee*, the *San Francisco Chronicle*, the *Los Angeles Times*, the Associated Press, a Reno radio station, and some kind of assistant to a tee-vee producer."

"No."

"Yes."

"Producer of what?"

"Productions, I guess. She was rude. I hung up. I think she forgot I was part of the story. She'll call back, I imagine."

I won't lie: I kind of liked hearing about all the ludicrous attention.

"How the hell did this happen so fast?" I asked—not asking Lloyd, really—just voicing the question.

"I'm sure someone in the building called the *Bee*, say, and someone else called the station in Reno, who called an affiliate in such and such, and pretty soon it's in everyone's computer."

"You have a point there. I just assumed—I still assume—it will be futile."

"Well, it will be futile, but it's still news."

"I didn't even think it would be news. So what did you tell them?" I asked.

"I told them what you were suspected of doing, and I told them I suspected you were taking a nap. They suspected me of being stupid or stubborn."

"Or both!"

"And they asked if I knew you were going to do it."

"And you said—?"

"I said no."

"And you weren't lying, really. You really didn't think I'd go through with it."

"Not today I didn't. I thought you'd do a dry run. Drive up, drive back. So anyway, there will be press at your arraignment tomorrow morning."

"And I'm being arraigned for what?"

"We'll learn at the arraignment, but at a minimum, trespassing, which doesn't sound serious but can carry a fine in the thousands."

"Oh."

"And I guess Reicher could sue you for interrupting the work-schedule—whatever the whole crew's pay is for a couple hours."

"I've put us in financial jeopardy. I'm sorry." He shrugged. "But the trespassing—won't all the fuss blow over by tomorrow—I mean, the press and everything? There's a whole globe full of news out there."

"I don't think it will blow over," he said. He stood up in the yellow light of the corridor. "It's the kind of story they like, you know. Husband arrests wife. Wife tries to stop dam. Woman lynched during Gold Rush."

"Husband gets events out of order."

"Here, put these on. I'll get you some slippers later."

He unlocked the cell, walked in, and handed me the orange "county clothes." He sat down on the metal chair again, having left the cell door open.

I began to strip.

"You call this 'by the book'?" I said.

"No, as a matter of fact. By the book, I would have had you change when I brought you in. A woman deputy would have taken you down to the shower room and had you shower and had a look at your body cavities."

"I see." I was down to my panties and bra. "Can I shower now? It's stuffy in here."

He shook his head. "No, it wouldn't do to have someone see me escorting you down to the showers this time of night."

"Not to mention examining my body cavities." I took off my bra. Lloyd was being ever-so-slightly-officious, and that made me ever-so-slightly-mischievous. He glanced at my breasts.

He scratched his head. I slipped my panties off.

"What exactly are you doing?" he asked.

"How about it, Sheriff?"

He glanced reflexively toward the outer office, and glanced back. He looked hard at me. He became stern, oh very stern indeed.

"Do you realize that if the night dispatcher—"

"—I guess I've gotten us into enough trouble today already. But I think you're chicken." I started to shake out the county jumpsuit, prelude to putting it on.

Lloyd got up and came in the cell. He sat down next to me and kissed my mouth, my breasts.

"I don't smell that great," I said. "It's been a long day."

He offered no opinion about that. He kept kissing. I glanced at his badge and got the giggles. He told me to shut up. He took off all his clothes, very deliberately. Socks and all, the dear sweet deliberate man. He stacked them near the bunk like a good soldier. We made love, and I suppose I should give some details, but I'm just Mary Herrera Bluestone, and all I'll say is we made love, expecting the dispatcher or the night janitor to walk in. We lavished a little panic and danger on our middle-aged bodies and our seasoned marriage. I do remember tilting my head back once and catching a glimpse of the stars through the bars of the window, through which scant fresh air puffed.

Afterwards, the Sheriff of Tamarack County got dressed rapidly, bless his thumping, badged-over heart, and I put on my orange jump-suit, no rush. I guess he figured we'd tempted the fates enough because he got out of the cell and closed the door and sat back down on his brown chair, heaving a big sigh.

"Close one, huh?" I said.

"Sometimes I wonder whether either of us has even one marble left," he said. "What happened to our common sense?"

"Well, if you think about it, there's nothing insane about what we just did. From a certain perspective, it's as sane as sane gets. Did you call Gabriel?" I asked.

Gabriel is our son—I guess I've mentioned that. He goes to Nevada-Reno University. Plays semi-pro baseball and works construction over there in the summer. My beautiful Gabrielito, into his twenties that summer.

"Yeah, I called him, just before his game."

"And?"

"And he asked whether I called in plenty of backup when I arrested you."

"He's quite the little smart-ass." I lay down on the bunk. "What happens tomorrow?"

"Tomorrow," Bluestone said, as if he were lifting a great weight. "Tomorrow morning I'll see that you get some breakfast and a shower. You're to meet your lawyer at—"

"—My lawyer?"

"Our lawyer. Tom Crimpton."

Crimpton was a former state bureaucrat who retired early, went to law school nights, passed the bar, and moved up into the hills. He was a jumpy chain-smoker who wore polyester dress shirts no one had seen since the Carter Administration. If life were school-recess, Tom Crimpton would be the kid on the playground the other kids tease, and more often than not, life tends to be school-recess.

"And then?"

"And then you go to court. You plead guilty or innocent. The judge sets the bail and a pre-trial hearing date."

"Will you be there?"

"Of course."

"And I'll be charged with...?"

"I met with the D.A., and he says trespassing will be the charge. Misdemeanor. Low—or no—bail."

"How'd that go?"

"The meeting? It went. He smiled that little smile of his, as if he thought I was squirming."

"Were you?"

"Nope."

A guy named Thom Matthews used to be D.A., a scotch-drinking, rawhide-grained man. He was kind to me and Lloyd. But he'd died of liver cancer two years earlier and was replaced by a shiny-faced, Chardonnay-sipping blond fellow named Miles Ward, out of the D.A.'s office, San Francisco. He seemed pleasant and polite at first but turned out to be ambitious, sneaky, and condescending. Big surprise.

Bluestone's face went slack.

"What is it? What's the matter?"

"You need to know Reicher sent their lawyer in today." —Reicher being the name of the construction company building the dam.

"And?"

"And he looked like a real lawyer, not like Miles or Crimpton. The kind of lawyer that doesn't fuck around. He brought a secretary with him."

"Goodness, that is serious. From?"

"Reno. Mary, he wants your ass bad."

I sat up. "Well, he sure must want something if he's hauling a personal secretary around the High Sierra. But what do you mean?"

"I get the feeling this guy wants more than trespassing."

"What more is there? That's all I did."

"I don't know. Conspiracy to conspire. They can make up anything. I think—I know—Reicher's running behind schedule and, if you believe the rumors, out of capital. I think the French investors are nervous. I know our Board of Supervisors're nervous. Everyone's tired of messing around with environmentalists and public hearings."

"And sheriffs' wives."

"Well, one sheriff's wife." I winced at that one. He continued. "We're all of us screwing around with their profits. They may not have budgeted properly—cost overruns—and they may need a scapegoat."

"Oh."

What Bluestone had been implying finally percolated through my thick skull: Reicher's lawyer would go after him, too, claiming the sheriff knew what his wife was up to.

I got up and went over and kissed him through the bars. We told each other to get some sleep, he dragged his chair out, and I sat on my bunk. Then lay on it. From my little incarcerated corner of the world, there was a lot to think about and a little to be afraid of, but fatigue and sex had pushed me into a clearing where I allowed myself to rest. It felt as if I moved into sleep sideways and quickly, like the motion of a hummingbird. And I imagined I smelled cedar oil in the night air, believed I heard the rush of owls' wings, a sound that's been with me ever since an owl flew low over Lloyd and me once at dusk—a thrilling whisper, and then it alighted on a cedar branch and fixed us with those eyes, which look at you from the abyss of time.

Did Juanita wake that night, the night José miraculously coaxed the men away from their shack? Or sleep straight through, waking to the pounding—pounding on the door? The big man Cannon yelling, meaner than a brushfire.... The morning air already scratchy, thick, close....

Cannon kicks down the door. Not difficult, since it's a cobbled-together thing, leather hinges. Without the door, the shack's nothing. Morning air and odor of muddy Claytonville pour in. José's gone, down by the river smoking, maybe—or, instinctively, walking away—away from last night's trouble. If José had been there, he would have taken the knife away from her. This is what I believe.

The knife.

Under the blanket? On a table? How big? Was it José's or hers? Bone handle or wooden? Made in Mexico or California? Perhaps blotches of rust. The blade-line wavy from sharpening and use.

Cannon's in the doorway—telling her what he wants to do to her. Calling her names.

Or: maybe not cursing but toying with her, staring, filling up her fear with his big body—belching, breathing. His cronies out on the street, grinning with their bad brown teeth.

Juanita's in a cotton nightgown. She needs a bath. Her hair's pinned up. She feels exposed, small, soiled. Where's José?

When the door came down, all came in: dust, evil, men, fear. The violence of the muddy, dangerous canyon.

The fragile, already meager civility of a mining camp disintegrates. Juanita wouldn't use the words "disintegrate" and "civility." My Spanish is so rusty, that I couldn't think of the words myself as I thought of her. She would though feel the terror of the wildness in these men. In Cannon.

Juanita sits up, clutches a blanket. She's stunned—then frightened, then enraged. Cornered rage. She feels smothered, as when the man tried to rape her in the village.

Now Cannon's in the middle of the shack, knocking things around, coming for her. He woke viciously hung-over—and drank more. Sour-mash whiskey, warm as bath-water. Ate a chunk of cold venison, if he ate anything.

Juanita either produces the knife from under the covers or goes and grabs it. Cannon laughs. His course red hair glistens with sweat. He's big, he smells—a rank, gold-camp odor, rotten and salty, clothes rotting on his frame. He comes toward her, grabs her by both arms, looms. He wants to pin her against a wall, but he's being careful of the knife blade. He doesn't want either of them cut.

He's not hurting her, physically, yet. She isn't crying—that surprises him. A ferocity in her black eyes surprises him: she's not afraid, he thinks. She's not struggling; her arms feel delicate. He relaxes his grip but does not let go, belches, doesn't know what he wants to do with her, to do to her. In all his rage, he has confused himself.

His eyes look like tadpoles in mud.

His hands and her arms are damp with perspiration, so when she wriggles and spins, she slips away—so easily. Cannon is surprised but feigns control. "Well, you little—"

She brings the knife up from thigh-level and sticks it in him.

It is done—done in a moment, a moment in which everything changes forever, even as California history rolls on, hardly taking note. Bringing up the knife from thigh-level is only a gesture, a movement of an arm through air, changing everything.

Lying on my cot, I focused on how much history, how much pain and change, course out of one gesture—the motion of one knife up, up from one woman's thigh to one man's abdomen.

—Swift and sure she sticks him—not so much savagely as reflexively: through his filthy shirt. The blade slips in below the ribs: this shocks Juanita. The horrible softness of the human body.

She lets go the knife as if it were on fire, steps back. He sees her back off, sees pity and regret in her eyes; it's her eyes that tell him he's hurt badly. They terrify him as much as he'll be terrified in his life, which is closing. He looks down at the knife. Feels nothing. Sees blood. Touches the knife, wants to leave it, believes if he does not disturb it, he will not die. Now comes pain.

He starts to die, sitting down carefully. Pain roars in his guts now. There is so much of the warm, thick blood. He calls for his friends— once, twice, three times. Juanita sits down, weeping. The friends hear. They rush in. Cannon's on his back, his shirt and pants soaked dark with blood, blood on his hands, on the wooden floor, blood everywhere. The wetness of it. The smell.

"Jesus," he mutters, "she knifed me." The men turn to look at Juanita, disbelieving. They fear her.

Cannon's dying, blood bubbling up from his stomach like red bile, reddening his tongue and teeth, his eyes rolling back, his breathing going raspy, his face a macabre storm-cloud gray. The men say nothing, do nothing. One of them puts a coat under Cannon's head. A stain of urine spreads on his trousers. He tries to talk but only gurgles and gasps. Juanita wails. He's dying, he dies, he's dead, his last breath leaving him with a ragged rattle and bright blood—and everyone in the room can hear the river. A fly lands on one of Cannon's boots. The river. Juanita weeps. The heat.

Someone says, "Hold this pistol on her. Keep her here. If José shows up, hold him. Shoot the sonofabitch if you have to...."

Seven

Attorney-at-Law Tom Crimpton asked, "What is it you want exactly?" The last word came out as a muttered afterthought.

He wore a yellow rayon shirt, a red tie, and a sky-blue blazer. I imagined the Reicher lawyer in a charcoal-gray Armani outfit with a shirt as sharp as a new hatchet, and I felt badly for my lawyer and me.

Tom Crimpton proved to be full of surprises, of a kind. The first surprise was that after minimal chit-chat, he got right to What is it you want?

"Well, I want them to stop building the dam, and I want to take the opportunity to talk about Juanita."

He looked at me.

I said, "The woman who was lynched...."

"—I know who Juanita was, for goodness sakes. I live here, remember? What's the connection with the dam?"

"In a word, power. Power destroying people and this canyon."

"I see." He raised his eyebrows. He lowered them. He sighed.

He sat in a brown metal chair outside my cell, his briefcase open on the floor. A yellow pad and a clipboard lay on his lap. Thinning brown hair. The nose was long, with the hint of a roundish nob on the end, not at all unattractive. A dime-size coffee stain on his tie. That was a bit sad.

"But they're not going to stop the dam," he said. "Soon there'll be a small lake there, and turbines and such." He put out his hands as if to ask, Any questions?

Now I saw he was truly perturbed, and closing in on exasperated; this, too, was a surprise. I'd always known him to be long-suffering. I knew he, too, had been against the dam. Was against it.

"I know that," I said. "But I wanted to speak out, act out. One last time. One time."

He sighed heavily; that is: parentally. "And you and Lloyd have talked this all out?"

"No, actually. I mean, we talked about it. But it wasn't a big plan we hatched. This is pretty much my doing. Obviously, Lloyd couldn't—"

Tom Crimpton winced and interrupted. "This could cost him his— it could cost him."

"He didn't do anything wrong. Or illegal. He arrested me, Tom. He did his job." I was leaning forward.

"Mary. How long have you lived up here? You know the way it works."

I shrugged tacit agreement. "Hell, Tom, most people don't want the dam. It's our canyon. I mean to say, it's nobody's canyon permanently."

"Our friends and neighbors are getting used to the idea of a dam.... And the canyon technically belongs to the federal government, and you environmentalists caught a bad break with the president and the Congress at the time. Sometimes awful projects go through.... All right," he said, sitting up as if to go to work. "I just wish you'd've thought about consequences before waltzing down into the river canyon."

I liked "waltzing." That was a good word for what I'd blithely done up at the dam. "What am I in for, Tom?" I asked, asking it in part because I wanted to know, but also because I wanted him to focus on his paper and briefcase, not on the haphazard way I'd "planned" to chain myself to Bar Rock.

"'In for'?"

"What's going to happen to me?"

"My hope is you're in for a bumpy but short legal ride," he said. "But I don't know. Shall we talk about what happens today?"

I nodded.

"We're going into court in an hour or so. Basically, the charge will be read, and you'll plead. Guilty or innocent. Or *nolo contendere*."

"Wow, what's that?—I like the sound of that one."

"A back-door guilty plea. It's a way of maneuvering for easy treatment, and it saves the County a lot of money."

"And what is the charge?"

He shifted in his chair and shrugged. "I'm afraid this is where it's starting to look unusual. The D.A.'s now going to press for felony trespassing."

"Felony? But tree-sitters have trespassed for months and not gotten hit that hard!"

He nodded, but he ignored my tree-sitter example. "It actually exists in the county ordinances. Up to two years in jail and a fifty-thousand-dollar fine. It's in there because of the ranchers over in the valley, protecting their livestock and water. It's rarely used over there and has never been used on this side of the mountain, as far as I can tell, and I know the history of county-cases pretty well. It's outrageous—

that they're thinking of clubbing you with it. It's an ordinance intended for potential cattle rustlers, or for animal-mutilators, for goodness' sake, not peaceful protesters."

"A year in jail. Two years. Fifty thousand." I repeated the phrases like a numb novitiate.

"The thing is, tree-fallers can cut every tree except the one people are sitting in, but you shut down a project."

"For less than a whole morning."

"Nonetheless.... Ready for more bad news?"

He didn't give me time to answer.

"Word is, the D.A.'s going to convene a grand jury and look into whether Lloyd acted improperly."

"Improperly? He arrested me."

Crimpton shrugged again. "It's just what I heard." He looked down at his legal pad and swallowed. I could see he was steeling himself to tell me something he didn't want to tell me.

"What is it, Tom?"

"Mary, I like you and Lloyd. You're good people." This is what Barker Updike had said of Lloyd and me. The phrase was starting to make me nervous. "I don't really agree with what you did—it's just not my style, that's all."

"Hell, Tom, it's not mine, either."

He ignored that, cleared his throat. "And I agree with you about the dam and all. But, well—"

"Go ahead."

"I'll be your lawyer for as long as you need me, Mary, but let me be straight with you. I think you need more help."

"More help?"

"More firepower. Another lawyer."

"Tom," I croaked, "Lloyd and I have complete—"

"Stop," he said. "I'm good at what I do. Wills, drunk-driving cases, living trusts. Clearing titles. This is a political dogfight. What I hear is that Reicher's behind schedule and under-capitalized. Reicher's looking for escape hatches. Ways to cover cost over-runs. It's taken them forever to get going up there. All that equipment, all those engineers...."

"But why would the D.A. play ball with them? It's not in the interests of the Board of Supervisors to have to pay for cost-over-runs."

"Oh, the Board won't have to pay. Reicher would probably declare bankruptcy."

"Won't the Feds cover cost-overruns?"

"Hell, no. Projects like this are designed to put money in corporate pockets and, theoretically, to generate electricity, but if the corporation screws up, the Fed's don't have to cover it. If they couldn't or wouldn't fix New Orleans, why would they care about a dam on a river nobody's heard of?"

"So the dam might be stopped? Great news."

"Just postponed, not stopped. Another company, another source of capital. That river never runs dry. But we're missing the real point. The D.A.'s nosing around for somebody to finance a run for the assembly. He doesn't plan on being in the County forever. He's no friend of the Supervisors. And frankly, he's got it in for Lloyd. I have to live and work in this county, plus I know my limits. I'm telling you straight out, get someone else."

I felt like I'd been fired. "Well, okay," I said. "I'll think about it. So how should I plead this morning? I mean, I was thinking 'guilty.' Because, you know, I did it. I did chain myself to the boulder."

Crimpton laughed. I think it was mainly a way to let off steam. He laughed some more.

"What?" I said.

"There is a certain logic to your position. If it's a misdemeanor, I'd say yes. If they hit you with a felony, no way we plead guilty. The bail should be minimal. I'm surprised Lloyd didn't try to get you out yesterday."

"He was trying to play it straight. This was my first night in jail. Ever. Where is Lloyd?"

"Dunno," he said, tidying up his briefcase. "Probably avoiding the cameras?"

"Cameras?"

"Yeah. Two or three TV trucks out there. Pulled in just as I was coming in to see you."

"Two or three?"

"Yes." He closed his briefcase, got up, moved his chair back to a corner. "What did you imagine would happen when you did this?" Tom Crimpton didn't ask this nastily. He was genuinely interested in my answer.

"Tom, I didn't. Really imagine. I got up that morning and did it."

What I couldn't disclose to him, what I could hardly admit to myself, is that I'd gone up there when I did mostly because of my mother. Accompanied by Lloyd's mother, Betty, my mother Eileen Herrera was out of town, on a cruise through Alaska's Inside Passage. I knew on the morning I drove up to the dam that if I was ever going to chain myself to Bar Rock, it was going to happen when my mother was out of town, out of state, out of reach of my acting out. It's a little embarrassing to admit, at my age, that your mother holds that amount of shame-inducing, what-do-you-think-you're-doing? power over you.

But remember, I'm technically Catholic.

Tom looked like he didn't know me at all, was starting from scratch with me. He rubbed his face the way only men do when plumbing breaks or women surprise them. Rub, rub, rub.

"Cheer up, Tom," I said. "It's not like they have a case against me or anything." He left, unamused.

I sat there for a while in the backwash of Tom Crimpton's visit. I guess I should have felt worried or scared, but instead I found myself working on defiance. I can't really say whether it was the felony rap or the grand-jury ploy to nail Lloyd—or whether I was just sick of moping, but I could feel myself hardening. It's funny how that works.

I'm always surprised when the world takes note of me. By "the world" I mean anybody Out There. Lloyd feels the same way. We're just accustomed to a certain invisibility. As Not Exactlys we're used to Not Mattering. Even at my gallery openings, I feel as if I'm living someone else's life. In one way, nothing that had happened after I sat on the boulder was out of the ordinary or unexpected. In another way, any reaction was unexpected—just because of how we were used to living in the world.

Now some of the world seemed to care enough to come after my husband and me. I was scared, more for Lloyd than me. I didn't know how I'd fight back. I knew I would fight back. A felony. Fifty thousand dollars. Two years. In prison. A lot of money. It would wipe us out. Two years!

I stood up on my bunk, stretched, and peered through the little barred window. Saw the TV trucks out there. I didn't see any on-camera types, just the funny-looking technicians with jogging shoes and khakis on and a kind of why-in-the-hell-did-they-send-us-to-the-sticks? air about them as they loitered and smoked and played with cables on a bright mid-June morning.

I sat back down on my bunk and thought of—Tom Crimpton's thinning hair. He would go completely bald, he would die, as would Lloyd and I, after the dam had been built and had crippled the river, and it seems I'd cleverly arranged for my protest to be too little and too late to stop a dam but more than enough to endanger my husband's career, our financial well being, my art, our son's college tuition, and our marriage. What an idiot.

Later I roused myself and convinced one of the deputies to bring me some pencils and paper. I ignored the paper and used the pencils to draw a crude mural of Juanita on the painted cinderblock wall. "Crude" may be an understatement. I'm a wood-carver, not a sketch-artist.

Eight

They must have put Juanita in a shed somewhere, or a back room. I've long had this image of her in the dark, in stifling heat, surrounded by the smell of hot, unpainted boards—raw, dry lumber. Flies. There wouldn't have been a jail yet, that's for sure. When she had to go to the bathroom, who took her, and where was the outhouse? Did they let her wash? What did they feed her? To me this isn't trivia. It's at the heart of what was Juanita's condition, if that's the right word. When you're a prisoner, imprisonment's not an idea. Imprisonment's right in front of you, no words. It's hot boards and a stinking crotch, for example. It's having to negotiate for essentials. It's the conditions. It's the specifics, like the rope.

For such a long time, during my time of considering the legend of Juanita, I had denied the rope. I could, it seemed, imaginatively conjure Cannon, his mentality. I could bring forth José, showing and hiding himself, a survivor, an ace in the deck, a marked-card of a man. The knifing—I could see that well enough for my satisfaction, if that's the word. The mob—the mob I could even smell, stinking with sweat and dirt and a diet of salt and beans, stinking of bad Fourth of July sour-mash whiskey and the symbolically bad breath of Senator-to-be Weller's stupefying speech.

The rope eluded recapitulations. Once—Lloyd himself only recently found this out, because his wife only recently 'fessed up—I went into the workshop and got a rope and made a noose and put the noose around my neck and snugged it up.

I needed to know about the rope. To feel it. I removed it very quickly because it was very creepy.

The noose taught me something. Or transmitted something, like a telegraph cable stretching back to and from 1850. It conveyed awe and the crudity of rope, the absolute aloneness Juanita must have felt. An execution is a killing, yes, but before it's a killing, it's a ceremony.

I'm guessing the rope was made back East and came round the Horn, with a shipment of fancy furniture, purchased brides, gold rushers, rats, new strains of syphilis, and so forth. Or mabye it was made in San Francisco—out of imported hemp.

Some of the men would have hunted up the rope right away, even before the "trial." Cannon's friends would have done so, would have wanted to lynch her right away; it's clear from accounts that hanging—and little else—was on everybody's mind. It's clear from my own prejudices that a trial was held only because New Statehood made people want to fake civility, "process."

Cannon's friends would have made and unmade the noose, would have argued about it—the way men quibble over the technique of things, talking it to death, the way they do nowadays with car engines and football. An entire family may be collapsing around them, but the men will be out there arguing over an out-of-bounds call or a piston-rod.

I think Cannon's friends would have joked, savagely.

Juanita stabbed Cannon on the 5th. On the 6th she was tried. On the 7th she was hanged from the bridge. To make a noose that will kill someone: doesn't this require a relinquishment of something substantial, something essential, in the noose-maker? Or maybe it reveals something substantial was missing all along.

Lynching's not a crime of passion. Nor is it, truly, "execution."

My argument: most immoral conversations are, at one level, purely technical in nature: This is so because the ones talking see no need to talk about anything except technique. "No, leave yourself more slack." Or: "It can be a bigger loop. You ain't strangling her, you know. You're snapping her neck." "How tall is she, you reckon?"

One who thought about larger questions was the doctor.

We don't have his name or description. In a couple accounts, there's only mention of "a doctor". A doctor who convinced the Kangaroo Court to take a recess while he examined Juanita to see if she was "with child."

Exactly what sort of doctor would he have been? —There, in a god-forsaken mud-hole in the middle of the Gold Rush? What kinds of doctor were any doctors then, even the best? Weren't they barbers with an attitude—literate men who weren't afraid of blood and howls of pain?

Was he young or old? Drunk or sober? Running away or toward? Nothing, there's nothing to go on. Still, he was there.

So I go on my vibrations, forgive the term, which tell me he was older and sober and—for some now-evaporated reason—there. Not hunting for gold, not gambling, not hustling for something. Just there—for some fateful carom-shot of a reason.

Being there, he saw. Seeing, he acted. Acting, he added a droplet of decency to Juanita's tale—but nothing else, not his name, not his words, neither a different ending nor effectual heroism.

I figure there are at least three ways the shard of the story concerning pregnancy could have materialized.

The simplest: Juanita was pregnant. I call this the "she oughtta know" theory. Was pregnant and said so.

Or Juanita, desperate, believed that if she said she was pregnant, they wouldn't lynch her. This is plausible, but somehow I doubt it.

Or, third, this doctor, this shadow of decency, looked at her and thought she might be pregnant or took a wild gamble hoping the examination would prove she was pregnant. Or, 3A, he just wanted to stall the mob.

Maybe he showed up at the "trial" and looked at Juanita and saw something in her face or her abdomen that indicated pregnancy.

...the room—the open space in a dry-goods store—is hot & airless, July afternoon, odor of dried mud, beans, salt pork. Twenty or thirty miners and merchants and card players are in there, lobbing tobacco juice, rubbing their stubble, staring at Juanita, who sits, fatigued—even traumatized—in a chair.

The doctor, known as Nathan in this telling, sits toward the back. Nathan's been in Claytonville for a while, knows how often miners get hurt—how, in the long run, gold isn't worth spit. Broken arms and fingers. Toes smashed by boulders. Fevers sucked in from rank mud, squalid tents, and human manure. Boils and sores from bad frontier diets. Broken teeth and gouged eyes from fights over money over claims over booze over nothing. Eye-gouging, in fact, was a routine way to fight. Scabies and rashes and scurvy and murky deep-down coughs that don't go away....

"*Donde esta José?*" Juanita asks the man who presides—the "judge."

The men in the room exchange glances.

"José ain't gonna save you," the judge says, as if he were talking to a dog—talking too loud, talking at her. Juanita understands English well enough.

She cries, therefore.

It is then that Nathan the doctor gets up from a table. His presence quiets the men. He is not a miner. He is a sober man amongst boozers.

"Jee-zzuss Christ," he mutters, biting off the second word like a chaw. Then men look up at him. Juanita looks up. Everyone in the room feels the blazing heat reflected off diorite bluffs, poured down from pale-blue sky.

"I want to take a look at her," Nathan says. He's a spry man who needs a shave. Gray stubble. Considering he's in a gold camp, his clothes are clean. This, too, brings temporary respect from the men. He is older and quieter than they, and his clothes are cleaner, and he isn't destroying himself digging for gold. All this counts for something.

So do his boots. Good boots, which impress the men. Also, his teeth—his teeth are impressive. That is, he has some.

The judge doesn't understand what Nathan means.

"In private," says Nathan. "The back room. And I'll need a basin of water, some clean cloth, and soap. Look here, I've treated plenty of women in my day. I have a hunch she's carrying a child."

This is the only time during the crucial three days when the men behave reflectively—behave as if their plans could, in fact, be complicated somehow. They exchange glances again.

Nathan receives the basin of water, the soap, and the clean rags. He asks for candles and gets them. Nathan and Juanita adjourn to a windowless back room.

He situates and lights the candles. There are two chairs and a small table. Naturally, Juanita is afraid of Nathan. Naturally, Nathan knows Juanita is afraid of him and sees her fear as the first thing he must address.

"I'm a doctor," he says. "Do you understand?"

She nods.

"Do you think you might be carrying a baby? Niňo, niňa." He rubs his own belly, then touches hers. "I'm thinking you might be. You have a look in your face I've seen before."

Maybe she smiles at how deliberate he's being. Why does he care if I'm pregnant? she might wonder. She shrugs. She looks at her own stomach. She looks at Nathan. She gets the implication.

She has just realized that, possibly, he can save her life. Her face opens to him. This terrifies him: He was afraid of this—afraid of hope ignited.

He asks more questions—about when she last menstruated (he calls it "bleeding"), how long she's been with José, whether she has had any children (she hasn't). Finally, he gets around to the subject of examining her, first by telling her she doesn't have to do anything she doesn't want to do.

Eventually, she lies on the floor.

She isn't wearing underwear in the modern sense of the term, of course; under her thick, hand-sewn gingham dress, a faded blue, she wears a cotton slip, patched and torn and re-patched. In cold weather she might wear women's drawers and stockings, but in summer she wears a dress and a slip and either plain sandals or leather shoes—small boots, really. These are what she wears today. She had to dress hastily, after all.

Something told her to wear the good shoes.

Nathan has put his coat under her head for support. Using three different phrasings just to make sure she understands, he tells her he needs to examine her. Examine her private parts. Each time she nods. Each time the nod is accompanied by resignation. Considering her modesty, he concludes she is not and has never been a whore.

Nathan has rolled up his sleeves and washed—out of habit, but also out of a desire to reassure her of his decent, if futile, intentions.

He begins to roll the dress and the slip upward from her ankles, slowly, checking with her at intervals. She gets impatient, sits up, grabs the garments in bunches, and pulls them up and under her buttocks and over her navel. This embarrasses Nathan: No professional expects a client to be the impatient, efficient one in the transaction. But he keeps his stone face.

Raucous laughter erupts in the next room, all the more rude for its uncanny timing. Nathan and Juanita look at each other. Nathan imagines he sees in the glance an embarrassment for the human race itself.

She tips her head back on his coat, pointing her nose to the ceiling, closing her eyes. She opens her legs.

He expects the odor—mostly briny, faintly fecal—that wafts up from her exposed legs and crotch.

As she closes her eyes more tightly, she scrunches her face like a child. He is amused. Gently, he pats the inside of her knee. "Easy, there." Too late he realizes how much he sounds like a horse-doctor. She unscrunches her face. She looks at him, glances away.

He does and doesn't know what he's looking for. He has examined many pregnant women and has that experience on which to draw, but he is, nonetheless, a doctor in the American West at mid-nineteenth-century.

Mostly he's looking for a fullness, a swollenness. He is looking for a sign. He is looking for something to keep the woman from being asphyxiated by a rope. He knows from experience that the hanged rarely die of a broken neck.

The only thing he's come up with is pregnancy. In broken Spanish-English, he asks about her time of the month. How long has it been?

She doesn't know. Please, try to think back. A while. But how long? A month? More than a month? He is getting angry, and she sees him getting angry, and mostly out of hopeless fatigue, she cries. *No se.* I don't know, she doesn't know, she doesn't know, she's sorry, she's sorry, I'm sorry. *Lo siento. Lo siento mucho.*

Nathan knows he should be apologizing. Should be the one able to convince the men she's pregnant—bluff a bad hand.

He says to Juanita, "No, no, no. Don't worry." Then he shuts himself up because he can't stomach saying 'Don't worry' to a woman about to be lynched from a tree. He assumes it will be a tree.

Unless a person's a certified saint, decency must eventually give way to despair, chronic grief for the way people treat each other.

I'm thinking Doc Nathan was decent—but that day felt despair, especially when Juanita muttered *Lo siento* and *Gracias* to him. Victims with good manners drive a stake into a decent person's heart.

Seriously, decently, he tried to figure a way—there in the small, stuffy back room—to get her out of town. There was no way. If he tried, he'd hang, too. Or get a bullet in a kidney and bleed to death. That didn't frighten him—he was numb to death and ready for his own and felt he should have died many times already. But I'll be goddamned, he said to himself, if I'll be strung up by the likes of this filth, shot by the likes of this drunken toothless shiftless vermin, gold prospectors.

One of the likes of them rapped on the slab-of-pine door.

"What in Hell's name's goin' on in there, doc?"

The rest of the likes of them laugh crudely out there in the bigger room.

The words that come out of Nathan's mouth aren't just shouted. They're propelled—by a kind of divine rage, propellent made of purest disgust and frustration. Jeremiah lashing a wicked city.

"Get back, you sonofabitch! Get away from that door!"

His words go through the door and like a snake strike the likes of them.

His yelling scares Juanita. Around his mouth, his skin goes white and twitchy. But the rage he blasted through the door also cleansed her every bit as much as the wet cloth she'd use in a moment to wash herself. Nathan sees the cleansing effect of his words, sees it on her face, does not know what it is, what it means, exactly.

Exactly it means that for a moment Juanita feels unburdened, stood-up-for. Not protected, too late for that. José, after all, is at least two Sierra Nevada ridges and canyons away from there by now. But stood-up-for: Somebody gave a damn about her damnation. Somebody hated the godforsaken mud-hole and mud-men as much as she—as much as they hated her.

The men are in a hurry. Gold is waiting, they believe. Juanita must be killed because she killed Cannon, they believe. They believe.

Nathan's pregnancy-gambit goes for naught. Even if she were three, four, five months along and showing, he reasons, they might hang her anyway. There's nothing to stop them, Nathan knows. The canyon is an island. There is no sheriff, no marshal. The "state government" is just the old territorial government, with the added focus of everyone getting rich off statehood and the gold rush. What is Juanita, and a child if she is carrying one, to such people? Why on earth would they know or care?

The "judge" is a grizzled cuss with dirty hair. Less than a year later, he will die from an abscessed tooth gone toxic. Fever will cook his brain in its pan of bone.

The jury is eight. A few other men slouch and yawn in the "audience," but the most alert out there are Cannon's friends.

Who "testify."

Damned right she knifed him. As cold as a hog butcher. "He died hard."

Cannon was a good man. Fine fellow. Shared some venison jerky with me before I could get my grubstake together. Leant me a shovel once.

Others in the audience, not Cannon's friends, whisper, "Who'll get his claim? He have a pard'ner? Heard when they buried him this morning, someone took some of the dirt to see if it panned out!"

Nathan remains. He stands once and asks about the door—Cannon kicking it in. The judge barks, "That don't mean she had a right to kill him!" And one of Cannon's friends says, "He didn't kick it in. It dropped off the shack. Goddamned José never took care o' the place."

"This ain't no trial," Nathan says. A juror stands up, his face gone purple.

"I've heard about enough from you," he says. "You got you a look under her drawers. That's what you wanted...."

"—You shut your goddamned mouth," says Nathan. "I think this woman might be pregnant, and this isn't a real trial. Why don't you take her to Sacramento, where men at least pretend to govern themselves reasonably?" If Nathan has been to Sacramento, he may realize how weak this argument is.

The juror moves around his fellows, moving toward Nathan, and Nathan moves out to meet him.

"Grab him," the judge says, meaning the juror wanting to fight. Two men do grab him, hold him, his face tight like a mad cat's.

"You," the judge says to Nathan, "you best get out of here, unless you really want trouble. I think we've heard enough from you. You go to Sacramento if you love it down there. We're givin' her more of a chance than she gave Cannon."

"That's stupid. That's not how a court operates."

"I said shut your mouth. And you can't prove she's carryin' a child."

Nathan calculates. It goes back to the question of whether he wants to die in this canyon or elsewhere.

Elsewhere, he decides, and he decides to make a clean cut of it, as he would on a leg that needed to come off. A decent man, he knows he must look at Juanita. He looks. She looks. He nods. She looks away. He considers whether he should stay in Claytonville long enough to see about the burial, but it's not worth the risk—the woman already dead and enraged men ready to kill him and throw him in the grave with her. The cut must be clean. Delay and feigned sentiment are cheap. They'd only insult her and make him feel soiled.

"Curse you all straight to Hell, all of you and this rotten business," he says, leaving—and leaving only a paltry whiff of his ever being on Earth—a vague mention of him in clippings rotting in the Bancroft Library of the University of California, Berkeley, or some other hole in an academic cupboard.

From that moment to the following morning, at the bridge, it is as if, for the men, Juanita disappears. They talk, they posture, they spit tobacco juice, they talk, they spit, they drink, they find "her" guilty, the judge says "she" must hang by "her" neck until dead, they find "her" a little food and water and put "her" in the back room and take turns guarding "her" as "she" sleeps or does not sleep, as "she" carries or does not carry a child, as, shocked, "she" stares into the abyss of dying. But they are not really seeing Juanita. She sees this.

Deputy Mike Cussler came in and, sheepishly, told me I had to wash off the mural. He had a bucket of soapy water and a sponge. I told him I understood—no special treatment for the sheriff's wife. While I was scrubbing, I experienced—I don't know, a revery?

Whatever it's called, it started with a phrase. The phrase repeated itself—like a maddening line from a pop song that sticks in your mind, popcorn between molars. The phrase was Juanita comes to me…Juanita comes to me…Juanita comes to me across…comes to me across, across, across…what?

Juanita comes to me. I kept scrubbing, charcoal-darkened suds darkening my hands. Juanita comes to me across….

Juanita comes to me across years and mysteries. Juanita comes to me carrying not even a last name; she's traveled far, so far I used to think of her arrival as a flag of my will, my I-will-not-forget, my I-will-honor-Juanita. Juanita (maybe) comes to me because she willed herself into my memory. She comes to me across mysteries and years. She wades underground rivers, elbows aside more famous ghosts. She crosses memory's border and History's official map-lines and claimed territories. If I smell the sweat, if I imagine I smell the sweat in her long black hair; if I hold her, if I imagine I hold her hand and feel its callouses; if my tongue tastes, if I imagine my tongue tastes odor of alum from her cool skin; if I finally come to read her eyes and know the fear and ferocity, the obsidian resolve that clenched the knife and did in Cannon, then it's all right if I say Juanita comes to me and I'm here to greet her at the end of her trek, which began when they marched her ahead of the mob to the bridge:

Post-Television, who can know how the hanging proceeded? Too many films, too many movies-of-the-week, have poured our imaginations into cookie-molds, especially where mob-scenes are concerned. I imagine it was more solemn and sullen than movie versions. I imagine someone pretended to wake Juanita, who wouldn't have slept.

Probably he just tapped the door and retreated. Perhaps she'd wept all night or prayed all night or sat stunned and nauseous all night. Maybe her whole body shook. If I were going to be hanged, I think my whole body would shake. Perhaps she spent all night believing José would show up.

I imagine José having made it to another gold camp by that morning, rolling a cigarette, thinking of her, taking a deep breath of mountain air and admitting to himself he was glad to be alive, just as simply and guiltlessly as he admitted, at the end of a poker hand that he enjoyed winning...*Adios*, Juanita.

They would've fed her something—biscuits and salt pork and water, perhaps. She would've nibbled at a biscuit, sipped some spring water, left the pork alone. She would've seen the folly in this and every minute event of the morning. Eating just before death—what exactly is the point? If decency's the point, then don't hang her.

The fear that goes beyond fear would have overtaken her. Her weeping would've become a shaking, a trembling, an illness—a spectacle of grief that would have sickened at least one or two of the self-appointed, stayed with them the rest of their lives more grimly even than the sight of her body hanging from the rope.

The short procession from the dry-goods place to the bridge: A man on either side of her, a man ahead of her—the one who served as judge, the one who would have located a Bible—the Bible, as is the case so often, made to be an accessory after the fact.

Quickly a crowd gathered, coming out of shacks, coming up out of the mudflats, the sun just over the eastern ridge above the camp. A murmur, a buzz—louder. Adrenalin. Disbelief. Belief: She should be hung, she must be hung, she will be hung, it is only right that she be hung. Titillation. At least one of the 49ers would have yelled out something vicious, a verbal club like Hang her, goddamnit, hang her, hang the murdering bitch. One of Cannon's friends.

What accounts for the calm Juanita exuded once the procession reached the bridge? Each story of the hanging remarks on it.

Trauma? Sounds and sights must have blurred. The sight of the men around her—if there was one woman, I'd be surprised—must have roared in her ears; and the river below, already muddy from morning placer-mining, must have reached up with its noise. And if a bird sang or a man coughed, the sound must have echoed in the gaping canyon of her state-of-mind.

The one who served as judge—his name, his face, his presence, his words: all have been erased, forever. He must have tried to silence the gathered—putting an arm out in that official, "civilized" way. And now we must invent for ourselves a last name for Juanita. Mercado? de Santos? Abelar? Hernandez? He would have said the name—Juanita Mercado, the jury has found you guilty of the murder.... The jury has sentenced you.... Hung by the neck until you are.... The Bible, the trusty Bible, would have appeared. King James.

Even if she could read, doubtful, she couldn't read that version. And yet, if it wasn't trauma that calmed her, maybe it was God. Not God the Father so much as God the Explanation that's left when all other explanations have departed along with the good doctor and mercurial José. God who made the sight of the crowd roar and the sound of the river rise up to blind her. God who had saved her from being violated in her village. God who'd placed Cannon the Bad Man at her door and the knife in her hand. God who made her bleed from between her legs, God who stopped the bleeding. God who flung bits of gold before men, these men who writhed in mud and played their cards so stupidly with José and came back to reclaim losses in full in the form of her. God who not only made these mountains, the biggest she would ever see, but God who lived in them—in boulders and springs, in rattlesnakes and brush, in wind and snow and adobe-white sunlight. God who wanted something from her. God who wanted her. God who wanted everything. It was like falling into His arms, perhaps. Resignation. A giving over of defiance.

The rope. Tossed over one beam of the bridge.

Juanita stood on a crude platform—one rough-milled board set upon two stacks of board-remnants. For the sake of "modesty," someone bound with twine her skirt to her ankles: Another weird splicing-together of murder and politeness. One of the men slipped the noose over her black hair. She stood still. He tightened the noose. The river. The mask-like faces of the mob.

Two of the newspaper accounts note her stoicism at this moment. Chin up. Eyes straight ahead. They say her final remark to the Earth was Adios. True? Why not? God wanted her.

Two men each kicked one stack of boards. Her body dropped. Some of Cannon's friend's cheered. Some men turned away. Most of watched silently as she choked to death, her face purple and contorted, her body writhing, the image cooked onto the hide of memory like a brand.

From Lloyd, who spoke with a friend of a friend of a friend who observed a hanging in Washington State some years ago, I've gathered hanging is a deadly science, in that the body must drop a certain distance in order for the neck to snap and for death to be "instantaneous."

"Once the idea of whether hanging's right or wrong is out of play," Lloyd said, "and it comes down to this person will hang, then there's a right way and a wrong way to hang the person. It's physics—weight and distance."

Juanita didn't weigh very much. They didn't drop her very far. They did it the wrong way.

She choked to death. It takes a long time to choke to death—her hands, trained to save her throat, tied behind her. The river roared. The men stared. The sky went white, went red. Went.

I couldn't wash her image from the wall yet.

Nine

Deputy Andee Munro came to escort me to my day in court. Andee: sturdy and stout; short, thick brown hair; her stance in the black deputy's boots, wide. I'd always thought of her as the well established Andee and felt glad that morning to be moored to the dock of her solidness.

She let me out of the cell, not hand-cuffing me, and led me through the office. Brenda MacDonald the dispatcher and a couple deputies smiled wanly. Red-haired, big-muscled Mike Cussler was there. All stared.

"'Morning," I said.

Like piglets heading for a trough, they stumbled around and fell over themselves rushing to say "Good morning" back-at-me. I was not used to making people nervous. I was not used to a great many things; these included wearing an orange jumpsuit.

And we were in the hallway. I assumed we'd swing left and up the staircase to the courtroom, but Andee said, "We're early, wanna get some fresh air?"

"Sure."

"Don't be trying to make a break for it."

Out we went through the doors and onto the steps of the courthouse on what was already a hot day. Sunlight ricocheted off a waterfall of concrete steps, off corrugated-iron roofs and clapboard houses of Claytonville.

At that moment, I became a celebrity, of the small-town kind. There was a crowd of maybe fifty. A gaggle. There was applause and shouting—which stopped as quickly as it sprang up. There was staring. There was the murmur of the gaggle. And the different, constant murmur of the river.

To be stared at as if I were a stranger by people I saw nearly every day of my life was—not exactly weird but both appropriate and surprising, like a satisfying dream. There was this wrinkled face I knew as Joe (the retired plumber) and that younger pinched face I knew as Rae (the chain-smoking waitress, single mother of three, bad blonde dye-job, black roots)—and so on. Some faces smiled. Most just stared guardedly. The television van had drawn most of the people there; television-the-business, as opposed to the signal, so rarely made it up into the canyon; usually it took at least a murder, or a forest fire out of control, and even then the story would end up late in a Sacramento newscast, bumped up against weather or sports or the story about a lost dog returned or the Lodi man who covered his entire house with flattened aluminum cans.

Baseball caps, cotton shirts and blouses, bluejeans, outlines of round tobacco cans, work-boots—I saw it all so sharply; the scene seemed burnished by the sun, stylized—maybe because I'd been in the cell, hard to say. Maybe I lifted a hand and waved. Don't know. I remember feeling as if I were in pajamas (in a way I was), feeling shy. I saw two men and a woman each grab microphones and speak with their camera people and make a move toward me.

"Well, Andee, what do I do?" I said.

Tiny drops of perspiration sat atop Andee's freckled nose. She knew I was referring to the TV people. "Up to you," she said. "What do you want to do?"

I didn't have time to answer.

Up the steps bounded Sybil Burns, fiftyish and impishly muscular, close-cropped bleached hair, one dangling lapis earring, hiking shorts, a black polo shirt, pristine hiking boots. Sybil Burns, force of nature—with a blue-chip portfolio that dwarfed the county's annual budget.

She came at Andee and me so fast that out of reflex Andee stepped in front of me, body-guard fashion. Sybil nudged her aside.

"God-damn, woman, I never knew you had it in you!" Sybil shouted in her easy Oklahoma drawl. "You sure as hell keep your light under a bushel-basket." As if I were ten and a boy, she hugged me and roughed up my hair.

"All right, back off a little," Andee said to her.

"Oh, for Chrissakes, get the bind out of your shorts," Sybil said.

Her Sybilness had summered in the county for ten years, running a hiking/self-esteem/feminist-consciousness camp for middle-aged women who were sick of men in general, sick of certain men in particular, and in possession of expendable income they had accrued in spite of men and lawyers and because of other lawyers.

The Buffalo Gals—as the camp/organization was known— did help out the underfunded: something, at least, to mollify liberal-guilt. I think they were called Sisterships instead of Fellowships.

La Syb herself had divorced an oil tycoon when she was 35, flung herself out of her Tulsa-Baptist-corporate life and into a West Coast, New-Age, carrot-juiced bisexual adventure, the epicenter of which had been Santa Cruz. Her rebellion had energized her. That much was clear. And she was not boring; almost everyone in the county was willing to give her that. In the lingo of the county, she had a butt-load of money.

Of course, things like the Buffalo Gals make California seem like a state of self-parody, rolfing and channeling its way toward a yogurt-brained, fiber-boweled mantrafied stupor. But Sybil was a real person.

Through the years I'd kept my distance from La Syb, mainly because I keep my distance from anyone that full of herself and set on organizing others.

Sybil was courageous, in her own way. A few religious fundamentalist types in the county prayed for her to drop into a burning cauldron, like Axel's mercury, and I wouldn't want to guess how many times she'd been called a dyke or otherwise insulted. —Not to mention her automobiles being messed with—slashed tires, smashed windows, sugared gasoline. Nasty little tricks.

Whatever she did up there for middle-aged women seemed to work. They came down off the mountain in possession of themselves, tanned and triumphant, lungs full of alpine air, hair infused with clean sweat and aroma of fir branches. Only once had Lloyd had to go up and retrieve a Buffalo Gal. She'd tumbled on loose shale, broken a leg. They were careful, well-prepared woodswomen—more likely than men to give mountains due respect, to pay attention to crucial details of map, terrain, season, hydration, gear. In Lloyd's book of practicality, they were preferable to the Boy Scouts, who tended always not to be prepared, as it happened.

The Buffalo Gals weren't my sort of thing, but I had always given Sybil her due.

Still Sybil Burns was not the one I wanted to see scaling the mountain of courthouse steps that day. As to ensuing events:

They're a little too confusing to sort out because a lot happened at once; or, so much happened it had an all-at-once look to it.

For instance, Sybil said, "We're goin' up there, too, Mary. We'll stop that fuckin' project. You had the balls to lead the way." I glanced at the group she'd been standing with. Middle-aged, muscular women. Awfully tan, terribly stylish, full of energy, not mixing with the rest of the Claytonville crowd. It was classic Slick vs. Hick.

My literal mind couldn't handle the "balls" reference. Also, Sybil's show of solidarity worried me. Lloyd with a jail full of the Buffalo Gals? One of the last things I desired in the slammer was company.

Then television-people came at me with mikes and cords, clipboards, questions, makeup, and sharp clothes. The crowd folded in behind them.

I was about to say something to La Syb when the reporters' questions started coming. Andee held my arm, as in a prom photo.

"Did your husband support your decision?"

"How will you plead?"

"What are the jail conditions like?"

I responded with flat, terse answers, which they didn't seem to like. I knew I was bad television, so I tried harder. "Like many of the County residents, I'm opposed to the dam. It's unnecessary. Conservation could make up for whatever power the dam generates." For me, this was getting to be a long speech, and I was getting desperately self-conscious. I looked over the roofs at a stand of conifers. "Also, I want to honor the memory of a woman known as Juanita, who was lynched in this town, from a bridge over this very same river, about a hundred and fifty years ago."

"Who was Juanita?" a TV-woman said.

"She was a Mexican woman, a resident of this County." I failed to mention that the County hadn't been invented yet. "Powerful, lawless men lynched her. Powerful men are trying to lynch the river now." Lynch the river? What was I saying?

Sybil looked like she was about to leave, so I yelled her name. The crowd around me parted. Everyone swiveled to look at her.

"What?!" she said.

"Don't do anything until you talk to me!" Only after the words were out did I realize how conspiratorial they sounded. All I wanted to do was to make sure she didn't run up to the dam with her posse and get arrested.

Sybil stared at me. She was surrounded now by the other Buffalo Gals, all in khaki shorts and the black shirts. "Who's that?" a reporter asked—the woman from Sacramento's ABC affiliate, I think.

"Nobody," I said. I looked at Sybil. "Promise?!" I yelled.

In the intense sunlight, Sybil smiled mischievously. We had been polite acquaintances for years—hello/goodbye in the post office or the grocery store. A wave on the highway as our cars passed. She'd bought one of my carvings, bless her heart. Now in a matter of minutes, we were "close." She thought I'd pledged allegiance to eco-feminism by chaining myself to a rock. By chaining myself to the rock, I'd stepped onto her theatrical turf.

She wasn't going to let my gesture go to waste, let me back away from the gesture. She was going to help me even if it killed me: She was an organizer, a born publicist and trouble-maker, and—perhaps most lethally of all—a born camp-counselor. Why, I asked myself, hadn't I had the good Tom Sawyerish sense to talk her into parking her kiester on Bar Rock?

"I promise, Mary." There was something smug about the smile on her lips. "Be talking to you later, honey!"

She turned and led her group away. The clot of reporters and gawkers cinched up again around me, though I think one newspaper guy took off after the Sybil. I could tell the television people yearned to follow her. Sybil was Good Television. But the logistics weren't right.

Hanging back were Ralph Grimley, grizzled editor of our own *Mountain Weekly*, and an Asian-American reporter I'd seen before—Ron Kuwara. With the *San Francisco Star*. He'd done a story on Lloyd's getting elected the first time. Salt-and-pepper hair, slicked back. A chain-smoker. A leather jacket in that heat—Lord! A deep radio-baritone—how funny that he wasn't in broadcasting. A look that said, "I don't really give a shit about anything." It was as if Ralph and Kuwara were waiting for the rabble to clear out.

Then suddenly everyone was looking behind me, and they got quiet.

Lloyd.

"What in the hell are you doing, Andee? She's due in court!" It was close to a bark. Lloyd and I exchanged cold glances. I started to speak up for Andee, but then the reporters shoved microphones between Andee and me and into Lloyd's face.

"What was it like to arrest your wife?" someone asked.

"What was it like?" Lloyd repeated. He worried up his brow; he was toiling at an answer. He was my husband, and I didn't want to see him struggle for a simile.

"What the hell do you think it was like?" I heard myself saying. I'm not sure that qualifies as Good Television.

"Let's go," Lloyd said. He grabbed Andee and me and pulled us away, but the little clot followed us. Andee's face was ashen, as if she felt she had really screwed up in front of the boss. The clot followed us right up to the courthouse door, where Lloyd stopped and turned slowly. He held up his hands to quiet everyone.

"Look, let's not all troop through the building, okay?" He was trying to talk loudly, but the loudness stuck in his throat. "There's no need. We're going into the courtroom, second floor. We'll all get there eventually."

I felt better for him and me and Andee when he said that, even though it brought sour, recalcitrant looks from the reporters, who still kept asking questions.

Someone started yelling. Someone at the back of the crowd, a man. In my gut I sensed something ugly was happening or about to happen—

there's just that feeling a person gets. The yelling got closer. There was jostling. That electric sense of a crowd in panic.

A tall, bearded man shoved the woman reporter aside, hard, and came for me.

Mainly what I saw was a brown-and-gray, close-cropped beard, orange rodent-teeth, and a green cap. Striped cotton "railroad" shirt. Logger's suspenders, red.

"Fucking bitch!" he yelled. A breeze of bourbon came with the curse. Gasps all around. The face of the woman reporter lost all color, I remember.

All of this happening in seconds, of course—then Andee said, "Hey!" and the guy, who was at least Lloyd's height and big-boned, shoved Andee in the chest. Andee grabbed his arm, he tried to punch her with his other fist, and Lloyd knocked me aside coming at him. The crowd peeled back, except for cameramen, who stuck their cameras into the ruckus like big insect heads.

The guy half-tripped, half-shoved Andee down to one knee. He went for her gun. He'd unsnapped the security strap and had a good grip on the butt. Frozen, I stared and thought, Oh, shit, he's got her gun and people are going to die.

Lloyd was on him fast. He hit the guy hard between the ribs and stomach. A sharp, crisp punch, up high. The precision of it startled me. I'd taken the sheriff's professionalism for granted. A lot of air came out of the guy. Then an arm went behind the back, and Lloyd was driving him down to concrete in front of the doors. Someone—some many—screamed, not me. Andee was up then and on the man's back. The guy was trying to squirm and cuss, but Lloyd got one handcuff and then the other on and tightened them. Andee got off the guy as Lloyd cuffed him, as if she and Lloyd had done this dance before. They had.

The man vomited: This development moved the crowd back further and even gave the cameramen pause.

Andee and Lloyd hauled him up and marched him into the courthouse; he grunted and cussed and drooled pink saliva. "Fuck you all," he said, efficiently. He was sweating in the heat. So were Andee and Lloyd. Me, too.

Over his shoulder, Lloyd said, "You better get in there, Mary, you're late." The flat calmness of his voice got everyone's attention as much as if he'd fired his pistol, I think. Also, in this situation there was something absurdly domestic about the remark. I glanced at the faces. They seemed to be reassessing Lloyd Bluestone, as indeed I was. I was bewildered and couldn't even bring myself to answer. I was standing in an orange county jumpsuit, without an escort.

Cameras kept running, scribbling kept getting scribbled. Nobody talked. They looked at me. I looked at them. There I was, Alice down the rabbit hole. I saw the vomit and looked away. Beneath my feet, concrete seemed insubstantial.

I walked toward the courthouse. Reporters and a few others followed me respectfully, as if I were a grade-school teacher leading a group on a field trip. It wasn't until we got to the door that Ron Kuwara from the San Francisco paper appeared beside me like a leather-clad ghost.

"Do you know that man?" he asked in his deep voice. I'd opened the door.

"No," I said. "Do you?"

Ron Kuwara laughed. "Uh, no," he said. "Don't think so."

"I know him." It was the voice of Ralph Grimley, our hometown editor. "Name's Kelly, I b'lieve. He used to set chokers for Robertson Timber." Everyone turned toward him and his information.

"What's a choker?" someone asked, and still someone else asked, "What?—he tried to choke her?"

Ron Kuwara rolled his eyes at his journalistic brethren and muttered, "Say goodnight, Gracie."

I took the opportunity to scoot inside and shuffle upstairs toward the courtroom, grateful to be brought to justice, whatever that meant. I hoped it meant I could get back to carving. I'm embarrassed, looking back, at, among other things, the unwavering selfishness of my need to carve.

Ten

I put up my hand to push through old, heavy oak swinging-doors of the courtroom. The hand trembled a wee bit; my stomach became heavy; a wad of revulsion had gathered there. Lloyd says people who don't get in physical fights much, and that's still most people I guess, often get sick after an altercation. Something about a big dose of adrenaline having been dumped into the system.

I seemed still to smell the man's bad boozy breath. A video-loop in my head kept replaying the scene, my husband slugging him, taking him down to concrete, warm concrete giving off bile-stench, the sound of the crowd in panic.

The old wood-paneled courtroom sat empty. Clouded high windows let in milky light. Benches seemed like pews.

Between the pews and the judge's perch sat two long tables, just like in Perry Mason's old courtroom—justice in black-and-white, but without the nifty camera angles and Hamilton Burger's defeated hound-dog face. When Gabriel was still in diapers, *Perry Mason* reruns used to come on during his nap-time. To this day I associate Raymond Burr's mug with a young mother's brief psychic respite and Gabe's sweet baby-face.

The County had put down some ugly brown durable carpet. Otherwise the room had a 1940s feel to it. It smelled like President Truman's hat, that's for sure. In fact, the room was probably built in the Thirties like the rest of the courthouse complex: Works Progress Administration money. If it weren't for Roosevelt and Carnegie, I don't know how many small county-seats in the U.S. would have either a courthouse or a library.

I took a seat two pews back from one of the tables at which I'd sit when the party started.

I told myself I had to face facts, or at least admit the existence of some unpleasant ones. Whatever I'd started by sitting down on

Bar Rock had now become an event-of-its-own. The odd collection of players included Andee Munro, Sybil Burns and her Buffalo Gals, a D.A., the furious foreman Wade Landers, my unlikely sepia-complected, locksmith-accomplice Rupert Williams, a drunken attacker known only as Kelly-who-set-chokers-for-Robertson-Timber, reporters and cable-feeds from another planet. The Reicher Corporation. The thing wasn't mine anymore. It was publicly held.

Not being utterly dense, I did know that that was, in part, the point of protests, and I told myself my sit-in had worked, sort of.

Into my musings walked Mavis Everson, court reporter.

She was one of those super-efficient people about whom other (inefficient) people like to gossip. She was always sharing recipes, taking her kids to summer church-camps, developing new ways to get nasty stains out of carpeting, crocheting doilies, taking hot meals to shut-ins, writing a who's-doing-what-column for Ralph Grimley's Mountain Weekly, in which she used too many exclamation points. It never seemed to do any good to tell myself I had no right to judge her that way, to sum up her life so slickly, to assume I knew what was going on inside her. I wasn't a big enough person yet not to judge her.

She wore a cranberry rayon dress suit, a cream blouse that needed to be sharp white—or not white—so as not to drain the rest of the color from her already pale face. Her auburn hair was cut and sprayed into immobility. I watched her wheel out a metal table with that mysterious little silent recorder's typewriter on it. She didn't see me, so I shifted myself on the pew to make noise. She looked up but kept her surprise well-contained.

"Well, Mary. Hi. I hate how this wheel squeaks." You would have thought we were at the grocery store. She kept herself busy setting up her work station beneath the judge's bench. Which isn't a bench, so I don't know why they call it that. It's a pulpit, if you ask me. A little knoll of wood, in this case deeply stained valley oak.

"Hey, Mavis."

Her eyes flickered in my direction.

I said, "So how long will this take?"

Flicker. "Take?" she said.

"This—my appearance or whatever it is today. I've never done this before."

She had sat down and was feeding paper tape into her machine.

"Oh, it varies."

"I see."

I heard a blower kick on somewhere in a hidden chamber of the courthouse. The courtroom was muggy. Then a fighter jet roared down the canyon and over the courthouse, buffeting glass in the old windows. Mavis glanced at the trembling ceiling and sighed.

As the jet noise dissipated, Mavis said—still not looking at me—"You know, I'm not saying the dam should be built. I don't necessarily have all the facts. But you know—"

"Go ahead."

"Well, it's just that, you know, people do need the jobs."

I was exasperated, mainly because I thought she was talking about Wade Landers' crew, who were all imports and would be working somewhere else anyway even if the North Meredith dam weren't happening. I wasn't about to argue with her.

"I know," I said.

"It's just that Jerry has a chance to get on with them up there when they start pouring the concrete. You know, here it is almost July 4 and Jerry can't find—"

Her throat caught. Jerry was her husband. They had three kids and needed more than one income. She fiddled furiously with her machine and swallowed hard.

"He's been out of work since January." She finally looked at me. "We're broke, Mary"—it came in a startling rush, more startling because Mavis was the last person in the county from whom I'd expect such a venting, and she swiveled in the chair to face me—"Jinny the youngest had to get these braces, my dental doesn't cover her completely, and—"

She wept. After a stunned beat, I got up and went to her, kneeling down, patting her. She didn't want to hug me, but she leaned into me like a big dog, her stiff hair scratching my cheek, her perfume and makeup molassessy in the humid courtroom.

"Jesus, Mavis." Jesus/Mavis sounded odd to me. Mavis's eyes darkened briefly, I guess because I'd taken the Lord's name in vain. I said, "I don't want anyone out of work—except maybe the Reicher people themselves. If the dam's gotta go through, I hope Jerry does get on up there." What was I saying? Of course the dam was going to go through.

She nodded, sniffling. "I know. I'm not mad at you, Mary. But these other environmentalists—you know, most of them are on welfare."

She was expressing one of the most deeply held prejudices in the canyon, one that so far had not tainted me and Lloyd in our anti-dam quest—but only because we'd lived there so long.

The assumption of the prejudice was that people who looked out for Nature, so to speak, or wanted to slow down Development, so to speak, were usually outsiders or newcomers who didn't have to or didn't want to work for a living.

I remember feeling chastened or humbled—I don't know how ex-

actly to put it—by Mavis, her falling apart in the muggy July courtroom. She had her troubles, she had her rough life, I didn't know everything there was to know about her, I had been arrogant, God bless
the child who's got his own, *etc*. In some indirect way I'd hurt her. I
was sorry.

But I thought, "Yes. This is what the bastards do. They dangle the
promise of work in front of these hard-scrabble, well-meaning, vespers-
saying canyon people. Then they come with an outside crew, throw
out a handful of short-term jobs, build their dam, and get the hell out."
I kept this earnest little speech to myself, of course.

I sat there with her because she needed comfort for a minute, and
she had to go to work soon. She put herself back together and was
ready to go. By God, I liked her.

I'd gone into the courtroom with the idea that it would be the hotspot,
that my gesture for the river and Juanita would somehow be formally
recognized there. I'd seen too many Jimmy Stewart movies on TV. I'd
make my point, find my local stage, take a bow, bow out. That's what
I thought.

The courtroom filled up around Mavis and me. Mostly people I
knew, people from the crowd outside. The press took up positions in
the back. I glanced back once or twice and saw the reporters sizing up
the courtroom and the people, as if they were in Eastern Europe or
Tasmania, not in an American canyon.

The courtroom suddenly filled, and I was suddenly self-conscious—
the "orange pajamas in public" reflex. Mavis put her bland mask back
on and never looked at me again during the whole proceeding, except
when I spoke my words, and then she looked professionally at my talking lips. The officials were the last to take their places.

One of the younger deputies came in and stood like a soldier next
to Mavis. Acting bailiff.

Murmuring grew louder, the way it does in a classroom before the
teacher comes in.

The D.A. Miles Ward strode in and dropped his black briefcase on
the table opposite me. I'd forgotten how stout he was—so blocky that,
no matter what, his trousers always seemed tight. The tight trousers
that day were navy blue, part of a blue suit, white shirt, red tie com-
bination. Old Glory. I'd half-forgotten about the dirty-blonde mous-
tache, too. It made him look in-costume. He flicked a glance toward
me but would not smile. He wanted to seem tough but was clearly
nervous.

The man who had to be Reicher's corporate lawyer slipped in, sat down behind Ward. Silver hair, pinstripes. Thinly concealed disdain, most of it—I suspected—for Miles himself. He crossed his legs grandly and looked at his watch. Yawned discreetly.

Then came my lawyer, Tom Crimpton, dressed all wrong, perspiring. I hoped I didn't hear one of the press people in the back titter at him. But I think I did.

"Well, here we go!" poor Tom whispered, opening his battered briefcase. I smiled.

And then in a scene with some off-key echoes of High Noon, my unforsaken darlin' Bluestone strode brusquely through the doors, quieting the Big Murmur as he did so. He was in no rush, but he wasn't dogging it, either. He came up behind the table, nodded at Tom, took my hand, and helped me up.

"How are you?" he said in a stage whisper.

"Okay," I said, puzzled. "You?"

"Fine. Got him fingerprinted and jailed—the guy."

"Who is he?"

"Carl Kelly. Logger. Your new jailmate. We'll hang a canvas partition between your cells for privacy. Before evening, I hope. Things are crazy."

"There is only the one jail, isn't there?"

It was the kind of clipped conversation he and I often had, but here we were in public with everyone staring at us like we were toads in a terrarium. I was unnerved. Not Lloyd.

"Well," he said, "I love you," again in a "whisper" everyone could hear. He kissed me, quickly but full on the lips.

There was nervous chuckling. An old geezer of a courtroom-barnacle named Sid Nash, sitting in the back, cried, "Play ball!"

The room broke into laughter. Bluestone strode out coolly. It seemed as if all the heads in the room—including the D.A.'s—had turned to watch him. As the laughter died down, the young deputy shouted, "All rise!"

Me, I was already risen, playing ball. The judge strode in—and did a double-take when he realized everyone was looking not at him but back at the oak doors through which Bluestone had just vanished.

"You may be seated," the judge mumbled. And everyone turned around and was seated—except for me. Tom Crimpton had to nudge me. Still tasting Bluestone's kiss, I sat down and saw that some other hardened criminal had once carved in the oak table, "Jesus was guilty, too." I was surprised no one had sanded and varnished over the observation, but I was grateful for the distraction.

The judge cleared his throat. "Is the County ready?" he asked.

"Yes, your Honor," Miles Ward said, trying to take his voice down an octave in his role as Ready County.

"Mr. Crimpton?" the judge asked.

Poor Tom had been fiddling with the lock on his briefcase just then. The lid flew open. It was like an unfortunate magician's trick. Again the tittering. Miles Ward and the Reicher bigshot glanced at Tom and glanced at each other. Smug.

"We're ready, your Honor," Tom said, recovering. I put my hand on his forearm briefly. I leaned over and whispered, "Fuck 'em if they can't take a joke, Tom." He reddened, grinned thinly. I looked up, and the silver-haired judge was looking at me.

It was then I chose to remember that, depending on how one looked at it, the judge either owed me and Lloyd one, or the judge was perfectly positioned to exact one from us. Actually, it depended on how he, not "one," decided to look at it.

I saw that, looking at me, he may have been in the process of deciding.

Our eyes met for a gnat's-cough of a moment too long. Too long in the sense that each of us knew what the other probably was thinking. He glanced away, picked up his gavel, got out his glasses, put them on, glanced down, banged the gavel. His silver hair was magnificent.

"Proceed," he said. It did.

Eleven

One blizzardy January night in the High Sierra, a sheriff's deputy named Bluestone arrested a Superior Court judge named Peat.

To about the same extent Lloyd and I are, or consider ourselves to be, misfits, we consider Carstairs Peat to be a fit-well: wealthy, well-schooled, white, and Episcopalian. Not that Lloyd and I have a tough life or anything; the observation's not personal or envious. If anything, Carstairs Peat, because of, not in spite of, his alleged privilege, has had his problems. Privilege is privilege, but still the carom-shots can be hard to figure.

And he'd ended up in Claytonville, just like us, so how different was he from and us? And by definition, by residence in Claytonville, he was eccentric. The route to and reasons for his being here had been different from ours. That part is for sure.

The differences began in the late Thirties, when his father, William "Billy" Peat, a real-estate man from San Francisco, bought up mines and chunks of private land the National Forest and Southern Pacific Railroad had overlooked or, in the case of the railroad, unloaded. Bought them at Depression prices, too. He made a little money with the mines, sold them, then sold the raw land after WWII and made a bigger lot of money, which he turned over to smart brokers who—and so on.

The 1950s or early 1960s: William, wife, and young son Carstairs summered in Claytonville, living in a refurbished but still drafty white Victorian on a hill, three stories. They wintered in the Bay Area, where Carstairs went to private schools while his parents cruised to Portugal or Hong Kong; eccentric travelers, they preferred freighters.

Eventually Carstairs went to Stanford, then to Bolt (U. of California) law school. He was awkwardly tall, looked like an old-fashioned preppy from those black-and-white movies set at Hollywood's Stock Ivy League Campus—hair oil, striped sweaters, gangly gait, out-of-date slang.

Of course I couldn't have known him then, but I gather there was always something ineffectual about him. There were allergies, asthma, migraines. His parents and everyone else treated him like an expensive, well-groomed pet.

Growing up, he threw himself into learning how to fish, how to prospect for gold, how to drink whiskey, how to pretend to seduce tourist girls, how to work on vintage Ford coupes—all of that. He wasn't stupid, certainly; but he was strangely clumsy in both body and mind. Not just the usual clumsiness of youth—and I know I must tread humbly here, having been the clumsily deflowered Virgin of Willow Creek.

The sense I always got from hearing people rehearse their Carstairs-Peat stories is that watching him trying to be a mountain boy—trying to do or be anything, really—was like watching someone attempt a foreign language just by using a dictionary. Or, as one of my art-critic friends once said to me in Oakland as we stood in front of an overwrought iron sculpture, "All vocabulary, Mary—all vocabulary, and no idiom."

At Stanford, Carstairs squeaked by with C's, got into Bolt because of Dad. Meanwhile, Ma and Pa Peat got decorously potted on gin every day in their San Francisco apartment. They almost never came to the mountains anymore. Carstairs got his degree, failed the Bar exam two or three times, finally passed it, but could not get on with any good firms in San Francisco. So Dad got him in at the D.A.'s office down there, where he worked for three years, and then Dad pushed him to run for D.A. of Tamarack County. How desperate the Martini Set can be for heirs-apparent to succeed! Carstairs did as he was told, and he won—and hated the job. Why shouldn't he have hated it? All his choices had not been his choices.

He got elected Superior Court judge—there is only one in the county—and hated that. —Twice married to and divorced from strange, willowy women, themselves vaguely connected to money but also awkward in the world and about as suited to the Sierra Nevada as British royalty or Broadway stars might be.

All dressed up, nowhere to go, stuck in a place he just used to visit in the summer, trying then hearing cases about drunk driving or shooting pistols in the town limits or stealing beer from the grocery store: that was the adult life Carstairs found himself leading.

Why didn't he leave? He didn't exactly have Kennedy or Vanderbilt wealth, but he had honest-to-god money and could have bought a cottage by the sea somewhere and collected...collections. Who knows what haunted him sufficiently to make him stay, spiral into self-loathing, keep doing what his parents said—doing it far past the point at which he could easily have said no?

The Father Billy Peat died of a heart attack. Ma Peat died of cirrhosis. Carstairs followed them into gin alley, getting juiced at lunch, then during court recesses and all weekend, and then all week. He changed from a lean preppy to a big paunchy man with a puffy, ruddy face and early gray but thick, mane-like hair—a kind of boozy version of a central-casting TV judge: thus a parody of what Dad had always wanted him to be. Carstairs Peat, cartoon heir, wet brain. But it was his misfortune and none of our own. Until one snowy night.

Because he was a judge, because he was rich, because he was in an odd way a local boy, the sheriff, any sheriff, never arrested Carstairs when he drove over fire hydrants or threw canned goods at grocery-store clerks or cut down his neighbors' trees in a booze-fantasy property dispute. Carstairs was always known to "make amends." He'd come around when he was sober and apologize stiffly, dig out cash or put a little more money in the William "Billy" Peat Scholarship at Claytonville's tiny high school. He'd make nice and take himself through a rinse cycle. Then go get drunk alone in the white house on the hill and start it all over again. I guess that, in the modern parlance, the County enabled Carstairs.

That night that January he drove through a snowbank and munched a telephone pole.

Deputy Lloyd Bluestone came by in a sheriff's four-wheel-drive rig, stopped, saw if Carstairs was all right, saw he was, saw he was drunk, smelled gasoline, turned off the car so it wouldn't explode, got Carstairs out. Arrested him for driving while impaired and damaging public property while impaired.

Thinking about Tamarack County, past and present, I realize just how much liquor plays a role in so many tales. I don't know that we're that much different from other American counties in that way. American history itself is booze-saturated. This is just an observation, not a temperance-rant. I like to sip my Merlot in the evening, when I'm not in jail. Anyway, it's not all that easy to think of a troubled life in this county that wasn't troubled, in part, because of booze, which was certainly a main player in that summer I sat down on Bar Rock.

And in that winter, years ago. Now, the sheriff then, Dick Cooper, had never in so many words said not to arrest the Superior Court Judge of the county. It was one of those edicts that didn't need any words, let alone so many. Bluestone wasn't naïve. But there are times, I guess, when a young deputy decides to take society at its word, holding it to its own rules. This was one of those times.

Later that night Bluestone told me the judge didn't seem to grasp he was under arrest until Lloyd had got him all the way back to the courthouse and put an Army-surplus blanket around his shoulders and started to fingerprint him. Before that Carstairs just sat in the car staring at the blizzard like a lunatic, making garbled small-talk.

At the courthouse, Carstairs in his green Army-surplus cape cussed Lloyd, called him a fucking stupid Indian and vowed to get his job and told him he should be glad to have any job let alone working for the county and what right did any goddamned Indian have to tell him he was drunk since everyone knows Indians take one whiff o' the stuff and want to screw goats and kill each other and this and that and Carstairs topped it all off, so to speak, by barfing up a Prime Rib dinner on a chair and then taking a poke at Lloyd. It must have been a big, slow-motion, underwater roundhouse you could clock with a sundial. "Usually," I remember Lloyd saying, "drunks take a swing at you and then puke. It's kind of like Carstairs to get it backwards."

Generously, Lloyd did not book Carstairs Peat for trying to assault a deputy. He wiped the vomit off Carstairs' face and shirt with a cold, wet towel. He got him some water. He put him in a cell for the night, with a pail next to the cot.

One of the small county's taboos had been broken. You weren't supposed to arrest the judge. The sheriff sat Bluestone down and blistered him. Claytonville was abuzz and afizz. But the D.A. at the time, good old ruddy-cheeked Thom Matthews (quite a boozer himself, ironically), stood by Bluestone.

The thing is, it saved Carstairs Peat's life, that arrest.

Not that he had himself a religious conversion in the cell or anything. He got the DTs bad and had to be sent to a hospital in Reno—God works in unmysterious ways, in some cases.

And not that Lloyd saw himself as a life-saver. He just happened to be the deputy that night.

Carstairs, at any rate, got dried out, joined AA—in Reno, not in Tamarack County, where the second A would always be a lie. Toward Lloyd, he remained cool as a shady pool, never bringing up the arrest, hardly acknowledging Lloyd around the courthouse.

What was he thinking? We didn't know. It couldn't have been just embarrassment, for AA was all about getting over that—wasn't it? And if he'd met the demon drink head on—admitted his problem, as they say—then why would he have a problem with the guy who helped him to that point? We didn't know. We knew there was some resentment.

It was one of those times when Lloyd and I just had to call a halt to the figuring-out and look at each other and shrug and say, "Let's move on."

After District Attorney Miles Ward said The People would seek to convict me of felony trespassing; after the gallery rumbled and mumbled; after Tom Crimpton argued, sensibly, against the felony charge; after Tom unsuccessfully asked for a delay in the procession toward trial; after he and I whispered back and forth; after I rose with him and told Carstairs Peat and Claytonville that I intended to plead Not Guilty Your Honor—then I sat down and looked at Carstairs Peat, whose look softened: a slight shift in the light of the eyes.

Then I knew that, at bottom, whatever tangle of emotions he felt or didn't feel toward me and Lloyd, a thread of gratitude stretched back to that snowy night.

And Lord, as if I needed reminding, I was reminded again that almost every glance in Tamarack County has a history; the most casual of hellos at the Post Office can be connected to a mine cave-in distant decades ago.

The gratitude in the glance was something I would test sorely. Immediately.

After I entered my plea, Judge Peat said he wanted to see the D.A. and Tom Crimpton and me in his chambers. He declared a one-hour recess, a sly move since it meant hardly anyone would come back to the stuffy courtroom. The fun's over; go thee forth, citizens, implied Carstairs Peat, to gossip and eat and nap in the heat. Leave the law to the professionals and the accused.

Peat's office was cramped but orderly: Almost fussy—things in little cups and holders and shelves. He had some not-bad Western art in there (as in American West, not Donatello), a few framed photographs, and an odd print of a portrait of Judge Learned Hand—a name Bluestone says sounds downright Indian.

Tom Crimpton perspired, the D.A. was arrogant in a twitchy, stiff-bodied way, Judge Peat seem placidly perplexed.

Carstairs said, "Mary, if I may speak directly to you—feel free to jump in, Tom—I wonder if you could say more about why you're pleading Not Guilty."

"That's a fair question," I said.

"Are we off the record, Judge?" Tom asked.

"Yes," Carstairs said. "None of this may be used in my court of law." Miles Ward cleared his throat but didn't speak.

I said, "Basically, I guess I want the trial because it might publicize the opposition to the dam, and also I want to get something off my chest about Juanita."

"Juanita? Our Juanita?"

Our Juanita. I liked that. "Yes. Before I die, I'd just like it out there that they were wrong to lynch her."

"I think everybody already knows that," Carstairs said. He wasn't being argumentative.

"I know. This is just a gesture on my part. A one-time ritual."

He let the oxymoron pass. "And how do you intend to introduce Juanita into a trial concerning trespassing?"

Tom Crimpton looked almost lovingly at Judge Peat, as if to say, Now you know what I'm up against....

"I don't. But when anybody asks me about the dam, I'm going to bring up Juanita. Two outrages, different centuries. That sort of thing. A woman hanged over the river, a dam built across it."

The D.A. guffawed bitterly. He said, "Your Honor, I don't see—"

Carstairs put up a hand. "Hold on, Miles. I'll get to everyone in a moment." To me he said, "Well, it's poetic, I have to give you that, Mary. On the other hand, it's poetic—and not much else."

"I agree with you," I said. "I don't exactly feel effective."

He shrugged. To Tom, he said, "And Mr. Crimpton"—he was back to formal-talk now—"you're comfortable with taking the case to trial?"

"Yes." He didn't sound very convincing, but he didn't tell Carstairs yet that he wanted to dump me as a client.

"Mr. Ward," Carstairs said. "Talk a bit more about why you're pursuing a felony trespassing."

"Simply because what we allege Ms. Bluestone—I'm sorry, Herrera—to have done falls squarely under the statute."

"Simply?" Carstairs said.

"Yes, judge."

"It's Bluestone," I said—"my legal name. I just carve as Herrera." All three men ignored me.

"I suggest that you reconsider, Mr. Ward," said Carstairs. "Mary has no criminal record, and she is a well established, well respected citizen of the county. I don't see how the felony is entirely appropriate."

"From the people's point of view," Ward said, "it may deter others from protesting."

Carstairs shrugged. "If there are others, a felony is still an option for them."

"But there would be a precedent."

"New crime, new arrest, new arraignment," said Carstairs. "Not really a precedent. This isn't case-law." He smiled, and Ward smiled. Ward wasn't budging. All four of us knew that the people he was representing were the Reicher Corporation, not the County. With a felony conviction, Ward would look like he was being tough on crime, but he would actually be delivering Reicher an excuse to screw over the Board of Supervisors and seek payment for cost-over-runs. I guessed they had something set up in the contract, ready to be triggered. Ward didn't care whether he offended the Board or broke the county because he'd be off running for office from another district in California. He wasn't a native of Tamarack County, of course. With some Reicher money in his pocket, he could find a ripe state-office to pluck, probably one in the Central Valley that had a divisive environmental issue going.

"I suppose I could rule against the felony," Carstairs said.

"And I suppose I could go to the Grand Jury," Ward said. "The famous 'indict a ham sandwich.'"

Carstairs, I could tell, was about to argue with him, probably pursuing the line that more people in the county were friends of mine than of Ward's. But the Judge held back. I was glad, because once people get on a grand jury, I'm not sure how much friendship counts, so I didn't much go for that argument myself.

"Well, I encourage both parties to give some thought to their positions. Trials are expensive."

"Not as expensive as dams," Ward said.

Again Carstairs appeared to bite his tongue. I had to give Ward grudging credit. He did have *los cojones* to make such a hypocritical statement. He knew we knew what he was up to. I was calm for a moment, but then I heard myself say, "You're so full of shit. You're helping Reicher make the dam more expensive." Ward wouldn't look at me. He looked at Carstairs to see if he was going to do anything about me. Carstairs had to do something about me, of course, but he waited a few beats, smiling ever so subtly.

"Mary, please. This is informal, and we are in chambers, but it is a legal process. Some decorum, if you please."

"My apologies, Judge," I said. I was looking at him when I added, "I meant no offense."

"None taken," he said.

"I took offense. I take offense," Ward said.

"Noted," Carstairs said. "It's time for lunch. Mary," Judge Peat said, looking over a pair of reading glasses, "I think you've made your point. This, this act of civil disobedience—it is not undeserving of respect."

"It is a crime, not an act—" Miles Ward began, and then faltered—"a criminal act—the County maintains."

"Mr. Ward," said the judge; it wasn't quite a bark, but close. "These are my chambers. I will not be interrupted."

Ward reddened, Crimpton whitened. I stuck to the color that had brought me there.

"Mary," Judge Peat continued, "I think the D.A. and I could work something out here, despite his protestations. Fourth of July is coming up. Lloyd doesn't need any added distraction—he'll have plenty of tourists and... misfits to worry about." He had almost said "drunks."

I started to speak.

"No, now wait," he said. "Also, I don't cotton to wasting the court's time on a long felony trial. Ours is a poor county." He stared at Miles Ward, looked back at me. "Tom, Mary, think about a plea. A plea of guilty to a misdemeanor. I think everybody would feel pretty good about that."

I was surprised that Miles Ward didn't say anything.

Tom spoke up. "As Mary's counsel, I would strongly urge her to accept the advice which the Court has given." Tom nearly broke his leg tripping over that stump of rhetoric.

It was hot in there. The men were sweating. They all seemed to lean toward me. If we'd all been eight years old on a playground, they would have pinned me to the dirt and made me say I ate snakes, I think.

Carstairs looked at his watch. "What else surprises me is that Tom didn't get you bailed out yesterday."

"I stopped by your office," Tom said. "They told me you weren't available for a rush-bail-hearing." Poor Carstairs, I thought. The only superior court judge in the county. So many hats.

"I'm always available when locals are involved. Well, some locals are more equal than others." He smiled. He looked at me. I looked away, thinking of the night Lloyd had arrested him. It struck me, suddenly, that the longtime sober Carstairs was a terribly sweet man, and I was so sorry that a chill persisted between Lloyd and him, and that Lloyd and I hadn't gotten to know him better over these years.

Carstairs continued. "At any rate, bail can be the absolute minimum, as far as I'm concerned, and as long as you give me your word you won't go back up to the dam. Essentially, Mary, you'll be on your own recognizance."

"That's all right, Judge," I said. "I'm not interested in bail right now. I'll remain in jail."

He laughed. He thought I was joking. He realized I wasn't. "Indefinitely?"

"I think so. Yes," I said.

"But Lloyd may need all those cells during the Fourth." I don't think Carstairs even knew yet about the logger who'd try to throttle me. There was exactly one empty cell left in the courthouse. I suddenly realized I'd probably have a room-mate soon. I hoped for a she.

"I know," I said.

The men, all three, looked at me. As if they did not know me. As if they had never laid eyes on me before.

Carstairs sighed pleasantly, as if to say It's your funeral. What he said was, "I really must get a bite to eat. Enjoy the afternoon, all of you. I don't think there's a need at this point to reconvene. I'll have the bailiff inform the court."

We all got out of the judge's chambers. Back in the empty court-room, Tom said, "Mary, you know how much I like you and Lloyd. But I think you need to look around for another lawyer. This is a bit much for me." He face was flushed, partly from anger, partly from heat. He had a right to be angry. I put a hand on his shoulder.

"I understand, Tom. And I didn't mean to make things tough for you. But I guess actions have consequences."

"Yes, they do."

"You're a good man. Send us a bill."

"Thanks. But I'm not not your lawyer yet. And it isn't about the money."

I laughed. He laughed. "I know. It's not about the money. Except maybe for Reicher."

"And the Board of Supervisors. And Ward," he added.

"If it was just about the money, I don't know how many of us would have stuck it out here in the canyon," I said.

"I hear you," he said, rolling a shoulder inside what had become a vintage jacket. Andee Munro came through the oak doors, ready to take me back to jail. "If you change your mind about bail—," Tom added.

"—Thanks. Go get some lunch," I said.

Twelve

… "You cunt! You goddamned cunt!"

I was back in my cell, and my jailmate was screaming—a lacerating, raspy howl. "Bitch! Fucking bitch!"

I froze, wanting to pretend he was just having a bad dream. I heard him get up. "Hey!" he screamed. I thought: I will not look. I will not look at him. Thought: What is it with this Cuntspeak all of a sudden?—the canyon filled with it. First the dam-foreman, now the logger.

"You hear me, lady?!"

I got mad, and I got up. Enough of this shit, I thought. What have I ever done to him?! The steel bars reinforced my bravery, especially since one empty cell made a space and made for more bars between us, although no one had put up the privacy partition, also known as a piece of cloth, yet.

I walked to the far side of my cell, clutched the bars, stared at him; he clutched his bars. Primates in a zoo.

"My name," I said, "is not cunt or bitch or you. My name is Mary. What is your name?" The acoustics off the concrete blocks were good.

"Oh, just fuck you, lady."

"Now stop that. I'm a person. My name is Mary. Look at me. Don't call me cunt again—ever. My name is Mary. What is your name?"

"What the fuck you want to know for?"

"It's Carl, isn't it? Carl Kelly?"

"Yeah," he said. "So fucking what?" Fuck was a good thirty per cent of his vocabulary.

"So I'll call you Carl. You call me Mary, okay? We got off to a bad start on the steps."

"Goddamn sheriff cheap-shotted me. Sucker punch."

"He was worried you were going to hurt me—or the deputy. Were you going to hurt me, Carl?"

This proved to be a tough question for him.

"I was drunk," he said. Well, then, I thought, why didn't you say

86

so?—all's forgiven.

"You're out of work, huh?"

"Goddamned fucking right I'm out of work. No goddamned trees to cut." He belched bitterly, involuntarily. He looked awful, gray around the mouth, dehydrated. "I feel like shit," he said. "I'd gawdamn kill somebody for a beer right now." He paused. "So, Mary, what exactly did you do up there?"

"At the dam? Nothing. Just chained myself to a boulder. Got in their way for, oh, five minutes or so."

"They threw you in jail for that? Shit. Where's a cop when you really need one, huh?"

There we were, just two cons commiserating about the System. A regular Alcatraz. Machine Gun Kelly and Wood Chisel Mary.

"Well, when I need a cop, I talk to my husband. The sheriff."

"No."

I shrugged.

"Shit. Well, no wonder." I supposed he meant *No wonder the sheriff got on him so fast.* He laughed. "Fuck...me," he sang to himself. "I'm fucked. I'm really fucked. I go and try to belt a sheriff's wife."

"Fuck," I said. "Fuck, fuck, fuck."

He laughed. "And you tried to choke me," I said, "not belt me."

"I'm sorry," he mumbled.

"Apology accepted."

For the moment, I felt as if I'd unhooked the wires inside a homemade bomb called Carl Kelly. I was pondering this when a pain in his guts—or so I surmised—doubled him over, and he lay down. He looked like he was suddenly sweating inordinately. He cried out in pain. I started yelling for a deputy. What came through the door was a sheriff, a husband—a cop when you needed one.

With a toothpick tucked in a corner of his mouth, Bluestone looked his old laconic self, except perturbed. "Now what?" his eyes said. I pointed and said, "He's hurting."

Lloyd glanced and departed, returning with Andee, latex gloves, and a gizmo for giving CPR the hygienic way. Unhurriedly, he told Andee to stand at an angle and hold her pistol on Kelly from outside the cell. He unlocked the cell, went in, sized up Kelly, who was moaning. Bluestone felt for a pulse at the neck and glanced around the cell—looking, I guess, for some instrument of self-torture somehow not found in a body search.

"We were talking, and all of a sudden he doubled over," I reported. Neither Andee nor Lloyd bothered to look at me. "I don't think he's faking it." Routine procedure, I gathered, called for their not believing a word from any jailmate, whether you've plighted your troth to her or not.

I sat back down on my cot. Andee pulled her gun and calmly aimed it at Carl as Lloyd opened his cell and went in. He cautiously approached Carl and checked around for a weapon, keeping out of Andee's line of sight and fire.

"What's going on, Carl?" Lloyd said.

"My guts," Carl said. "Bad ulcers."

"Okay," Lloyd said. "I'm sorry, but I need to handcuff you."

"I know. In front, maybe?"

"I think so." Carl put out his hands, and Lloyd put the cuffs on.

Finally they got a stretcher for Carl and hauled him out. I saw there was blood in his spittle as they took him past my cell. When the door to the miniature cell block shut and everyone was gone, I felt indescribably alone.

Okay, describably. My heart went out to Carl but came back into itself. Carl's rumpled cot looked sad, called up a feeling of shabbiness in myself I've never been able to exterminate, even on days when I really seem to have gotten the better of life.

That day wasn't one of those days—not just because it was so strange but because a thick listlessness overtook me. I lay on the cot looking up at the cracked, cob-webbed ceiling and confronting the fact—it seemed a fact then—that Lloyd and I really had no friends. Well, friends, maybe—but not the kind of soul-mates I imagined most other people had. Not many people stuck it out in the canyon for as long as we'd stuck it out, so we'd seen some good people come and go. Also, for the first time ever, that thing Lloyd and I took so much pride in—our self-sufficiency—seemed barren to me, a kind of joke. I thought again of Carstairs Peat, a nice man I should have known better. I prayed for Carl Kelly.

My mind spun off in crazy loops.

For instance, though in my head I knew the Fourth of July week-end was coming up, I'd kept thinking of it only as later, forever later. When I realized the obvious, I panicked. That weekend always over-whelmed the sheriff's office. The worst. Drunks, fights, hiking-calamities, dirt-bike pile-ups, mountain-bikes going over cliffs. The canyon choked with tourists. Fire danger as high as it would be all year, with the charming addition of contraband fireworks.

I'd heaped my protest on top of Lloyd's worst seventy-two hours of the year. I felt ashamed.

I learned later I was having something called an "anxiety attack". News to me.

I got cold sweats and huffed and puffed as if I'd run a mile. I sat up and got dizzy. My chest hurt. I stood up and considered puking in the steel toilet. Nothing happened. I sat down and crouched against the bars, couldn't decide whether I wanted to yell for help, weep, or never see anyone again ever. So I just kept sitting, my stomach a county-sized pit.

I had no name for what I felt besides terror; or, was so terrorized I didn't think to name it. How long I sat there I don't know. When you fall into panic you fall out of Time. I know when Lloyd came in, I felt no relief. The strange, fearful look he gave me only scared me more. I couldn't speak. I wanted to die—no that's not true—I wanted someone to shoot me with a tranquilizer dart.

The floor of that cell in our little Podunk mountain town seemed like the place the universe had selected for its drain—and everything was draining out there now, taking me with it, down the pipes, through Bluestone's beloved diorite strata, filtering out of clay banks and washed gravel into the North Meredith river, where one or two of Juanita's atoms, housed in moss, might greet me: "*Que tal, hermana?!*"

And Bluestone said, "What's wrong, honey?"

After helping to load Carl Kelly into Claytonville's one ambulance, Lloyd had returned—just to check on me, it seems.

"I feel like shit, that's what's wrong." My way of dealing with the panic seemed to be to complain. "I'm scared and tired and sweaty. I hate your jail and I want to burn this orange jump suit. Why can't I have a book to read? Why isn't there a TV in here? Even guys on Death Row watch TV."

The "I's" I was uttering began to hurt even my ears—cheap lids of Ego's tin pots banging together. I was shouting to keep up—or to find some of—my courage.

My husband raised his eyebrows—slowly, as if they were operated by a pulley-system. He spoke calmly. "You can have a book. You can't have TV because the Board outlawed it two years ago. That crackdown on crime. Remember? Said we were too soft on hard criminals. Like yourself."

"Was that the same year they froze your budget?"

"Mmmmn—all part of the same crackdown. All of a piece."

He looked not good. I'd seen him less tired after he'd spent twelve hours in the woods looking for a lost hiker. He sat down outside my cell, leaned back against the concrete blocks. I knew what his body would smell like if he were just coming home and I'd set down the chisel to hug him—briny, with a dash, faint, of cinnamon or nutmeg. Ah, the particular odors of our lovers. In this case the only lover, incredibly as it may seem, I'd ever had.

It was hard for me to believe my Bluestone was getting significantly middle-aged, but there they were, those determined creases in his face, deepened by fatigue the way seasons of heavy rain deepen ravines. My head was against the bars shared with the middle cell.

We talked to each other, Lloyd and I, but did so without moving our heads or looking at each other.

"Everybody wants to see you," he said.

"Every-who-body?"

"Oh, like Sybil and her Buffalo Gals. A guy from Earthlife or River Rescue or River Life or one of those groups. He had a pony tail, a pocket pager, a laptop, and a cell-phone."

"A well-armed environmentalist."

"Yep. Reporters, too."

"So why didn't they see me?"

"I didn't let 'em. I thought you'd like some time alone. Plus the whole Carl Kelly thing."

"Isn't that my decision?" I didn't raise my head or my voice.

"No. It's mine. You're in jail, you goof-ball, not summer-camp. I told them all to come back tomorrow and take a number."

"Are you in trouble?"

"What do you mean?"

"Miles Ward. The Grand Jury."

"I guess. I just want to get through the Fourth."

"I picked a helluva weekend."

No response.

"Maybe I'll just take the bail and get out of here, Lloyd. Carstairs wants me to get out. And I've had it."

"Had what?"

"I don't know. All the fun I'm going to have, and I haven't had any. It all seems stupider by the minute."

He shifted his weight and looked at me—I could feel him doing it. He said, "It seems to be working. I mean, what do you want? People are stirred up. Oh—I almost forgot—word is a bunch of loggers are coming to guard the dam site up there. Actually, truckers. Logging trucks."

"What do you mean—guard?"

He shrugged. "A deputy picked it up on the CB. Said they're coming in from all over, even a couple from Oregon, going to park their trucks up there, stand guard. So they say."

"Guard against what?"

"The likes of you, of course. So see what you've started? Be glad! It's becoming an event."

"What's the dam have to do with logging?"

"What's Juanita got to do with the dam?"

"Good question, and screw you," I said.

My question to him about the dam and logging had been rhetorical. I knew that in the minds of Western loggers under seige, as they felt themselves to be, one environmental protest was the same as another, all part of The Threat. Meanwhile, Weyerhaueser and Georgia Pacific continued to "diversify," to shut down "unprofitable sectors," to "consolidate divisions" and "down-size," tip-toeing quietly away from the fight between tree cutters and tree lovers, moving on to greener profits, leaving labor standing there. I'll stop now before I break into a verse from "Joe Hill."

I heard Big Lloyd shrug, or imagined so. I looked up. He continued. "And you've flushed everybody out. Reicher, Miles Ward. They're exposed."

"So are you, my dear."

A jet, maybe it was two this time, cracked the canyon's serenity once more

"God *damn* those planes! What is it this summer?!" I got up and looked for something to kick, but everything was steel or concrete.

"It happens every year," Lloyd said, using a fatherly voice that bothered me no end. "Gabe called from Reno. Said the big air show's back on for this year. They're practicing, that's all. You just notice it more 'cause you're not up home, lost in woodcarving."

"Practicing? Jets, practicing? Give me a break!"

"Well," he said, and got up, "we are at war."

"We're always at war."

"I'm sure as hell not going to top off my day by arguing with you. Sleep well."

"Goddamn it, get back here."

"What?" he said flatly, and turned around.

"What are you so snotty for?"

He stared. "Well, if I'm snotty like you say, maybe it's from all the pressures of a new millenium, or maybe it's from having roots in a noble, primitive society that was the victim of genocide. It could even be intestinal gas."

"Or maybe it's having roots in primitive intestinal gas," I said.

He bowed at the waist. He did it with a smile. We were old warriors. I sat on the cot and gathered myself to apologize. "I really didn't realize this thing would slop over into the July Fourth weekend, Lloyd. Honest."

"Mary."

"What?"

"Bullshit! For twenty years or more you've been talking about Juanita getting lynched on the Fourth of July."

"I have? I have. That doesn't mean I scripted all this. Whose side are you on?"

"Nobody's. The sheriff's. You didn't have to script it. It's in your damn brain somewhere. You were going to do this. We'll ride it out, wherever it goes."

"I love you. I do!"

He moved toward the bars, determined, like a raccoon heading toward a creek to look for a meal.

I got up and met him at the bars. We kissed modestly. There was something metallic but not unpleasant about the taste of the kiss. It reminded me of our very first kisses. "I need something," I said.

He backed off warily, still inhabited by cautious raccoon-spirit, obviously thinking about the erotics of my first night in the slammer. "Not that," I said. "What I need is a shower—and that book you promised."

"I'll get Andee on it. We have quite an extensive library. Oh, and your new lawyer's coming in the morning."

"But Tom said—"

"It's not about Tom. It's the Ol' Buffalo Mama—"

"Sybil Burns?"

"Yep. She hired her—the new lawyer. From Sacramento. Sybil says she works for a big law firm that she—Sybil—keeps on retainer. Are you with me so far?"

"So you've talked to Sybil?"

"Yeah, I told her it was okay with me, except her paying made me nervous and I said we'd work that out. But hell, Tom doesn't want to be our lawyer no more."

"He talked to you, too? And it's anymore—doesn't want to be our lawyer anymore."

He rolled his eyes.

I said, "—and why didn't you discuss this with me?!"

No response.

"I'm just real busy, Mary. Things are crazy. New Fiscal Year. The Fourth. I'll send Andee in so you can get your shower. I'm going home to clean up. Then I'm going to the Jazz Society."

He left.

Sturdy Andee Munro came to fetch me, carrying a paper bag of "things," cotton panties and such. Whatever fatigue Lloyd exhibited was going around the sheriff's office, a little plague. Weariness lapped at Andee like small waves around a dock piling.

"Couldn't I just have one small piece of wood and a carving knife?" I asked, as we walked the little road that curled around behind the court-house and led down to where prisoners showered. She let go with a belly-laugh.

"That's the first time I've had a prisoner come right out and ask me for a knife," she said. "Thing is, if it were up to me, I'd give it to you."

A breeze puffed up through the canyon. We both felt it.

"Oh, I hope there are no fires this year," I said. "Is that too much to hope for?"

"Prob'ly. I hope we can find fireworks before they set 'em off. That is too much to hope for."

Andee had that slow, ambling walk all cops, it seems, adopt, except with her it was cute somehow. She was big but delicate, young but oh so serious.

"So how's my husband?"

"We're all kinda worried about him. He's even quieter than usual. You know, the department used up a lot of overtime this spring, so, you know, over the Fourth, Lloyd's decided to work double-shifts himself."

It pained me a little to get this news from Andee, not Lloyd. I doubted whether she was so crafty that she was trying to make me feel guilty. But there the guilt sat, a lump of wet dough in my gut.

The showers in the outbuildings—down in a little hollow below the county courthouse—were those old rusty but unbreakable metal stalls—pre-fiberglass, pre-plastic, prehistoric in a way. The plastic curtain was mildewed. The shower head was misnamed; water came out in a torrent, and water must have come from one of the old springs close to a mine tunnel: something part sulphuric, part metallic filled my nostrils. Blood of the ghost-miners. Ghost of that mercury used to amalgamate gold-dust.

Tainted by long-ago mining though it may have been, the water was hot. I scrubbed me and my anxiety twice, let that bad, beleaguered water beat on my neck and shoulders. Andee bent the rules, letting me indulge. She sat on a bench outside the stall, reading an old *Reader's Digest*—at least that was what she was doing when I stripped and climbed in the stall.

After I shut down the torrent and stepped out to towel off, I saw Andee had fallen asleep. An endearingly deep sleep, mouth open, nose making noises that were not yet a snore.

It was one of those moments when I knew that even if I'd been the best carver the world had ever seen, I couldn't have represented what I saw. I'd have needed to be a—painter, a great painter and an earthy one, a Breughel, a Vermeer, let's say—to capture this large, sweet earthy woman asleep in eery light, wearing her law-enforcement get-up, a *Reader's Digest* open on one ample thigh.

The History of the Visible Canyon, I thought, consisted of explorers like Mr. Meredith and Colonel Clayton; miners and mining companies; a line of gray-headed county supervisors stretching back toward Gold Rush days; and so on. The History of the Invisible Canyon included the small native tribes who lived on fish and blanched, detoxified acorn-flour and hardly left a whisper in their wake; it consisted of women like Andee, who deserved better but did all right. Staring at Andee, I thought, "She deserves better," although I didn't exactly know what I meant, what her betterment might look like.

I fished out clean things from the bag she'd brought along, put them on. She woke up—a little embarrassed. And we walked back to the courthouse, the canyon dimming in twilight. Bats flapped against an odd shade of blue. A breeze massaged the manzanita heat.

"This Jazz Society that Lloyd goes to—what is it?" Andee asked.

She had the look I'd seen on so many faces in the canyon when minds the faces belonged to were bumping up against the fact they'd known Lloyd for a long time and didn't know him at all.

"Well, he and three or four other guys—most of them from up in Tamarack—started it ten years ago. They meet in the town hall in Tamarack, listen to records. CD's, now, I guess. iPods."

"Listen to records? That's it?"

"Yes and no. They listen to records and talk about jazz. Sometimes they have a meal and a couple drinks, Diet Squirt for Lloyd. There are no dues and no officers. I have no idea how people join or leave. I think they're up to around ten members now. At the moment, Lloyd's obsessed with Neil Hefti and Duke Ellington. And the big Agenda Item is whether to invest in a new sound-system. That argument should carry them through the year twenty-fifty.

"You ever gone?"

"Oh, no. The more mysterious it is, the better—the better for Lloyd, I mean. I guess it's like Masons or Elks or The Order of the Secret Hand-Signal, or whatever men belong to."

Andee was only more bewildered. We were near one outer wall of the jail. I looked up at my cell-window, felt a terrible regret.

"But," Andee said, "how do you know...."

"...that they're actually doing what they say they're doing? Well, it's too weird to make up. Plus sometimes the other wives call and chat with me and say they've peeked in at them."

"So it's no women allowed?"

"No—I know Lannie Cheever was a member for a while, before she sold the bar and left. It was Lannie who brought in one of the rare guest speakers."

"Who?"

"Can't remember his name—he'd played clarinet in Buddy Rich's band once. Somehow Lannie knew him and knew he'd be in Reno with some casino band, so she had him come over. The boys were thrilled. Must have been the weirdest night of that guy's life."

"Lloyd and jazz," Andee mused. "Lloyd and jazz."

"Yep, the Tamarack Jazz Society."

We rounded the corner of the building. Andee's posture got more official. I didn't pay much attention to the figure on the courthouse steps until we were close enough to make out the face.

Gabriel Bluestone. Rare Gabriel, my only child! —Sitting on the steps, as quietly as the steps. He had his father's ability to go into an eery motionlessness, like a deer who suspects something wrong in the wind.

It was like Gabrielito not to call out.

But when I knew it was him, I made him pay. I ran up to him, calling out, grabbed him, made him stand up, and kissed him, hugged him, rubbed his hair.

"God, Mom, get off me."

Andee laughed.

Me in prison clothes and wet-haired disturbed him. Not the way Moms are supposed to look. He looked afraid and embarrassed for me both at once.

Gabriel, college-aged in the canyon's twilight, so strangely mine and not mine. So handsomely strange and familiar, my child.

His showing up was to change everything—or rather to mark how everything changed—as did the arrival of The Lawyer. Maybe I sensed as much—then and there, at dusk, as Juanita's spirit seemed to hover in the air, deft and menacing, like a hawk.

Thirteen

The shock of the scene with Carl Kelly and the soothing arrival of Gabriel seemed to cancel each other out, at least so far as getting some sleep was concerned. I made it to morning anyway. In the meantime, it seems Lloyd had turned himself into a human dam that held back a stream of people who wanted at me—wanted to get me on video, or audio—or just get to me. From this distance of time, why they wanted at me seems understandable. I was the center of gossip, broadly defined.

I greeted my first visitor around 8 in the morning—and that would have been a Thursday, I believe, the second of July.

And that would have been a half hour after waking, going to the steel toilet, washing in the steel sink, and wondering why the steel hell Lloyd had selected *The Guns of August* by Barbara Tuchman, whose last name I pronounced at the time, I am embarrassed to say, "Touchman," as the book to have a deputy leave on my cot the night before—and on that night before I had butted my eyesight against a few pages of the first chapter, where an Edward gets buried (after dying: no news there), and a Germany feels encircled, and a Mary Herrera nods off, drooling on the county's mattress.

My visitor wasn't a visitor. It—he—was Ed Porter, a gentle, decent, short, hard-of-hearing former deputy—whom Lloyd Bluestone had, it seemed, made a current and temporary deputy deployed to chaperone my visits with visitors.

A decade earlier, something had happened to Ed Porter every cop fears almost as much as death itself: A big drunk had taken his weapon away. The incident turned out all right—nobody got shot—but it changed Ed, permanently. He resigned. No one could talk him out of it. He withdrew into retirement like a reptile into dormancy, retreating into vegetable gardening and placid hearing-loss.

Lately Lloyd had taken to hiring Ed for non-combative law-enforcement errands: Giving talks to the PTA, riding in an ambulance, sitting in the jailhouse while lawyers talked to prisoners. Deputy Emeritus. It was a practical move in a short-handed sheriff's office. It was also good for Ed Porter's soul. And his pocket-book.

Maybe the Sphinx had more worldwide fame than Ed, but not more composure: Ed's nervous system had processed his career-ending "failure" into a Buddha-like distance from all things ambitious. Emeritus status seemed to have helped the process along.

I doubt Ed Porter's peace had passed all understanding; indeed, maybe it was just that his hearing aid malfunctioned all the time; anyway, he possessed enviable serenity. "Poor Ed" you sometimes still caught people saying in the post office or the bar, but they were talking about the incident and their own secret fears of humiliation and failure—they weren't really talking about Ed Porter, who'd moved on.

So there was "poor Ed"—sitting in a freshly pressed uniform topped off by a freshly buzzed gray crew-cut—when my brand-new lawyer and my brand-new longtime friend, Sybil Burns, just about ran me over with support. They burst in around nine. Ed fetched chairs for them, returned to his perch.

Sybil's skin looked particularly tanned and lotioned; she wore pre-faded bluejeans, a western belt with turquoise ornamentation, cowgirl boots with silver toe-guards, a teal-green oversized blouse, dangly-bangly silver earrings. Oh my goodness she was full of energy—the kind people get when they pass through therapy too fast and come out having "gotten themselves together" in such a togetherly way their headlights are always on high-beam. She and Ed made for quite the little contrast. Mrs. Liberace versus Father Theresa.

I was glad my lawyer, who I didn't yet know (but suspected) was my lawyer, was so—how to phrase this?—hard-assed: solicitous toward Sybil Burns, but thinly so; otherwise both focused and bored: the way predators of the forest fuse those qualities. She didn't look at me as her prey, but she did seem to look through me at her prey, which seemed to be everyone else in the county—including my former lawyer, Tom.

Name: Laura Klein. She worked for one of those law firms with a string of names—like Candlewax, Horsehair, Rickshaw, and Grime. It was a Sacramento firm—not LA or San Francisco—but in a way, as I was to learn, it was more powerful for being low-profile.

Laura Klein had the kind of well-put-together face that stays that way even when the hips start accruing interest. She had the kind of thick, honey-blond hair men take for granted and women envy.

But the skin of the face covering the marvelous bones was ashen, anemic. Fingertips of the right hand were stained orange. A serious smoker. The hair had seemingly suffered through many style changes, maybe even some ill-advised frosting. ("Hair is not cake," my mother once asserted.) Laura Klein's body was playing second fiddle to Laura Klein's drive to survive. Career.

The fact I worked up a cheap psychoanalysis of her before we'd exchanged the simplest words told me a collision between us was unavoidable. She checked me out, too—in her predatory half-bored, half-intense way. Sybil prattled on. Ed Porter had opened folding chairs like origami flowers.

"As I gather you know," said Laura Klein, after preliminaries, "the arrangement is unorthodox in that Sybil is actually retaining my firm—me—to represent you. I want to make sure you are aware of the arrangement and agree to it—in writing."

"Do I have a choice?"

"Yes. You may refuse to be represented by me and ask Judge Peat to appoint a lawyer for you. Tom Crimpton has met with Judge Peat and written him a follow-up letter indicating he has ceased to represent you."

"Oh," I said.

In this mode the woman talked in paragraphs, and with a firm, almost-too-loud delivery. Sybil's face went a little slack. This wasn't quite the female-bonding experience she'd had in mind. I was being my mulish self. Laura Klein had no problem letting the mule know who was wagon-master.

"You're my lawyer," I said, getting in harness.

A smile appeared on Laura Klein's face for less than one second: the time it took for her eyes to look down at her legal pad and look up at Sybil.

"Sybil, give her a dollar, free and clear."

Sybil fished cash out of her jeans, pealed off a one, handed it through the bars. Ed watched.

Laura asked her, "Is that dollar Mary's?"

Sybil: "Yes."

Laura, to me: "Mary, if you wish to retain me, say so. My initial fee is one dollar."

"But I thought Sybil—"

"Your paying me a dollar makes me your lawyer. The firm is in a financial arrangement with Sybil that does not impinge upon your legal relationship with me and the firm."

I gave her the buck. I can't remember where she stowed it.

"Fine. We have a lot of work to do. The only thing not disastrous about the so-called hearing was your not-guilty plea. Thank God for small favors."

I shrugged. "Well, it all seemed routine. I was charged. I plead. Pleaded? I refused bail. Tom did all he could."

"I'm sure he did," she said, "I don't doubt that. He should've asked for a delay, raked the prosecution over the coals with regard to evidence and the felony charge, and entered several motions—including one for dismissal of charges and, failing that, one for a change of venue and one other for Judge Peat to recuse himself."

Wow. I felt like Dorothy over Topeka, with vertigo and the ruby-red hiking boots of a mountain sheriff's wife. Laura's fierce competence scared me more than Tom Crimpton's well known limitations.

Effortlessly, Laura shooed Madame Burns away. She gave her a legal errand that sounded plausible—looking up the number of times felony trespassing had been prosecuted in the county, and why, and how effectively. After Sybil disappeared, Laura turned to Ed Porter. "Is it absolutely necessary for you to be here?"

It took a while for the sentence to percolate through Ed's hearing aid, during which time he cocked his head like a robin listening for earthworms. "Oh, no," he said. "It's not absolutely necessary. But it's sort of how we do it here." He sat back then, a Buddha-glaze coming over his eyes. Laura Klein rolled her eyes for my benefit.

"There's usually a practical madness to my husband's methods," I advised her. "Ed is the perfect jailhouse guard." I winked at him.

"Whatever," Laura said, letting her glance lie on me a couple extra beats—sizing me up—different from checking me out, believe it or not. "I'm gonna give you some tasks," she said.

"Okay?"

She handed me a fresh legal pad and a pencil.

Ed Porter noticed. "Is that absolutely necessary?" he deadpanned. Laura was not amused. From that point on, I had trouble concentrating on what Laura said. In my greedy little mitts, I had charcoal and paper. All I could think about was sketching ideas for carvings. The law could go hang itself, so to speak.

"First, I want you to write down everything you remember about the day you went up to the dam site. Nothing—I repeat—nothing is too trivial. I don't care how many pages it is."

"Okay."

She started nibbling at her upper lip with her lower teeth. Smoker's nerves. I had a feeling we'd soon be wrapping up our business. The nicotine clock.

"Next, I want you to write a statement. For the public."

"The public? What public?"

"The public," she said. "Irritably," I believe, would be the word to go with it. "Either you or I are going to read it on the courthouse steps out here—to the newshounds and all. The timing is right. The *Cutting Edge* people are here."

"Who?"

"*Cutting Edge.* The tabloid show. Syndicated—produced out of San Francisco? They'll be interviewing you shortly."

"What should the statement state?"

"It should state nothing about what you did or did not do up at the site. That's all for the courtroom. Instead, it should say why protest in general was necessary. It should state your beliefs—about the river. The environment, yadda-yadda. One page, max. I will edit."

"My beliefs. One page. Max. Gotcha."

"Don't leave your husband out of the account you write," she said. "As far as we're concerned, he's the arresting officer."

"No, he's my arresting husband. And all he did was what he had to do—arrest me."

She didn't like back-talk, not one bit. "Look, you just hired me to represent you. I know only one way to do that. Full-bore. I agree your husband's in deep shit, but that's another matter. It's your case I'm working on."

"My case is his case."

"In the sense that he arrested you, and in the sense that he can't be compelled to testify against you."

"No—more than that. I want you to look out for him, too. If Sybil won't pay you to do that, I will."

"You can't afford me."

"You don't know that."

"You can't afford me, I do know that, and it's a conflict of interest, anyway."

I laughed a mean laugh. "Oh, what horse shit. Lloyd's interests and mine do not conflict."

"Legally, in fact, they do."

"Fuck the law."

"Most lawyers do."

I flung the legal pad and the pencil against the back wall and walked away from her. Ed Porter rustled and rearranged himself.

Laura said, "Feel better?"

"Just go."

"I'm gone. I don't much care who you're mad at, as long as you're mad—"

"'Whom,'" Ed muttered, out of the blue. "'Whom you're mad at'"

"—As long as you're mad at something," Laura finished. "And besides, when I get through with the D.A., he probably wouldn't be able to identify your husband in a lineup." She said this gathering up her stuff and coughing a cigarette cough. I turned around.

"I'll see you," I said.

"You bet you will. And do your homework."

"Do you smoke?" she asked, fishing a cigarette out. Camels. Filtered.

"No. But thanks for asking."

"Outside," Ed muttered.

Laura put the lighter and the cigarette in her left hand. With her right hand she scuffed Ed Porter's gray crewcut. Ed Porter was mortified: the Buddha of Tamarack County blushed! My lawyer left. I picked up the pad and pencil.

As instructed, I wrote up the account of my crime—an account my lawyer would presumably use to acquit me of the crime. What a country. I committed a sin of omission by not mentioning my erstwhile locksmith accomplice, Rupert Williams.

I took a half-hearted stab at the "Statement for the Public" but soon turned to sketching plans for woodcarvings; pencil sketches on yellow legal paper carpeted the jail-cell floor.

Sometime after lunch, Ed Porter came back, and a jailhouse parade materialized.

Headstones in overgrown graveyards of California's gold country feature more Italian and Sicilian names than you might imagine, assuming your imagination has even visited these mountains. —Family names like Costa, Lavaroni, Giumara, Figone, Distafano, Tannura, Zerga, Luchessi. Some came from burnt hills of Italy because they had heard of burnt hills of California. They came to mine, to farm, to ranch; to work in trades—precise carpentry, artful smithing. For a few Prohibited years, some bootlegged wine.

And so I give you Myrna Lovetti.

She came from the Carbone family, and they pronounced the long 'e'; it rhymed with baloney. Mainly they worked in drygoods and hardware, settled in the timbered, wet side of the county. Myrna married a guy from the Lovetti family, who were ranchers in the Sierra Valley on the dryer, sagebrush-side of the county.

The terrain was dryer, the Lovettis were not. They drank—especially the men. They fought. All comers—and if no one came, each other. After September hay was all in, barned up, or sold, everyone in the Valley said or thought, "Look out, here they come," and everyone hoped the Lovetti men would head for Reno, where cops and casino bouncers handled that sort of thing with one slot-machine-arm tied behind their back.

Frank Lovetti was his name—Myrna's husband. They were married for five years and had one son, Tony, who from the beginning wasn't right in the head, to use the phrasing of the County. When Tony was four and Myrna & Frank were in that fifth year of marriage, Frank disappeared. Took off in the family car, a black Buick. Vanished.

Myrna wore black—a shade darker than the Buick's—for a year—and another year. In that sense she mourned Frank's departure as if he were dead but in another sense she talked about him as if he'd just gone out for cigarettes. She was devastated by his disappearance—warped by it, turned into a sour, eccentric creature.

Tony grew up to be gangly, always "not right," and picked on. There was an "episode" with a janitor at Claytonville school—a teacher found Tony and the man in a closet. Tony was either raped or about to be raped; the facts were cloudy; the general idea wasn't. The County threw the janitor in jail, and then out of the County.

Tony's contemporaries left him alone after that. He acquired a peculiar dignity he had not had before. Myrna, on the other hand, took on even more shame, martyred by misfortune. She transformed herself into a kind of breathing folktale character: When her black labrador, Shadow, died, she bought another black labrador and named it Shadow, and when it died, she bought and named the third Shadow. You get the idea.

Tony grew up, after a fashion, took radio-repair and electronics courses, moved down into the foothills, got a job in a little electronics shop, lives there still, alone, walking down the thin, solitary road of his own life. He took up collecting old radios.

Myrna, meanwhile, did things such as keep what came to be known as the eternal pot of sauce on her stove. That is, she always saved a bit of the most recent red pasta-sauce and used it to start a new batch. Some said she started doing this the week Frank left, so the sauce was like a witch's brew and a curse and an eternal flame all in one. Not to mention a tasty meal. It was all very sanitary and above-board, mind you; the part she saved was just a token spoonful. Myrna's kitchen was obsessively well-scrubbed.

Nonetheless, on rare occasions when she had dinner guests (Lloyd and I have been there twice), the guests knew they were eating part of her sorrow—a home version of the communion game.

Such pathology added to a gray aura she brought with her to the jail that day.

The message of Myrna Lovetti (age 65 or so) to me was simple.

"You're out of line. You're only hurting yourself—and your husband."

"What do you think of that dam up there, Myrna?" I really wanted to know.

"Think? What do I think? I don't. Not about a dam. Men will build dams. Always have. You must protect yourself and your family. You've changed."

"How?"

"You want something. What is it you want?"

"What do you mean?"

"You make trouble—get yourself arrested. What is it you want from this trouble?"

She saw it as a transaction.

"I want to say No. Haven't you ever wanted to say no, Myrna? To shout it? To stop nonsense you see?"

Myrna Lovetti got a wild, wicked grin on her face. "Oh, believe me, I have said no. To all the ways the world wanted to change me, harm me."

"And you think I'm off base."

"Yes. There is too much display in this. You must think of your husband. Too much display." A waggle of a knobby-knuckled finger.

And with that, she left. Myrna the Magpie, prophet bird, dancing with the color black. She'd come to say her sooth, arriving like a force of nature from her overheated, sauce-smelly house. Display. She said that word like she owned it. She balled it up like a fist and thumped me. I took deep breath and stared at the Juanita mural.

The parade of County Eccentrics continued with the famous novelist whose fame had eaten him.

I was standing before the back wall of the cell, lost lovingly in an elaboration of Juanita's #2 pencil-mural, when I heard the voice.

"Lloyd lets you do that? Our very own artists-in-the-slammer program. How uplifting, so sociologically sweet."

Immediately I pegged the whisky baritone and thin bravado of that voice. Gary Stad Fromm.

Gary Stad Fromm was an Author. Twenty years earlier, he'd written and published a novel called *Indifferent Angel*, with which he hit the trifecta: splendid reviews, massive sales, prizes up the ying-yang. It was optioned by Hollywood but never produced. He made enough money to retire to the hills—namely, a house on a hill overlooking Claytonville: Though, of course, when he moved there from Oakland, "retire" was not how he would have described the maneuver.

G.S. had been at work on his second novel for a good fat twenty years. If you are a wood carver, "at work" means digging into wood with a chisel. If you are a writer, "at work" means whatever you want it to mean. I'm not being anti-writer here. In fact, I think wood carvers have it easier because the wood says to you, Well, are you "at work" or aren't you? Writers have to face that blank page, that blank screen, a vacuum to fill, not a thing to carve.

Until I started carving, I knew Gary Stad Fromm no better than anyone else did, for he held me at a distance. Lloyd and I might see him at a restaurant, in the store or post office. He dressed in a "writerly" way—courderoys and vests, berets in winter, odd straw hats in summer. He carried a well-worn leather briefcase by a shoulder strap and let people imagine that in there were magical pages of a next novel, fancy pens, big words, inspiration, all the rest. Schtick is not a word I use much or am sure about, but I think it applies to how G.S. Fromm carried on.

After I became known as a carver, I felt as if I became both a problem and a curiosity to Gary. A curiosity—in that I was something he hadn't assumed. A problem—in that there was another "artist" in town. Believe me, I never imagined myself in his league. In any league.

My work was seen in a handful of galleries. His book was forever in print—around the world! But dances of the ego are not rational, obviously. Because I was smaller than he and knew I was smaller and simply moved straight ahead with my work, I was a problem to him, and he was not a problem to me.

I was a problem to him because he could not move straight ahead with the work and I could. Stature didn't figure into it.

The work was eating him and eating itself. One summer a few years back, he caught me on the street in Claytonville and essentially forced me to walk with him down by the river. He'd been drinking. At the river, he wept and confessed that every time he sat down to revise the second novel, it got shorter. At one point he'd had a manuscript of 500 pages. It was down to 150 pages and shrinking.

"You must know what it's like—to want to carve but not to be able to—to over-carve something, carve it to death."

"Yeah, sometimes it doesn't go so well," I admitted. His eyes told me he loathed the casualness of my admission, the absence of terror in my relationship with my "art." "But—maybe this is where it's lucky to be a carver," I continued. "—I can just move to the other side of the shop and work on something else. Always more wood, you know." I think I might have glanced up at the forest looming over Claytonville.

"And there are always more words, too! That's the problem, you see. Which word? Which sentence? Which story?! A wicked labyrinth of choices. But what am I talking to you for? You're—"

"I'm what? Too dumb to know the difference? A woman? A novice? A hick?"

"Nevermind."

Later he apologized for his drunkenness but, like most drunks (and artists), tried to cover the tracks of what he'd revealed. "The work's going well now," he'd mutter to me in the post office—a glancing mutter as he high-tailed it out. Of course he was lying. I didn't care. Or I should say I cared that he was lying to himself—cared because I never never never wanted that to happen to me. I prayed I'd always be able to look wood in the eye, as it were.

He didn't have to say a word, or even lie anymore, for me to know his second novel had kept shrinking. It was probably an outline now. I could smell the writer's block on him. We pretended to pretend, he and I. We had reached a truce, and, bless his heart, he'd bought one of my carvings—not to show off or patronize me, but just because he liked it.

And now: my Bar-Rock protest and jail time had drawn him out of his architecturally splendiferous "cabin," drawn him to me just as they'd drawn Myrna Lovetti, a frustrated artist of another kind.

Ed Porter had returned by then, though Gary Stad Fromm did his level best to pretend Ed wasn't there. Gary sat—and sat his writerly leather shoulder bag down beside him—a bag which had taken on a Black Magic aura. After a lot of conversational this and that, G.S. weighed in with Wisdom.

"You know, Mary, Yeats said that all the important arguments we have in life are with ourselves."

I was in no mood. "I'll take your word for it."

Continuing the argument with himself, G.S. let his eyes turn ceiling-ward and said, "All artists are tempted by politics. Politics is one of the great seductresses."

A sneezing fit overcame Ed Porter. He sneezed something like five times in a row. Like a Gatling gun.

What on earth a Famous American Author was doing there perched between me and my mural and a sneezing, deaf, retired deputy I do not know—a Higher Power arranges the seating at such tête-a-têtes.

"They're waiting for you," he said.

"They?"

"TV people. Outside. Apparently, your husband has given them leave to conduct a jailhouse interview."

I glanced at Ed, who with a nod confirmed the news.

"Goodness," I said.

"Badness," said Gary. "Tabloid TV. The prostitute's most garish disguise for the Great Seductress."

"You mean politics." I was trying to keep up.

"Politics."

"I need a ghost writer, G.S."

"Oh? Shall you pen a quicky jailhouse autobiography?"

"No, but my lawyer wants me to write a statement for the public. To be read on the courthouse steps."

Melodramatically, he brought a hand to his forehead. "What is happening to my fair backward province? Sad Tom Crimpton has become Clarence Darrow, Melvin Belli, Johnny—

"—No, not Tom. I have a new lawyer. Courtesy of Sybil Burns. She's an ass-kicker—the lawyer I mean."

"The plot congeals, I see. Positively gelatinous."

"Will you help me?" I asked.

"Yes," he said.

He opened the Author's Valise. Ed Porter and I sat very still, as if we expected the Earth to tilt, as if Myrna Lovetti, having changed into a bat, might fly out of that dark leather bag.

Fourteen

Jennifer Rosamund was both "the talent" and the producer. Danny Little was the photographer. I was "the story."

Friday, the morning of July third, I felt more left out than locked up. Ed Porter, in civilian clothes, brought me breakfast but left before the first munch of wheat toast broke the morning calm. There didn't seem to be much activity in the sheriff's office. Where was Sheriff Husband? I'd grown accustomed to a murmur out there beyond my bars and the one door—and to Bluestone's ambling in when he got to work.

I'd made myself happy by imagining Lloyd and Gabriel joining forces to make themselves a breakfast in the kitchen near the river— Lloyd mumbling questions to his son about college and baseball and women, Gabriel mumbling noncommittal answers right back at the Old Man. Me not there to improve communication.

And of course, the parking lot out there was quiet because most of the county employees had started their long weekend.

The honeymoon phase of Protest was over, I noted, looking at cold scrambled eggs. Claytonville was at work or gone-fishing. The sluggish, massive onslaught of RVs, station wagons, mountain bikes, and yuppie-guided Harleys now inched its way, I knew, up from the Central Valley—a thick vehicular anaconda of vacationers. In just one of these weekends, more people would invade the foothills and mountain canyons than all of the Gold Rushers combined.

Someone over in the cafe—I heard the exchange with perfect pitch in a day-dreamed scene—was saying, "Mary Bluestone still in jail?"

"Don't know. Think so. My understanding is she refused bail. But then someone—I think it was Bob—said, no, she posted bail."

"I hear she got herself a lawyer from Sacramento. It's what I heard, anyway."

And the waitress would swoop down on that little formica counter, coming after gossip like an eagle diving to a lake's surface, saying, "I don't see Mary staying in there more than one night. You boys okay on coffee? I bet she's home carving, or watering her squash."

Then something else, some little beige tile in the village's beige mosaic of conversation, would be reported or remembered, offered, contested, denied, put to rest, or recycled. Rarely a mention of the river, dam, or courthouse proceedings.

It's about equipment, not news or entertainment or finding things out. Equipment. That's what I learned, on July 3, about TV.

A short, swarthy guy with a rooster buzz-cut & L.A. casual clothes came through the outer door carrying silvery equipment cases and black nylon bags. Except for brushing me with a glance, he behaved as if I weren't there. He dropped off a load, went for another, brought it back, and had enough stuff to halfway-fill the space in front of the cells. There were coils of extension-cords, although I guessed they weren't really called that. I thought ruefully of my obsession with the rope they used on Juanita.

Breathing hard, sweating (he had a paunch), hands on hips, he looked in my direction, then up, then down. I was on the cot.

"Hi," I said.

"Hi. You draw that?" The mural, he meant.

"Uh-huh. What are you doing?"

"Setting up. Boy, is the lighting weird in here."

"Setting up for what?" I knew, but what the hell.

"Oh, Jeez, thought you knew. We're from *Cutting Edge*. Shooting a story on you."

"But why are you in here?"

He looked at me as if my family tree hadn't ever branched.

"Uh, to interview you?" Suddenly, he'd become snotty. He started unpacking.

"I don't think so."

"That's what they all say." Unpacking. Grunting. His L.A. jeans were way too tight: cookie dough wrapped in cellophane. "Actually, almost none of them say it anymore. Anyway, take it up with the talent. I just take the pretty pictures."

On cue—why can't I ever make entrances *con brio* like that?—the Talent arrived. Thin as a sunflower stalk. Black hair in a shortish cut that might have cost as much as one of my carvings. A wonderful pale-lemony linen suit—not wrinkled. Every piece of linen I've ever worn for ten seconds looks like a relief map of the Rockies. In my orange jumpsuit, I looked—contrasted to the talent—like a highway caution-cone.

Jennifer Rosamund was her name, it turned out. She whipped off those Armani sun-shades. Her lip-lacquered mouth said, "Gawd, Dan-o, what an ugly room." I felt like reminding her it was a jail cell, but I didn't.

"You must be Mary—is it Bluestone or Herrera?—I've heard both."

"*Buenos dias, senorita*," I said in a Tijuana barmaid accent, looking at her cow-eyed. Incredibly, she took the bait, looked at Dan-o the Grunter, who was getting a tripod on its legs like a newborn calf. He paused and said, "She's jerkin' your chain, Jen."

"Oh."

"Bluestone's the name on my driver's license," I said.

She introduced herself. We shook hands through the bars. Her hand was wet and hot. Overheated Talent.

"What we're gonna do is," she said, "—is that Danny will set up and then we'll do an interview, but then, like, we'll do some extra shooting, too."

"I don't feel like being on camera," I said. "I feel fat and dirty. I think I'll pass, if you don't mind."

It was as if, from the recesses of my county jumpsuit, I'd produced a pistol. Dan-o stopped what he was doing and looked at Jennifer. Jennifer looked back at him. Then came the old soft-shoe. Or is it soft-sell?

"Gawd, I know what you mean, I mean I've been doin' this for seven-eight years, and I still get panicky about how I look."

A little more twang had seeped into her speech. I thought I heard Texas in there, maybe Oklahoma or Missouri. You would have thought Jen and I were long-lost sorority sisters. But I thought, Not so fast there, Little Missy.

"I wouldn't say I'm panicky about my looks. I just don't want to be on camera."

The twang disappeared. We were back to the California newspeak tones:

"But wouldn't you like 35 million Americans to hear your point of view about this dam? And the—the woman?"

I waited. They waited. Dan-o wasn't about to assemble one more blessed piece of equipment if he wasn't going to be able to use it. The altitude had gotten to him.

"How do you know 35 million watch?"

"Is that a yes?"

"A maybe."

"Contingent upon—?"

"Upon a shower and makeup." I felt superbly shallow. "Also, the story's got to be about the dam and Juanita, not a hick sheriff and his wife."

"Well, as a matter of policy, we don't let subjects of our stories dictate content, but of course the dam will be a big part of the story. And the woman. Juanita." A "yeah, right" grin touched Dan-o's face, and he recommended the screwing-together of aluminum tubes and cable connectors; several large black cords, I saw, snaked through the doorway: The little jail of Tamarack County was about to be up-linked.

"After my shower we'll talk more."

"Who do I see about this shower?" Jen had a whatever-it-takes-to-get-the-story bounce in her voice.

"Anybody out there in the office?"

"There hardly is anybody. Just the blonde girl."

"Brenda MacDonald. Nobody else?"

"Just a funny little man in plain clothes."

"Ed. Ed Porter. Jesus, where is everybody?"

By everybody I meant mainly my husband and my son. Why hadn't they stopped in at least to say good morning? I should have known that I should have known enough to have been worried.

Ed Porter toyed with the idea of accompanying me to the shower—in an official capacity, that is. But I think he took a hard look at the situation and saw the silliness of it, got me a towel and a new jumpsuit, and (apparently) told Brenda the dispatcher to fetch me some underclothes from the stockpile Lloyd had brought from home—and from home Lloyd had, of course (husbands!), brought my least favorite, least comfortable underwear.

Having showered, walking back up toward the courthouse out of that little hollow where the outbuildings sit, I felt myself elevated into a classic summer day in the Sierra Nevada, every shade of green displayed on mountainsides, the air hot but clean and dry, the sky a blue so deep that if it went one quality-level deeper it would seem weird, not exquisite. I was aware of the North Meredith River's narrow murmur and thought, naturally, of the dam site: Had Rupert Williams blown up Bar Rock? No one had said a word about it. I'd been so busy with lawyers and looney jailmates, Myrna Lovetti, Sybil Burns, the attorney Laura Klein, and the novelist Gary Stad Fromm, and murals, and memory and now *Cutting Edge*, that I hadn't thought to ask this basic question. Had the famous rock been blown to bits?

A notion announced itself abruptly: Okay, enough. Let Juanita rest. Accept what you have not changed (the dam), get back to work, to Bluestone and Gabe, to morning weeding and evening reading and carving in between.

Back at the cells, the Talent and Dan-o were gone, but who should I spy on my cot but my lawyer, Laura Klein, asleep, with The Guns of August spread open on her chest.

She woke up because the cell door squeaked as I opened it further.

"I feel like Goldilocks," she said, "commandeering your bed."

"Commandeer away."

She looked not good—in the face, that is; pale, weary.

"Reading Tuchman—'zat part of the torture in these parts?"

"It's pronounced Tuck-man? Three pages is all I could manage. Seems more like a Winter book, in spite of the title. What's going on?"

"I couldn't sleep—I mean, all night. It's so goddamned quiet up here. How do you stand it?"

She wasn't expecting an answer. "So I thought I'd drop in on my client. And dozed. The altitude."

"Make sure you drink a lot of water." I found a place to park my kiester. Settled, I asked, "Why did you take this case?"

The answer wasn't snapped, but it was impatient. "Uh, money? Remuneration. Profit."

"I meant this case. Surely you have a choice."

"I do and I don't," she said. She sat up. "I don't really want to go into it. I'm more interested in making an ounce of sense of why you chained yourself to a rock."

"Oh, well, by all means, let's talk about what you're interested in."

"My, aren't we cranky."

"Yes, aren't we."

One of those moments ensued—where both parties realize they've just had a miniature, immature quarrel, a spatlet, without setting out to have one.

"As I see it," she said, recovering for both of us, "I'm technically the guest here, so I think I should apologize."

"The host accepts and apologizes right back."

"I took your case because I'm an associate who is first in line to be a partner, and because I work the criminal turf—as opposed to civil. The associate who's second in line takes most of Sybil's work, but he went on vacation. One of the partners kicked your case to me. Nothing personal, but I had better things to do than to drive up here and live in a shabby motel. Sybil offered her place, but I can't stand those women. But I took the case cheerfully. It'll seal the partner-deal. I could lie, if you want, and tell you it was your cause that attracted me, or the legal complexities, which aren't very complex."

"So, how is the case?"

"I'd characterize it as amusing right now. I wouldn't call Miles Ward the most imposing adversary I've faced."

"I'll be darned."

She yawned. "I've laid the groundwork to make the felony charge evaporate. I've petitioned Judge Peat and the Attorney General to remove Ward from the case because of his dealings with the Reicher Corporation."

"Dealings?"

"When he ran for D.A., he accepted a campaign contribution. A small one—proving he's both corrupt and stupid."

"Holy shit."

"Not the legal term, but I think you're getting the drift. Which brings us to Judge Peat. I've petitioned him to remove himself from the case."

"What?"

"He was arrested for DWI some years ago. Your husband was the arresting officer. Conflict of interest. If that doesn't work, I'll go for change of—"

"—You can't do this!"

"—venue. Why not? Besides, it's done."

"You don't understand—it's a small county—this'll look so personal. It's because Lloyd arrested him that you mustn't do this. There's a history there."

"Oh, I know all about histories and counties where everybody knows everybody. Sacramento County's the poster child, believe me. It can make Chicago look like a monastery. Although I have my doubts about monasteries."

"You don't get it—Judge Peat's leaning over backwards for me. It's the opposite of holding a grudge. When we met in his chambers—"

"It's done."

"Undo it, goddamn it!" I paced, I stalked. She lit a cigarette.

"Okay if I smoke?"

I shrugged. "Look, Lloyd and I have to live in this place after you leave. Carstairs isn't just a judge. He's our friend." Admittedly, friend sounded hollow as it came out. He wasn't a friend, but he wasn't an acquaintance or family or an enemy, either. Most relationships in small towns can't be categorized cleanly.

"All the more reason he should recuse himself."

"Well, then say it's because he's our friend, not because Lloyd arrested him."

She just laughed.

I said, "Has he read this petition-thing yet?"

"I doubt it."

"It's with the Clerk? Shit, I'll just walk down the hallway and get it."

"No, you won't."

Jennifer Rosamund and camera-boy returned.

"Oh, God, cigarette smoke," Jennifer mourned. "Could you put that out?"

Laura: "No."

This exchange was among many reasons the two took an immediate dislike to one another.

"Okay, let's get this thing over with," I said.

"Thing?" Laura said.

"An interview," I said. "*Cutting Edge*. Ten billion viewers."

"Be vague in your answers," Laura said. "I'll stay to make sure you're vague."

Jennifer, attempting to ignore Laura, said to me, "I probably won't ask this on camera, but isn't there some irony in an environmentalist being a wood-carver, or vice versa?"

"Do you mean 'hypocrisy'?" I said.

"Yes."

"I suppose so, if you stretch the point. All my exotic wood comes from plantations, not rain forests. From around here, I use oak that's dead and down. Or fruit-wood from the old abandoned orchards."

"Oh," she said. She got out a compact mirror and looked at herself with a cold, hard eye.

Months later, when I finally looked at a videotape of the "piece," I would marvel at how completely unlike the experience of the interview the tape was. To dispense with my vanity first, I'll mention my face on tape looked like the mug of a submerged body. Then, to get more objective, I'll say that "I" was a very small piece of the electronic story. The anchor of *Cutting Edge* crooned one of those melodramatic introductions, as—in slow-mo—the image of the sheriff my husband was superimposed over the image of me in the jail jumpsuit. "It seems even the most remote California communities are not immune to strange California justice" ... Husband arrests wife... Jennifer against the backdrop of the dam site... Jennifer on the bridge that was a stand-in for the bridge on which they hanged Juanita... Me... Maybe ten seconds of talk about Juanita, "lynched during the historic Gold Rush"... My puffy TV face saying, "If we don't need the electricity, why do we need the dam?"

And "The question is, do any other creatures have a right to live on the planet besides us?" I actually said that: how mortifying. My talking-point: "They lynched Juanita over the river, and now they want to lynch the river." Jennifer Rosamund: "A spokesman from the Reicher Corporation declined to be interviewed on camera." Not only on camera, but off. Borrowed footage of the scuffle with my accoster, Carl Kelly: This, it turned out, was the center of the story—a camera being bumped! Poor camera! Lloyd on top of Carl, me looking only mildly pained, as if I had gas.... Jennifer in a wrap-up, standing on the bridge, trying desperately both to include Juanita and make sense of my connection to the lynchee; she made it sound as if Juanita were my great-great grandmother, "roots in Old California." And that was that.

Sometime after lights, camera, interview but before Judge Peat roared in, I chatted again with Laura Klein in my cell.

I could tell Laura was going to ask me about Lloyd. It's a look people get, even jaded lawyer-people. A mixture of curiosity, patronage, and politeness.

And in that instant before Laura asked about Lloyd, I thought of what I might tell her; in such moments time stretches. Or maybe the mind just calls up memories all at once: You feel as if all of what you could say is laid out before you and there's no rush to speak.

I thought I could tell her about "us"—the LloydandMaryness of us—Willow-Creek-teenage-sex-and all that. Could explain how at age six Lloyd was orphaned, his Indian-carpenter-father and waitress-white-mother killed on a Nevada highway, which that night had been just one semi-trailer-truck from not being deserted enough to let Lloyd's life go forward on its highway ordinarily: Where the highway curved around a sage-brush hillock, the driver of the semi was just enough asleep to let his rig drift left, and around the bend came the Bluestones' gray Chevy pickup...Hours later, after the trucker had willed himself conscious and radioed for the Nevada Highway Patrol and the trooper showed up and looked at it—debris of the worst wreck he would see in his life—and after the trooper realized that he'd have to tarp over everything and have it hauled to Reno, bodies and all, and after he looked for skidmarks to measure and found none—only then was it clear Lloyd's mother and father had rounded the hillock and died before they were surprised, force and light, awareness and death hitting them at once. The trucker, the state trooper, the Bluestones' friends, the coroner of Washo County, the tow-truck operator, and—when he got a little older—Lloyd himself were left to return and return again in their minds to the mathematical purity, the pristine, horrific unlikelihood of the accident. Its "impossibility." If the trucker had eaten one more french-fry at the grill in Wells, Nevada; if he'd shifted up or shifted down a little more or a little less efficiently fifty or sixty or two or eight miles away; if the Bluestones had left home sixty seconds—hell, thirty seconds—later; if they had almost hit a deer and stopped; if they had had a quarrel and stopped; if the trucker had popped some pills; if and if and if...there would have been a swerve, or the semi would have already roared into the sagebrush (the Bluestones, alive, stopping to help the trucker who would not have killed them but who killed them in this non-hypothetical life), and Lloyd would have kept that father and mother and they him, and the changes flowing like a watershed, coalescing like springs into rivers, would have multiplied, engulfing me and no-Gabriel and life after life after no-life. But there was no swerve. There was death, a flash, and Lloyd, orphan of a flash, foster-parented by the Kjellstroms, who adopted him eventually, keeping him and he them; Lloyd, who adapted eventually, but who almost never utters the names of his real parents; —Betty Kjellstrom insisting that he keep his own name—virtually a legal impossibility in those days—and the name is now my name, Mary...Herrera...Sacramento...Willow Creek...Claytonville...Bluestone.

I could, I thought, tell Laura how the Kjellstroms had not intended to keep Lloyd for long but were won over, if that's the phrase, not so much by cuteness or brownness or orphanness as by a haunting calmness in the boy. Betty: "He was seven going on eighty-seven. Even when he cried, and cried for them, for his folks, there was something adult about it, as if he understood what he was crying about, making it even harder to comfort him. To tell you the truth, of all the reasons we had for wanting to adopt him, and there were lots, I think the big one was Axel and I wanted to watch this grown-up boy grow up. Something very special about the lad."

Could tell her how Lloyd, a high-plateau, half-Washo-Indian kid, made friends with the Tamarack National Forest, or that piece of it which surrounded the Kjellstrom's place. Betty said by the time he was 9, she'd pretty much let him wander anywhere, as long as he stayed away from the river. "He just knew his way around, and I let him play in the woods like I'd never let any of the other foster kids do. He'd bring back everything—salamanders, dead birds, praying mantises, arrowheads, old coins, you name it. He'd always hold it up, whatever it was, like a present. And his face shined."

Could recall for my high-priced lawyer how Lloyd had entered, so to speak, my life, at Willow Creek—try to make her see how it was for us up here after that, how we were handed, had (not-meaning-to) handed ourselves, a life we didn't know what to do with, how we just "did life" some days.

But in that jail cell, sitting across from her in a freeze-dried moment, before she was about to ask about Lloyd, I felt that if I wouldn't be able to make her see Lloyd in a way she'd honor, I didn't want to say anything—felt as if Lloyd's life was, like the names of his real parents, better left unsaid.

"Your husband...," Laura said.

"Yes?"

"He doesn't seem like most cops."

I smiled.

Moments later, in roared silver-haired Carstairs Peat.

It was as if he'd been born again, sired by offences done him, his face ruddy-dark like pomegranate-meat.

Fifteen

The voice of the dispatcher Brenda MacDonald alerted me. The door to the outer office opened. I heard her voice quaver when she said, "Hi, Judge"—then Judge was past her and on Laura and me, his limbs all gangly and garbed in tan chinos, pink Oxford shirt, topsiders.

"Have you no sense left in your head, Mary Bluestone? Is it sunstroke from which you're suffering?"

He waved a paper, just—I thought at the time—like a TV actor playing angry. "What," he continued, "on God's green Earth do you mean by this insidious, insufferable, insulting document!"

I have to say, knowing Carstairs' past, I was proud of him, marching in there, all downright snarly, packing some serious alliteration.

Personally if not legally, he had me dead to rights. Felony or no felony, he and I had lived in the same county a good couple of decades. When you share a long past like that with someone, even if the two of you are more eternal acquaintances than friends, and even if your husband arrested him once, you don't haul off and go sending the person a letter like that—felony or not. Or maybe you do, in this day and age. But I don't and didn't think it was right.

Laura Klein got up to earn her fee. She didn't know what to do with her cigarette—a trivial concern, but how refreshing to know she could be even two per cent not-in-control.

Laura and I were in the open cell, she standing, me sitting. Just outside stood Carstairs.

"Judge Peat, I must—"

"Who're you?"

"Laura Klein, Mrs. Bluestone's current attorney of record—"

"So I surmised. One isn't supposed to smoke in this courthouse. Your idea?" He held up the offending document, which his rage made tremble like a dried flower. I looked hard at him and also sniffed, discreetly, to see if he'd fallen off the wagon. No. Good.

"Judge Peat. I must protest this confrontation—"

"—Must you?"

"Let me finish. My client is completely within her rights to petition for your recusal."

"Yes, I've been around the California Code a time or two, Miss Klein. Mary, do you want me off this case?"

I said "No" and Laura said "Don'tanswerthat" simultaneously. Tie goes to the lawyer, I guess, for Laura plowed on.

"Your Honor, with all due respect, sir, you are now dramatizing the very reason I filed the petition. Personal involvement."

"Counsel, there is a grand total of 3,000 residents in Tamarack County, one sixth of which live in this very burg." Burg was a nice touch. I was rooting for him. "The odds against my not knowing visitors before my bench are extremely bad—or good, depending on one's wagering vantage."

Laura's cigarette had burned down to her knuckles. She dropped the butt and crushed it. She lifted her chin a good half-inch. Highly carvable, that chin, I thought.

She said, "I'm willing to let the State Attorney General make that call."

A twitch gathered the skin between the Judge's eyebrows—a throwback tick, no doubt. Laura's threat to "tell on" Carstairs to the State Attorney General probably brought memories of tortuous teen years—getting harassed by hill-kids while his parents got crocked on the mosquito-clouded veranda.

"Sit," he said. "Please." She sat. He put his arms behind him, truce-like. He lectured, quietly.

"When I do have occasion to step down from a case, Sacramento can't usually find a replacement judge. What county court doesn't have a busier docket than this one, after all? So they send a retired judge. For the past five years that's been Granville Tuck. Granny, we call him. He thinks his mission in life is to nurture tender careers of young prosecutors. Like Miles Ward. And he doesn't work summers. So, about when your calendar's getting full in Sacramento—September, say—you'll have to come up here. And if Granny's on the bench, you'll lose because he and Miles will be playing kissy-face. Granny's brand of what you're perceiving as small-town justice makes me look like gaw-damn Louis Brandeis. Am I making sense?"

"I'm managing to follow your take-the-devil-you-know argument, yes." Her mouth was screaming at her to put another cigarette in it. "But a third alternative—pardon me, option—is a change-of-venue."

"No, it isn't." This was me speaking. A word in edgewise. "My wood-carving isn't portable." I was hoping the way Laura looked at me signaled she was miffed, not that she was surprised I knew what change-of-venue meant. Carstairs tried again.

"Name 'Buck Walters' ring a bell?"

"Used to be with our firm," Laura answered, resentfully, "—a partner—before my time. Investment banker now. Money-runner." If she could have spit these words on his pink shirt, she would have.

"I went to Bolt Law with his brother, Stu. We both flunked the bar the first time around. Stu's a senior partner in a cozy little Santa Rosa firm. He specializes in staying out of the way and fly-fishing."

"I'm just sure this is going somewhere."

"And Stu and Buck are about as close as two jealous, scotch-drinking, narrow-minded Republican brothers can be. I'm a Democrat myself."

Laura sighed, dramatizing her boredom.

"Buck still golfs with your people, I'd wager."

"My people?"

"The partners. Senior. Old farts."

"I suspect so."

"Well, Stu and I have kept in touch. I even invested in his winery." (In more ways than one, said me to myself.) "Failing the bar's a kind of foxhole experience, though I suspect you wouldn't know. I can see myself in a week or ten days calling Stu and telling him what a fine lawyer you are, and asking him to lean on Buck to put in a good word for you. I tend to find the term 'ball-breaker' disgusting on several levels, but it's part of Stu's lexicon."

"'Stu' can shove it. I don't need your old-boy network, Judge."

Carstairs was unfazed. "Nor do I. And I don't need Granny Tuck in my courtroom or belching green peppers in my chambers. If efficiency and going for the throat and knowledge of the California Code count for anything, then you've earned that partnership. Based on my limited knowledge of your work, that is."

"Gee, thanks. How did you know...?"

"Sybil Burns. There's no business that's not Sybil's business, apologies to Miss Merman. My talking to Stu, who will talk to Buck, who will golf with your people—I consider it merely a professional courtesy. Courtesy has been the theme of my admittedly rambling oratory here, and I thank you for your patience."

"I have to say I've never had a conversation like this in my entire professional life," said Laura. "A judge, my client—in a jail cell—I—"

"Yes, yes, in Sacramento the legal life is as pure as the driven snow," Carstairs said. "You've had plenty of these conversations. It's just that up here we can't afford the varnish. Right, Mary?"

"I guess, Carstairs. But I buy varnish all the time."

"Blessed are the literalists," Laura said. She and Carstairs shared a most superior chuckle, on my tab.

"Judge," I said, "I'd kind of like to take that bail now."

"And I would like to grant it to you, Mary. But that would require a hearing. It is a holiday."

"The felony charge is ludicrous!" Laura said.

"Please!" Carstairs put up a bony hand. "Now we are treading on inappropriate ground. Anymore talk of the charges will have to take place in chambers, with the D.A. present."

Laura guffawed. Carstairs didn't like it, but he took it.

"Ten o'clock, Monday morning," said Carstairs, tearing up the letter, wadding it, tossing it into what had been Carl Kelly's cell. Carl Kelly—what on earth had happened to him?

"Miles will be there," Carstairs continued. "This will be resolved. I have vacation plans that don't necessarily include turning Mary into a convicted felon."

"A plea bargain?" Laura asked.

"That's a Cadillac term for what I hope will be a Chevrolet conversation," said Carstairs, concluding cornily. He left, a lilt to his gait.

Laura rolled her eyes, lit a cigarette, took a deep drag, blew it out. "Get me out of this goddamned county!" she said, adding, "He's slightly more savvy than I thought. But what an ass."

"Carstairs is an odd duck," I said, "but he came by it naturally. The thing is, he has Miles' number. For you that's good. And for me."

She shrugged. "By the way, is he gay—Peat, I mean?"

"He doesn't live a 'gay life.' Or—well, you know what I mean. He's been married a time or two, but that doesn't prove anything. It would be just his luck."

"Meaning?"

"Meaning nothing bigoted. It's just that he's always led somebody else's life. Carstairs—I can't really think of anything important in his life that's been his call. Every day I see him, somewhere back in my mind I'm thinking, this man should be somewhere completely different doing something completely different. Gay but staying in the closet would be just one more example of that."

This seemed to get Laura thinking—about herself and her desire to be somewhere else. A glance at the watch. "If Sybil comes around, tell her I had to go to Sacramento. I'll be back Sunday night."

I must have looked curious.

"I'm not abandoning you," she said.

"Oh, I'm not worried about that," I said. "It's that you'll be driving against the traffic. Everybody and his dog'll be coming out of the mountains Sunday. You've never seen anything like it. Think of LA traffic crossed with a Tamarack County highway. I know you don't want to spend one minute more than you have to up here, but if I were you I'd leave Sunday morning."

She changed the subject. "I'd like to see some of your carving some-time. Sybil raves."

I gave her the name of a Sacramento gallery.

"You're gonna make me go to a gallery?"

"Drop by the house Sunday morning. Have Lloyd show you my workshop."

"I'm sure he'd be delighted."

"Maybe I'll be out of prison by then."

"How?'

"I don't know. I'll think of something."

She shook her head. The bewilderment seemed real. Between Carstairs and me, a fine legal mind had been turned, temporarily, into scrambled eggs. "I really have to get out of here," she said.

I was sitting on my cot, staring at the Juanitaless wall, which I'd finally washed. I heard several men.

Heard several men enter the sheriff's office—the door to out there, closed. I heard and knew, knew Lloyd was hurt. Gabriel, too? God, no.

Knew by how the group burst in; knew by a certain electrical current that passes between longtime loving partners. Knew.

Was out my unlocked cell and through the door. Did a stutter-step when I saw Lloyd–upright but book-ended by Andee Munro and another deputy. Blood all over the front of his shirt and across his forehead. Blood in his dark hair, darkening it more.

Sixteen

I rubbed away blood, dried and wet, from Lloyd's forehead. The gash was actually a crooked cut an inch above his left eye. Face-cuts just keep bleeding. Lloyd's a good coagulator, but the cut was damn deep so blood went on seeping. I tried to soak it up with some tissues I'd grabbed. The deputies had laid him on the floor and raised his legs. I sent someone to get some ice to put on Lloyd's neck. His uniform was splashed with blood, also his badge. Deputies and the dispatcher surrounded Lloyd and me. I was busy with Lloyd, who was conscious but stunned, so it took me a while to realize how quiet everybody was. No one had said what had happened, only something vague about Lloyd getting hurt up at the dam site. It took me more moments to jump to the right conclusion.

I looked up and asked, "Where is Gabriel?"

They just glanced at each other, like children in trouble, so I picked out big, brawny Mike Cussler and looked him the eyes. "Tell me," I said.

"He's okay—he's—"

"Tell me!"

"He got shot in the shoulder, but he's stable. He's—"

I didn't hear the rest. Lloyd held my arm. He said, "Mary, do you think I'd be here if Gabe wasn't all right? I had them bring me here so—" —But I shook off his grip and stood up and screamed. I found words and screamed them. "Where is he?!"

Andee Munro said, "He's over at Doc Loban's."

Lloyd started to speak again, something about his coming to the office, not the clinic, so Loban could concentrate just on Gabe, but I wasn't listening.

I'd bolted. Nobody tried to stop me, but Andee followed me. I tore past county workers and citizens, me in my orange jump suit, and it had to look like a jail-break. I heard Andee murmur something like "It's all right, folks" as she loped behind me, her pistol flopping against her thigh—odd that I remember that sound.

I got out of the building, flew down the steps, ran across the bridge that used to be the bridge that hanged Juanita. In blazing sun I ran across a dusty dirt parking lot to Loban's clinic, a remodeled old house, and bounded in there.

Inside I almost passed out, not so much from the run as from not breathing in the heat. Loban's receptionist look stricken but recovered, got up, and met me as I was about to burst past her desk. "Stop, Mary," she said.

"No," I said, and pushed.

"Stop! He's all right. He's awake. Doc is with him. Just sit—"

"No."

"Wait? A moment."

"A moment." I was out of breath and steaming with sweat. Otherwise I might actually have punched her.

She disappeared down the corridor, entered a room, didn't bother to close the door.

Murmuring. I heard Loban's voice: "Ask her to come on back." I didn't need to be asked.

I'm sure I screamed, instinctively, when I saw Gabe laid out on an examining table. I vaguely remember several "Oh Gods," and I remember weeping and trying to fall on him and enclose him in my arms, but Loban held me back and said, "You don't want to do that. Calm down."

"Is he bleeding...?"—I almost said "to death."

"No, he is not. It is going to be all right."

Eventually I calmed and took it all in. Loban had given Gabe something for shock, so he was glassy-eyed, stoned, and serene. "Hi, Mama," he said, as if he were six. Of course, I wept more. His shirt was off, and Loban had cleaned a wound at the base of Gabriel's neck. It seemed an awful ragged thing, and seemed somehow scorched, too. Loban told me to sit down, so I did. He checked Gabe's eyes. The nurse—skinny, blonde Kathy Butler—came in and took Gabe's blood pressure again. I felt as if I were watching it happen in an aquarium. I was in some kind of shock myself, of course, and a patina of unreality materialized. Finally Loban turned to me and explained.

"Your son is going to be fine. Miraculously. He was shot. A pistol."

"Who?"

"Apparently the foreman up there. At the dam."

The full force of unintended consequences struck me. I couldn't speak. I'd gotten my son shot.

That was the result of my adolescent caper on Bar Rock. I would deal with myself and my stupidity later.

"How bad?" I asked.

"Miraculously, not bad. Basically, the shot creased his neck, without hitting an artery. A gunshot wound is a gunshot wound, mind you. But I don't see any nerve, arterial, or vascular damage. I'm going to put in some stitches, the sooner the better. We'll bring antibiotics on board. Okay?"

"Okay. Thank you. May I—?"

"—Just wait in the office."

"I love you," I said to Gabriel. "I'll be right outside."

"O-kay," he sang. "That guy shot me."

"I know." I broke down again, and got out of there so I could get myself together.

And as I was doing that, a sheriff's cruiser pulled up, Lloyd got out of the passenger side, holding a towel to his head, and strolled into Loban's clinic. Andee, who had trailed me, helped him up the few stairs.

When he came in, I went to him and hugged him, and we held each other for a very long time. Lloyd was holding on with one arm; he still had the towel to his head. Andee was holding back tears. We broke our embrace.

Lloyd said, "Gabe and I are fine. So are you. The rest is gravy."

I agreed but broke down crying again. I think I would have broke down no matter what he'd said. He could have said, "Feathers," and I would have cried.

Doc Loban got Lloyd set up for stitching in another room. In the outer office, Andee sat next to me. She asked me if I wanted her to hold my hand, and I said, Thanks, but no. I told her not to go anywhere, though. I liked having the well established Andee Munro sitting next to me. She told me what had happened up at the dam-site.

Before noon, someone driving down-canyon stopped in Tamarack—the town where Lloyd had let me out to pee that morning, which seemed ages ago. The someone phoned Lloyd anonymously with a heads-up: Log-haulers had parked their trucks at the dam site.

The truckers appointed themselves protectors of the site. Most of them weren't hauling logs because the Forest Service shuts down logging over the July Fourth weekend—the highway slaughter is big enough without logging trucks being in the mix of traffic on a narrow alpine highway.

Not born yesterday, Lloyd had been content to let the California Highway Patrol handle the situation. The highway and its easements were the CHP's business, whereas Bar Rock and any woman chaining herself to it, hypothetically speaking, were county business, unless the

Feds had a vested interest, and in Tamarack County, they never did.

Lloyd knew he was just stalling, though, because there was only one CHP officer assigned to the county and if he—Harry Haskins was his name—thought he needed backup, Lloyd was both obliged and obligated, by honor and contract, to provide it. Not being born yesterday only postpones duty.

Haskins called, said he needed help. Lloyd took the sheriff's SUV. Lloyd let Gabe ride along, a decision he will regret the rest of his life. On the way up-canyon, Lloyd radioed Andee and told her to come by the site.

Everything was calm when Lloyd and Gabe got there: Logging rigs parked just off the pavement, drivers standing around jawing with Haskins, construction-workers ambling back to work after lunch, a big crane swinging material up, over, out, and down to the dam-site below.

Haskins: "Just telling the guys here they need to move the trucks out."

Lloyd: "Yeah, that'd be a good idea. So much traffic this weekend. Gotta give those tourists a wide berth."

A truck driver: "Well, the foreman here doesn't seem to mind us hanging around." He hooked a thumb toward the dam, as if to point to Wade Landers. "Helps to keep the protesting freaks the hell out."

Lloyd: "I'm glad he's made you feel welcome. But this is really Officer Haskins' call—a question of highway safety."

Another driver: "Shit, Sheriff, you gotta be kidding."

"I hope you'll help us out, fellas," Lloyd said, and I can hear him saying it with a bit of steel, just enough firmness.

That's about as testy as things got because Haskins told them all what a citation would run them. Money talks, *etc.*

Wade Landers arose from the canyon. He wanted to know what the fuck the CHP and the sheriff were doing there. The CHP and the sheriff explained, said everything had been ironed out.

Landers was drunk. He sidled up to Lloyd.

When Lloyd lowered his head to spit in the dust, Landers took a big step and swung. Lloyd saw it in time to try to slip the punch, but it caught him hard above the eye.

"My feet were close together. I went down like a tree," Lloyd reported. Before Haskins or Lloyd or anyone else could react, Landers took off for his pickup, some 25 feet away. Haskins assumed he was going to get in it and speed off, so he was going to get in the patrol car and get ready to chase him. Instead, Landers flung the door open, dove into the cab, and came out with a pistol. By this time, Lloyd was up, and Haskins was drawing his weapon. Gabe stood nearby. So did Andee, who had drawn her weapon. She told Landers to put the weapon down.

He stopped. He hadn't raised the weapon. Everybody stood still. One of the log-truck drivers said, "This is bad." Andee remembered that.

According to Andee, she saw Lloyd out of the corner of her eye. He turned his head toward Gabriel, who stood just in back and to the side of Lloyd. Lloyd was about to tell him to get in back of a vehicle and to keep down. At that instant, Landers raised his weapon and fired it, everyone assumed later, at Lloyd. But Landers was drunk and probably had no actual experience with the weapon. The shot creased Gabe's neck, though of course no one knew then it wasn't fatal. Gabe went down. Haskins and Andee fired, just as Landers—perhaps horrified himself at what he'd done—flung the weapon down. Haskins' shot missed. Andee's was low, striking Landers not in the chest, where she'd aimed, but in the hip, shattering bone. Landers went down like a sack of gravel, howling with pain.

"Andee, get his weapon," Lloyd said—automatically, I'd guess. Then he turned to see his son lying flat in the dust, motionless, bleeding from the neck. How the whole mountain range must have seemed to have collapsed on him then. Of course he believed the worst. Of course he got on the ground and staunched the bleeding with this big brown hand. Of course he spoke to Gabe—words that seemed to come from some other person, some other place. The blazing sun beat down on the site. Lloyd bled, too, blood streaming down his face, blood he didn't notice until he tasted it. Blood of a father, of a son, nothing divine about it. A bleeding father, my husband, bending over a bleeding son, my son.

...In the stifling hot clinic, Andee finished telling me the story. I was sobbing. Sobbing because I saw how close I'd come to losing my one and only son, conceived accidentally but providentially in Willow Creek Ravine; and I could have lost Bluestone, too. I was sobbing because I was exhausted; because I felt as if God had spared me. Andee was crying, too.

"And Landers?" I asked.

"The bullet shattered the shit out of his hip. Haskins got him in the CHP car, drove up to the Four Corners where the medi-vac helicopter can land. They got him to Reno. As far as I know, he's alive."

Moments earlier, when Andee had been telling me the tale, I'd wanted to kill Landers. Destroy him for hurting my baby. My emotions seemed to be careening. Now I heard myself saying a silent prayer for the recovery of Wade Landers, who had called me a cunt and shot my son. It seemed vaguely Christian of me. My hands were shaking, I noticed. Not just trembling, but shaking, like my grandmother's, when she suffered from palsy. Andee got up and got me some water.

❧

Eventually Doc Loban came out and said he didn't think Gabe needed
to be transported to a hospital because doing so would probably cause
more stress than keeping him here. Gabe's vital signs were normal and
stable; there was indeed no arterial or nerve-damage. The wound was
a bit like a scorch. Loban said he would transport him if I wanted it
that way, but he said that with the July 4 traffic, he'd prefer just to keep
Gabe in the clinic overnight. I went in and spent more time with Gabe,
until he went to sleep. I held his hand.

By then Loban had stitched and bandaged Lloyd's cut. Lloyd and
I and Andee got in the sheriff's car and went back to the courthouse.
Apparently it was a day for farce as well as violence, for there in the
sheriff's office was novelist Gary Stad Fromm, drunk.

Some problems with living in remote small towns are obvious. The
isolation. The hard winters. The tough terrain. The one that often
gets to newcomers, however, is that in a very small town, people just
show up at your place—your job or your home. So in the winter, for
example, you might come down with cabin fever one day, but the next
day you might be driven mad by people just showing up, dropping by
and dropping in. Too much privacy and no privacy—that's the vice that
squeezes you in a town like Claytonville. So here Gary Stad Fromm
was. He'd just shown up, precisely when everybody in the office was
trying to keep the last nerves from fraying after everything that had
happened.

Lloyd didn't see the need to lock me up just yet, so most of us
had found a chair. Lloyd looked. . . well, like he'd been slugged hard,
stitched, and bandaged, but also like he was bone-weary. Standing,
Mike Cussler said, "Gary, you look like you could use something to
eat." It was a kind way of suggesting he get the hell out, go home, and
sober up.

"Thanks, no," said G.S. "Haven't eaten all day. Not about to start."

Until then I don't think I understood how deep the famous novelist's self-loathing ran.

He was without the infamous leather bag but in possession of a
typescript. His expensive designer-jeans were soiled; so was his collar-
less, vaguely "European" cotton shirt, out of which he pulled a pair
of half-glasses. And put them on. And cleared his throat. And took
no notice of Lloyd's bandaged head or bloody shirt. So much for the
novelist's eye. Fromm looked at me.

"Mary, you asked me to draft some remarks. I have."

All eyes on me. Gamely, I tried to halt the runaway genius.

"Oh, that was just an idea the lawyer and I were kicking around—before those TV people showed up. Turns out I don't need a speech, Gary, but thanks anyway for—"

"—I think," he said, "when you hear this you may"—his head bobbed slightly—"revisit and readopt your earlier, uh, stratagem."

G.S. began to read the script. I don't remember particulars, only the general thicket of it. There was a lot about honor and civil disobedience. Something about the slow apocalypse of technology, or something like that. He stumbled around in it—a lost Boy Scout in a patch of manzanita. We all either turned or hung our heads or both. Bluestone finally spoke.

"Gary."

G.S. kept reading.

"Gary."

G.S. stopped reading.

I focused on the soiled jeans and soggy shirt.

"Well," G.S. said, then jutted out his chin, grinning smugly as if he'd just unveiled the Mona Lisa, "that'll give you the flavor of it, anyway." He was prepared to surrender quietly. I was surprised Lloyd didn't let him save face.

"Go home, Gary. If you brought your car, leave it. Walk. You're drunk."

G.S., though foggy, achieved enough clarity in his noggin to be surprised by Lloyd's directives. I've convinced myself I saw a flicker of appreciation on his face. After all, how long had it been since someone had been straight from the shoulder with G.S. Fromm? At some un-soused level, even he had to be sick of unrelenting deference.

He tried to manufacture some dignity. His way was to drop the script and grind its pages with a boot. That would have been better theatre if we all didn't think the pages had it coming.

"The Law-Giver has spoken," G.S. sneered. His eyes found me. "If you're in need of a speech, fair hobby-crafter, you know"—he gestured to the floor—"where one lies. The rest, citizens, is silence." He would have stomped out but out-stomping would've asked too much in the way of equilibrium. Finally, agonizingly, he was gone.

Andee picked up the script and tossed the pages in recycling. I swear not five minutes passed before Sybil Burns, of the Buffalo Gals, strode in. The groans were all but audible.

"Hi, all," said Sybil. "'Loggers've parked their rigs downtown and looks like some enviro-types, bandana-heads, are pulling in—should be quite a weekend in Sleepy Hollow. Mary—you're out! Myyyyyyy gosh, Lloyd, what happened to you?!"

She put her hands on her hips, around which a turquoise belt snugged her jeans. I filled her in on the afternoon's violence. The story actually made her quiet, pensive.

Lloyd dispatched Andee to have a look at Claytonville, now that loggers and environmentalists were adding to the crush of July 4 tourists.

"I wouldn't worry," Sybil said. "I mean, aesthetically, it's not pleasant—Buffalo Gals milling about with old gnarly loggers, granolas, and touristas. Felliniesque. Frankly, I doubt if push will come to shove."

"I'm paid to worry," Lloyd mumbled. I wished devoutly that he would go home and rest. He added, "Milling around plus booze and politics and heat. Not good." Sybil chattered away in response, I forget about what.

"By the way," Lloyd then said, "I don't know if all of you have heard. Carl Kelly—the guy who attacked Mary. He's dead." Even Sibyl stopped talking. In the reverent silence, Lloyd continued.

"They took him down to Grass Valley in the ambulance. He was doing okay. They were fixing to run some tests to see why he was bleeding inside, and he went into cardiac arrest."

The sadness that hit me surprised me, I must say. It wasn't so much that I pitied Carl Kelly. It was more like for a minute there I pitied everybody. Just like Gabe, Carl Kelly was somebody's son. Lloyd went on, more quietly.

"So now I gotta write a long report about the scuffle out here, try to remember how hard I hit him." His voice trailed off. "How many times... and such...."

Sibyl and I stood very still.

"You mean," I said, "they think one punch... did something?"

"I don't know. I spoke with a doctor down there. He said they'll do a full autopsy tomorrow. But he said there was some evidence of stomach and liver disease." Lloyd shook his head remorsefully. "I'm pretty sure I hit him in that Heimlich place, you know—going after his air. Up high."

Sibyl patted his arm. "Lloyd, it's not your fault." This embarrassed him. He hadn't been fishing for pity.

I said, "Let's us just wait for the autopsy. There were plenty of witnesses. Videotape. You didn't wail on him. He was napping a half-hour later, sleeping like a pup."

All the deputies got busy, and Lloyd headed out for the restroom. Over his shoulder, he said, "Mary, we'd better get you in your cell."

Sybil said, "My lawyer, Laura, is on her way back up here, by the by—tonight. She just cell-phoned."

I was about to ask why Laura Klein would drive down to Sacra-

mento only to turn around, with hardly enough time to file a brief or
comb her hair, and return to the hick-county that annoyed and bewildered her.

I didn't get to ask because there, in the outer office, stood big,
brooding Rupert Williams, my Bar Rock accomplice, who after we
greeted him, said, "I've come to make a statement, but I don't have all
day."

"So what kind of statement you want to make?" asked Lloyd, after he'd
returned from the john and gotten Rupert settled. I could tell Lloyd's
head still hurt like a sonofabitch.

"Short," said Rupert. "Not about the shooting. About what Mrs.
Bluestone did up there. I helped her."

Since Rupert kept glancing at me, I said, "Mr. Williams, you really
don't have to go to all this trouble."

"Who elected you sheriff?" Bluestone said.

"S'all right, Mrs. Bluestone," Rupert said. "I've thought it over."

"Call me Mary," I said.

"What do you mean you helped her?" Bluestone asked him.

Rupert took off his cotton cap, revealing the neatly trimmed, salt-
and-pepper hair. He looked at his watch.

"I'm headed home. Home-home. Lodi. I quit up there."

Instead of asking why, we just waited.

"It's a mess. 'Bout as organized as bucket full of eels. How's your
head?" Rupert asked.

"All right."

"That was terrible. How's your boy?"

"He's going to be fine. Unbelievably lucky, all the way around."

"Landers?"

"Haven't heard. I expect the CHP guy to check in and let me know.
I hope he's all right, Landers I mean."

"Back to why you quit," Lloyd said. "It's because of the shooting?"

"No. Reicher's a week behind in payroll. Material's not showing
up. Landers has been getting drunk by noon. Shit, you can't do that in
construction. I was on a job like this before. We was redoin' a causeway
bridge near Marysville. Money ran out. Union lawyers went after the
company. The company went Chapter 12. Ain't gonna do that again.
Plus I'm a long way from home. You know"—he turned to me—"we
never did blast that rock of yours."

"You're kidding," I said.

"I drilled it and was gonna set the charges, but then Landers said no. I heard Reicher's lawyer'd been by. Rumor was, they wanted to save the rock as evidence."

"That's really silly."

"Not so much evidence as something to point to when they sue the county."

"Say more," Lloyd said.

"It's just a rumor. But I guess Reicher could say with Mrs. Bluestone being your wife and you a county employee, the county obstructed the job."

"She represented her own little self up there, not the county."

"I've heard similar rumors around the courthouse," Lloyd said.

Rupert shrugged. "They're outta money. It's like, you know, they're losing the game, so they wanna tip over the board any way they can. I ain't gonna be a part of that."

"Bar Rock—still in one piece," I mused.

"And your statement?" Lloyd said.

"What I told you. Project was going down the tubes before Mrs. Bluestone showed up.... Besides, when she did show up, I helped her."

Bluestone raised an eyebrow.

Rupert explained.

"If I were you, I'd think about this," Bluestone said.

"What they gonna do—fire me?"

"What I mean is, as it stands, you'd be an accessory to a felony."

"Way I see it, she wasn't trespassing if I invited her to hang around." He stopped short of saying that he'd helped me chain myself to the rock. That was all right by me.

"The D.A. may not see it that way."

"Well, anyway, they hafta catch me first. I've made up my mind."

"I'd advise you to talk to a lawyer."

"Appreciate that. But I'll make the statement."

Bluestone sighed.

"Why don't you sleep on it?" I said.

"No, sir. I'm gonna crash in a motel here and get on my way before sunrise."

"All the motels are full," I said.

"Stay with us," Lloyd said.

"No—no way."

I pressed him. "Look, it's no trouble." Easy for me to say. I'd be in jail, probably, not hosting Rupert.

Ed Porter answered a call. Lloyd applied ice to his stitches. Rupert spoke:

"All right. I believe I will take you up on your kind offer. I don't feel like fighting the traffic. It's getting late in the day."

Seventeen

While Rupert wrote—in block-print—his report, Bluestone hauled me into his cubicle and had me get on another phone as he rang Judge Peat's house, catching the Judge on ring three, and broaching within moments the subject of my release. Lloyd's tone was taut. He wasn't used to asking for favors. And of course there was the history between him and Peat.

He told Judge Peat about the dust-up at the dam—Gabe and Landers shot, Lloyd battered.

Lloyd told of the brewing hubbub downtown, said he might need jail-space, promised I wouldn't leave town, let alone the county. He discussed Rupert Williams' statement.

Though I'd announced my presence on the other line, Carstairs spoke as if I weren't there. He took on a courthouse-insider's tone as he and Lloyd conversed.

He seemed to have company—there were sounds of elaborate cooking in the background: sizzling, chopping, running of water, clanging of pots. The questions were few and terse from Hizzoner. Bluestone answered briskly.

"Sheriff," Carstairs intoned, suddenly stagy, "your reasoning is entirely persuasive and characteristically pragmatic. I shall dictate a letter releasing Mary on her own recognizance for... seventy-two hours—but stipulating that she shall remain within town limits. And let me call Mr. Miles Ward, our D.A."

Bluestone and I said, "Thanks, Judge," in unison.

"You two have as restful a weekend as you can. Gabe is all right, you say?"

"Yes, Judge," I said.

"You two are amusing me with this 'Judge' business. It's usually 'Carstairs.' Take care."

"Same to you, Judge," Lloyd said.

We were about to ring off when Carstairs added, "Miles will not be amused by all of this, Sheriff."

"I know, Judge."

"There may be Hell to pay."

"There's always Hell to pay," Lloyd said.

"Yes, isn't there?"

End of conversation.

"You two sound so chummy," I told Lloyd.

"Bunk."

"You'd never know you once arrested the guy."

"Yes, you would. Now get outta here—you're free—on your own reconnaissance or whatever the shit that is."

"Recognizance," Ed Porter murmured.

Lloyd, out of the cubicle now, said, "Okay, Mr. Williams, I'll take that statement, if it's signed. Mary, take Mr. Williams—"

"Rupert," Mr. Williams insisted.

"—Rupert—up home and make him comfortable."

"You need to come home, too," I said. "You were in a fight, you're cut, and you're exhausted."

"No, Ed and I have something to do."

Ed's eyebrows raised.

"What's going on?" I asked.

"None of your business."

"Tell me."

"No."

Rupert shrugged at me as if to say, Well, we kept our secret from him, after all.

Thus was I dungeon-sprung into lengthening shadows of July 3.

Rupert fetched some clothes, *etc.*, from his pickup, which we advised him to leave near the courthouse. We set off across town.

Sybil had spoken truly: vehicular icons—log-trucks, with hauling parts unhitched and stacked over the cabs, and old mini-vans with curtains and lots of bumper stickers—had accumulated in Claytonville's middle. Most of the owners seemed to have dispersed.

Rupert and I turned to make our way toward the wooden sidewalks of the "business" district—and saw Haskins' CHP car heading up the gradual grade and out the western side of town. Rupert and I were no doubt thinking the same thing, wondering if Wade Landers had made it alive to a hospital in Reno.

The tourists, as usual, looked tired, bewildered, hungry—anything but happy about vacating. Seeing them always made me wonder why more of them didn't just stay "down below," as we provincials refer to urban and suburban California.

Calculating the self-consciousness per yard, I swear it was the longest walk of my life, because who didn't I see? Their hellos were slathered in meaning; their glances at Rupert the Black Man and me the orange-jumpsuited-one lingered on him and me like our own perspiration; the faces of some of my townsmen-and-women were often taut and grave, the most efficient small-town way of silently saying what I'd done at Bar Rock was out of bounds—and who are you, Mary Bluestone, who we thought we knew all these years?

We passed the one short street of shops, the post office, the lumber yard, headed up the mild hill along the North Meredith River... home....

Got Rupert settled. Made him a sandwich, poured him a beer, read "nap" all over the report of his face and told him to go for it and showed him his guest room.

Took a shower, put on real clothes.

Went out back, saw what I knew I'd see—Bluestone hadn't had the time to water or weed the vegetable garden, which I didn't have the energy to water or weed, which would soon be fried.

Avoided going out into the workshop. Once out there, I'd never come back. In one way I wanted to carve, but in another the image of myself picking up a chisel depressed me, no end. Didn't know why, didn't want to probe the why.

Began to muck out the house:

The effect of Lloyd and Gabe on the house (of most men on most houses?) had been flood-like. Eddies of debris had formed. Things had been lifted, as if buoyed by a slow influx. What had been low, such as magazines on coffee tables, had been moved to a higher plane—countertops, windowsills, backs of chairs. What had been high—dishes, glassware, opened cans of food, cereal boxes—had sunk. Most of the mess was waist-high, that level at which men can work on stuff quickly, like bears, and leave it, sniffing and snuffling it out later when they return in hunger or befuddlement.

Got some laundry going.

Began cooking. Tried to keep my mind off Gabe lying over there in the clinic.

Realized, while cooking, that I hadn't heard a jet rip across the sky since... when? Because of the air-show in Reno on the 4th, the frequency of jets usually increased on the 3rd.

Answered the door: And there stood my attorney Laura Klein, who didn't like saying what she was saying, which was that Sybil had told her to stay with us one night and then come up to the Buffalo Gals' Encampment; and which also was that she'd gotten to Sacramento, found that one of the legal aids had goofed up a batch of documents for another case, discovered that an old flame whom she emphatically did not want to fuel was in town and wanting to see her, and realized, with mortification, that something previously unthinkable had happened: Tamarack County suddenly seemed appealing.

I welcomed her warmly, told her she could find plenty of privacy in a den, where we had an extra bed (Rupert was in the guest-bedroom), found her towels and showed her the guest bathroom, told her to wash off the travel-dust, and—like Rupert—enjoy a precious gift presented to humankind, a nap. Told her a Mexicali smorgasbord, so to speak, of victuals would be ready for her and for all when she woke.

Laura had heard already from Sybil that Carstairs had let me out. Laura was too exhausted to be surprised, but not too exhausted to be amused. She found the bathroom, then the den, and collapsed.

I poured myself a glass of Merlot, went outside, listened to and looked at the river. I worried terribly about Gabe. Resisted calling Doc Loban's clinic. Resisted calling the sheriff's office to yell at Lloyd, Come home! Tried to calm myself. Sipped Merlot. Tried to process everything that had happened. Couldn't. Sipped more Merlot. Hoped my house-guests wouldn't want to come out and chat just yet. I knew that after dinner, I probably couldn't keep myself from visiting Gabe once more.

I looked at and listened to the river. The blessed river.

Concluded that jail is bad and home is good, that Gabriel and Bluestone alive meant everything.

Claytonville Cemetery lies north of town. Like most actual "boot hills," it's where it is not because of gothic ambience but a mundane concern—drainage. It's bad business to bury the dead in a hollow, a ravine, or a flat. Let souls go where they may, if not where they will, but bury their fleshly temples in firm, high ground.

In this case, ground over which black oaks and poised cedars preside, their deep root systems grasping, embracing, our entombments.

The oldest marked graves in the cemetery date from the early 1860s. The names include standard-issue Anglo-Saxon ones (Smith, Wilson). Also there are Cornish, Italian, German, and Swedish names. Of all the Chinese who moved through the Sierra Nevada—building flumes, cutting roads, laying rails, and doing other brutal work—only one secured a marked gravesite in Claytonville Cemetery. The stone reports only his nickname—"China Ralph." Not dates. In vain I've searched for Hispanic family names there. None.

The infants' headstones murmur implicit tales of diphtheria and whooping cough, influenza, cholera, pneumonia, and polio.

One miniature Washington's-monument marks an empty tomb, so to speak, of twenty-three miners killed in the awful Bourbon Ridge

Mine cave-in, 1903; once everybody knew no one could have survived, the fatal tunnel was sealed. To think of the bones still down there in the mine-tunnel cools the living marrow.

Axel Kjellstrom, Lloyd's father in adoptive deed if not in biological fact, is buried in Claytonville Cemetery, was buried there on a hard February afternoon. North Wind raked the canyon. His stone reads simply, "Axel Kjellstrom," with the dates, followed by "Stone Mason." He lies next to Bryce Wyrdell, an eccentric's eccentric, whose stone gives the name and the dates, followed by "I didn't ask to be born." Axel loathed Bryce for never working but also loved the man's unapologetic dislike of life and the living; for some reason misanthropy lifted Axel's spirits.

Who knows how many cups of coffee they slurped at the cafe, winters, when Axel might take a couple weeks off to let his cracked hands heal? He'd take young Lloyd with him, set the boy up at the counter for a piece of pie and a glass of milk, then go to Bryce's table, where a misanthropic rant would already be at gale force. If only Bryce had worked, had done something with his hands, he and Axel would have been friends, not perpetual acquaintances.

We can't see the cemetery from our house; a patch of woods blocks the view. Still we feel as though we're connected to the graveyard, not just because we knew many of the residents when they were above ground, but also because when coyotes lope by our house, as they often do, they're coming from or going to the cemetery. Nothing Transylvanian about this. It's just the way the trails seem to be laid out, according to requirements of coyote commerce.

Thus graves were on my mind the morning of July 4, when I got up before everyone else and took a cup of coffee outside and savored the air. I looked hard across the river to a hill above Claytonville. It's furnished chiefly with madrona trees. It's ground in which Juanita's body, supposedly, was buried. I thought of some things that should be true but aren't and some things that shouldn't be true but are.

I considered the sounds of the river, substantially the same ones Juanita would've heard and considered according to the matrix of her experience: That aural connection was the most specific link between me and Juanita. River-sounds, then and now.

I had called Doc Loban at home, and he said he'd already been over to check on Gabe, who was great except for some pain, so Loban had put a little more pain-killer in the I-V. He said he'd get Gabe home soon, with pill-versions of the pain-killer, and he suggested that we get him to a plastic surgeon sooner rather than later, for a consultation if nothing else. He said again how lucky Gabe was, how the scarring would be minimal, even without cosmetic surgery. I asked how Gabe's spirits were, and he said fine—Gabe didn't seem traumatized, just angry, when he wasn't asleep. I offered to go get Gabe, but Loban said he wanted to check him one more time, and then he'd drive him up to our place, it would be his pleasure. A house call, in a manner of speaking. At such moments, Claytonville seemed prehistoric.

Then, finishing the coffee, I thought some morbid thoughts, not about Lloyd (home now and sound asleep), Gabe (how many prayers had I said the night before?), or Landers (we'd heard he was alive and stable in Reno), but about Juanita. I'm no shrink, but forcing myself to ponder the distant past was probably a way of coping with a bad July 3 that might have been a fatally catastrophic July 3.

I thought about how they wouldn't have wasted precious lumber on a coffin for her; how they would've shrouded her in the most expendable hunk of cloth in the gold camp; how the men digging the hole, rolling her body in, and shoveling earth over her would probably have been drunk and may well have done something low such as open their trousers and urinate on her fresh grave.

A fine thing it is to be pulled back from grave-robbing thoughts by my husband's arms. I leaned back against him.

"Hey," he said.

"Hey." I turned, looked at him in his flannel robe. "How's the head?"

"Fine, except for this nasty cut."

"I'll change the bandage after breakfast."

"Think I'll let the air get to it.

"Anybody else awake?"

"The lawyer. Taking a shower, I think. Wonder how she did in the tent."

Laura had gotten a bee in her briefcase and decided she wanted to sleep outside in a tent—something she hadn't done since she was 14, she said. Fine, we said, we have close to an acre of ground, just pick a spot and put on some deet.

I'd shown Laura and Rupert around my woodcarver's workshop—sheepishly, like a teenager showing off her room. Then we'd fallen on dinner. Finally went out and put up the little dome tent, gave Laura a flashlight, insect goop, and our most comfy sleeping bag (with a foam pad), wished her well.

Then at last Lloyd and I lay in bed and had a chance to talk, talking mostly about Gabe at first.

"So what were you and Ed Porter up to this afternoon—after Rupert and I left?"

"Nothing."

"Come on."

"We set up a big flat-bed truck with a microphone and speakers."

"Where? Why?"

"Middle of town, cheek-by-jowel with the vee-dub buses and log-rigs. It was Ed's idea. All these people got a lot to say, so let them talk. We couldn't find any bunting."

"Not a bad idea."

"Bunting?"

"The platform."

"There will be ground rules."

"Like?"

"Nobody speaks more than five minutes. Ed's the timekeeper. No booze in the crowd or on the truck, of course."

On my way back to the kitchen, next morning, I ran into Laura Klein. Her hair was wet, and she was dressed in sweats. She desperately slurped coffee and fumbled with a pack of cigarettes.

Such a spectacle of nerves was she that I couldn't even say "Good morning"; it just didn't seem right until she'd found one of our stone benches outside and lit up.

She took a drag, blew it out, gulped coffee. "That's better. Hope it's okay I made coffee.

"'Morning."

"'Morning. Sleep all right?"

She regaled me with tales of the tent, how every sound had kept her awake 'til midnight, at which point she'd plunged into a sleep formidable enough for Jules Verne and his famous leagues. She woke herself up with a nightmare—something about a baby wailing. "Or maybe it was all those neighbors' dogs yipping."

"The baby was probably the dogs, and the dogs were the baby, and all of them were coyotes," I said.

"Sounds like Freud on acid. What are you talking about?"

"The coyotes come through here about every night, summers. When they cry, they sound too human. Then they'll yip-yip their way along the trail, up past the cemetery, 'til they're out of earshot."

"You mean, I could have been eaten?"

"No. They go in for birds, squirrels—maybe a deer. Never lawyers."

"I forget there's a sort of wilderness beyond all the off-ramps."

"Not much of one. Cable TV, cell-phones, four-wheel-drive cars, computers. I'm thinking the wilderness has become an interactive Website."

"Nonetheless. Wait 'til I call my Aunt Edna in New Jersey and tell her I slept in a tent and woke to coyotes. It will confirm her worst fears about the West. It's okay if I smoke out here, isn't it?"

"Well, we are sitting on what they call a powder keg," I said, gesturing at the mountains. "It's all fuel, unfortunately. Just put it out in the sink, and Lloyd'll be your friend for life."

And there we were at the sink, my lawyer and I, washing fruit, scrambling eggs. She leaned against the counter and set her eyes. "Have to cross-examine you for a minute."

"Go for it."

"I'm not clear on what kind—or what tribe—I mean, Lloyd—what is he?"

"Washo. W-A-S-H-O. Some people add an E at the end. They were a really small group. Not really a nation, in the sense the Sioux or Shoshone were. But they had their own language and stories and way of doing things, so I guess they qualify as a nation. They lived mainly in the great basin on the other side of the range, south and east of Lake Tahoe."

"First I've heard of them, not that I'm an anthropologist or anything."

"I remember reading in a book once, something like, 'The story of the Washo is very short and very sad.' At least the last chapter of their story's short and sad."

"Meaning?"

"The silver strike hit in Nevada. Right in the middle of Washo turf. You can imagine how long it took for the silver-rushers to overwhelm a thousand Indians whose idea of conflict is to chase a squirrel and kill it. There's a semi-reservation over there now, but you know, we're talking about fragments of a people. Leaves in the breeze. It wasn't that long ago."

"Does Lloyd think of himself as 'Native American' or 'Indian'"?

"I don't think you can look like he looks and be treated by people the way people have treated him and not think, you know, at some level, 'I'm Indian.' On the other hand, his Ma was white, he was raised from six or so by white parents, and his great-great-grandfather might just as well come from Atlantis, for all the sense of a past it gives Lloyd. I think he feels like Lloyd most days."

The timer for the biscuits went off.

I took them out. "Want one?"

"You know," she said, "I do. Maybe it's the mountain air or those coyotes, but I'm starved."

I slid one on a plate and found her a knife, butter, and home-made wild-plum jam, tart and ruby-colored. "So that was the cross-examination—Lloyd's origins?"

"What about my origins?" said the original Lloyd, arriving from provinces of our oddball, self-built house. He'd become Sheriff again—khaki shirt, plus badge; green trousers, boots.

"She wanted to know about the Washos and all that."

"The way of the buffalo," he said, picking up a biscuit, "except the buffalo are making a comeback, if hamburger meat qualifies as one."

Seated, we three became oddly reserved again: a lawyer and her reluctant clients. Laura spoke.

"The cross examination, part two, is—this Juanita person."

I sighed.

"Forgive the lawyerly question, but what if she did murder the guy?"

Lloyd chuckled.

"The sheriff and I disagree on that point," I said.

"And?"

"And I say it was at least self defense."

"That's certainly the case I would have presented. A man breaks and enters. There'd been a confrontation the night before. Afraid, Juanita defends herself. That's the story I'd tell a jury."

Laura continued. "Bear with me here—don't get insulted. Self-defense versus murder aside, what's the big deal?"

"In the end, I'm probably just sentimental, but I want her to stand for something. For a past gone wrong. They lynched her. When it's in my head, it makes sense. When I talk about her, it sounds weak."

I got up and pretended to putter with breakfast fixings. I decided to keep talking, to get it over with. "Okay. Look. If she wasn't the only Mexican woman in town, she was one of the few. A gold camp full of rough white men. California's steaming toward statehood because the Union wants the gold. Statehood as in more civilized, right? Rule of law? I don't doubt Juanita wasn't one tough *chiquita*. She defends herself. Against a thug. They do some kangaroo court thing and lynch her from a bridge, bury her in an unmarked grave. Rule of law, my ass. They cap off a July 4 celebration—we the people!—life, liberty, and the pursuit of a rope to snap a Mexican's neck!"

Lloyd looked at me as if to say, "Feel better now?"

Laura had set her chin on her thumb and put her index finger alongside her nose. Professor Klein.

She said, "Aunt Edna likes to say, 'It's not what you remember, it's that you remember.' She didn't mean that remembering somebody's batting average from 1940 was the same as remembering Treblinka. She meant you needed to pick a piece of the past that's right or wrong in some important way and remember it. Preserve its name."

"Juanita is Mary's 'understory,'" said Lloyd.

"Okay, I'll bite," Laura said. "What do you mean?" Lloyd set himself.

"In a forest, like here, all the brush and some of the trees are what's called the understory. The top story is the big trees—ponderosa pines, really old cedars, stuff like that. Before humans started suppressing wildfires, the understory was thick, full of lots of different species of brush and small trees."

Laura sipped her coffee, seemed bemused by this little lecture bubbling out of the usually taciturn Bluestone. He continued.

"See, take manzanita for example—the nuts it produces won't crack open unless they're burned. Manzanita evolved with fire. It's odd, but the understory depends on getting wiped out by fire, because the fire doesn't really wipe it out—it helps it propagate. And the health of the forest relates directly to the number of species—lots of different growth. A rich understory."

"What's this got to do with Juanita?" I said.

"Well, for whatever reason, you feel connected to Juanita's story."

"And it helps her propagate?"

Lloyd giggled. "No, but it fills out Mary's story."

Professor Klein homed in. "And how does the fire work in your analogy?"

He was about to answer when Rupert Williams emerged along with Rupert Williams' rather booming morning voice: "Are those biscuits I smell? Tell me those are biscuits I smell."

"Those are biscuits you smell," said Lloyd.

"Those are cold biscuits," I said. "I have another batch coming. Sit. Coffee?"

"Yes, ma'am. Thank you."

Now shyly, Rupert eased in between my sheriff and my lawyer. I heard what had to be Loban's SUV pulling up, with my Gabriel. I ran out of the house.

It was the Fourth of July.

Eighteen

I hung on to and squeezed my son so much and so hard between Loban's vehicle and the house that Gabriel finally barked at me to leave him alone. When he got in the house, Lloyd hugged him, and both of them teared up. So did Laura and I. Rupert somehow kept his game face, although I saw him working on a biscuit especially hard. Gabe settled in and started eating. His neck was freshly bandaged.

Breakfast-talk turned to the demise of Wade Landers, Reicher's money-woes, Judge Peat's willingness to let me loose, and our close personal friend, the District Attorney, stocky, mustachioed, ambitious Miles Ward. Of whom Laura said,

"I almost feel sorry for him. These kids these days—so political so early. He should be getting his trial-chops together, not messing around with corporate weasels. That can wait."

"Enough about Miles, let's talk about me," I said. "Where does my case stand?"

"Considering Reicher's red ink, Rupert's statement, Peat's improved mood, and so on, I'd say Ward'd be dumb to do anything but offer a misdemeanor plea. Light fine." She waited a beat. "He'll be extremely dumb."

"I didn't hear any of this," Lloyd said, "and I'm off to work." He said goodbye to Rupert Williams.

"Can't you rest?" I said. "Your head...."

"It's the Fourth of July," he said. "I got loggers, I got environmentalist, I got tourists. I got heat, and I got booze. Probably a little meth, too."

I expected Rupert and Laura to take off then, too. Him to Lodi, her to the Buffalo Gals. But when I told them about Lloyd's arrangements for July Fourth gab-festivities, they both said they wanted to stay in town until mid-afternoon.

It was close to noon by the time every one of the four of us—Laura,

Rupert, Gabriel, and I—got ourselves put together to walk "downtown." I tried to talk Gabe into staying home and vegging on the couch, but he said no.

I'll always remember Laura asking, as we strolled, as she smoked, "What happened to those jets I kept hearing—not that I'm complaining or anything?" and Rupert chiming in, "Every time they went over, I liked-to jump outta my skin," and Gabe saying, "They were just warming up for the Reno air show. They won't come this way anymore."

Also I felt a peace of sorts, looked forward to Sunday, the 5th, when Lloyd would be home, puttering around, and Gabe would be doing laundry, and trying to talk us into letting him to return to Reno for a baseball game (we wouldn't let him, of course), and I'd be back in the workshop.... The humidity was down, my spirits up, the dam on hold.

Claytonville was clotted up but cheery—kids, dogs, tourists, and natives; a sidewalk sale underway; odors of barbecue joining the clean breeze. The first thing to be heard coming from the tinny P.A. system as we approached the flatbed-truck-platform was something about if we don't re-center ourselves between the Sky Father and the Earth Mother... and then, from the crowd, you're not even making any sense! What the hell you talking about! Soon we joined the crowd listening to speakers. The sky was bright.

Ed Porter, an absurd yet effective referee, sat in a chair on the flatbed, beneath a parasol propped up (wedged between) crates. Before him stood a large cymbal on a metal rod. He'd tap, first lightly then resoundingly, when a speaker's five minutes were up. Brassy vibrations in July's golden air.

If someone really tried to push the limit, Ed turned into a regular Buddy Rich. The crowd giggled. He'd smile thinly, point his drumstick at the next speaker waiting in line down by the portable steps they'd erected at the back of the flatbed. About when the line dwindled to two and Bluestone's Speak-In looked like it would exhaust itself, two or three more people from the crowd would come out and get in line. The ratio of men to women speakers was about five to one.

Laura sidled up to me about that time—Gabe had disappeared for the moment. She'd fetched herself a Diet Pepsi from a makeshift hot-dog stand some Claytonville high-schoolers had set up at crowd's-edge. She lit up a cigarette and gulped Pepsi. I gave the crowd a good once-over, thinking a July Forth thought: What made these creatures especially American? After all, they were out in the noonday sun—an English affliction.

They were arguing about The Land—an especially American riddle-maker. God gave us the Land: so say some. God gave us to the Land: so say others. We own it. We don't own it. We steward it; it stewards us. It was made for you and me so we could do our manifold damnedest with our destiny. It's inexhaustible, God's bounty. It's unrenewable, our nest to foul. It's doomed, it's just fine, we know exactly what we're doing (don't worry), we know exactly what we're doing (the wrong thing, but we do it anyway), we stole it, we bought it, God gave us to it/it to us/it to it/us to us, and round and round and back and over again, quarry of quandries.

In their scruffiness and gleaming-eyed righteousness, the Greens and the loggers, bikers and the backwater natives were sometimes hard to distinguish from one another. There was a great deal of hair, just as there must have been in 1849.

A turn in the breeze ran some of Laura's smoke under my nose. I coveted a sip of her Pepsi.

Then one of the little spectacles provided by mere life-itself showed that life-itself was in charge. The spectacle, I cringe to report, involved two dogs humping.

The couple in question was a black-and-tan hound (the male) and a retriever-mix (the female). Their passion was ignited at the periphery of the crowd. The female, and who can blame her, seemed ambivalent—and put upon, not to mention set upon. While the hound thrust, staggered, and slobbered, she kept moving, walking into the crowd, which parted like the Red Sea.

The hound apparently belonged to a barrel-chested logger, who moved in to pull his charge off the female—"Mackie," he yelled, "goddamnit, son, get off her!" But a loose-limbed, pony-tailed, shirtless guy stopped him. "It's cool with me, dude, if it's cool with you. We don't mind if Ribbon has pups." Several spectators formed a human corridor. They clapped and cheered. Sybil, who had only just begun to speak from the platform, said, "Let the joy be universal."

Mackie the male, poor devil, lost his concentration for a moment, and his penis, as pink as strawberry sherbet, disengaged. Earnestly, he remounted, his face displaying that heartbreaking canine mixture of sincerity, embarrassment, and resolve.

"Don't tell me Lloyd arranged this distraction, too," Laura said.

"Well, he is good with dogs, but...."

Mackie finally discharged, shall we say, his duties. Ribbon seemed nothing if not relieved. The world was all before them. The crowd applauded; a truck-driver, predictably, yelled, "That's just what the sonsabitchin' environmentalists are trying to do to loggers!" Booing and laughter.

I said to Laura, "Now you know what we do for fun in our fair metropolis. Please join us in the spring when the trout spawn, won't you?"

"To Ribbon," Laura replied, toasting the air with her Pepsi can.

"Something tells me," I said, "she won't see a dime of child support."

"I'll give her my card."

I was so relaxed, even cheery, at that moment, so glad to be out of jail and in the sunlight, that I was completely side-swiped by Sybil's words, suddenly broadcast.

"I don't know about all of you," she said, "but I'd like to hear from the woman who's the real reason we're here today talkin' about these issues and gettin' our views out." I hated the way she was dropping her g's, all folksy and shit. "Mary? Mary Bluestone, come on up here!"

Greenies clapped, loggers and truckers booed, bikers... looked stoned, and I have to say I sided with the boo-birds. I didn't particularly want to hear from me, either. But I knew I had to speak.

I was, graciously, allowed to go to the front of the line, which was represented by a grass-blade-thin young woman in a purple tank top and bluejeans. She greeted me with a smile—and an aura of body odor so massive as to be operatic and, like the aroma of alpine skunk-cabbage, not wholly unappealing. "Go get 'em," she said.

"Thanks," I squeaked.

Out of the swamp of her b.o., I ascended the makeshift steps and hit myself with anxiety in the chest. Ed Porter rather obviously set down his drumstick, as if to say, "The clock's off," and Sybil engulfed me with a hug. She smelled of Chanel, of course. I stepped up to the mike and was terrified. Afraid that if I didn't start speaking I'd never speak, I spoke.

"Well, I didn't expect to come up here," I said.

"Louder!" someone shouted. I moved my mouth closer to the mike. The loggers and truckers out there in the pond of listeners mostly folded their arms or slouched, whereas most of the Greenies turned their faces up to me expectantly, and the bikers... looked stoned. I gave it another whack.

"You know, going up there to that dam site—that was mostly a personal thing."

"The personal is political!" a woman shouted, echoed by "Right on!"—which came, I think, from Ribbon's owner.

"I didn't go up there planning to cause such a stir.... For me"—my throat was already parched—"it's just that—the dam never made sense. If we don't need the electricity, why should we build the dam?" Scattered applause. "But even if we need electricity, should we be damming these small rivers? Now, I wanna say something to the truck drivers out there and the loggers. I've been around construction people all my life—my Dad—he built highways." That got some applause. The Greens seemed to forgive my working-class roots. I continued. "The people from Claytonville here—you know I care about working people. Jobs." I was sounding to myself like a politician. "And I know that if we keep building houses and using paper, we can't very well turn around and say, 'Don't cut anymore trees.'"

The loggers loved that one. The Greenies looked like they'd caught a whiff of pandering. I guess they had.

"But you know, we have to work this out somehow. We tried every way possible to make our case against the dam. A reasonable case. To me it felt like, if you have the money, you can build whatever you want whenever you want it." This perked up the Greenies. "Who does the river belong to? You? Me? Us? Reicher? I think we need to treat the river like it's just on loan to us. Before Ed gongs me up here, I just want to say a couple more things. To the people from River Rescue and other groups, I'd say try to understand what loggers and construction people go through. They're trying to make a living. And to the loggers and truck-drivers and such, I'd say, think about—well, generations to come. These so-called hippies and greenies—I know you don't see eye-to-eye with them, but they're trying to save the land and water for people not born yet. That's not such a bad idea. To everybody, I'll say, thanks for coming out; it's a great day for Claytonville. Thanks."

It's a great day for Claytonville? I said to myself, trying not to fall off the truck. What the fuck does that mean? At least I'd sort of followed my high-school speech-teacher's advice: "Stand up to be heard. Step down to be appreciated."

Gabriel and Laura greeted me at the bottom of the steps. (Where Rupert had gone to, I didn't know). From Gabe I expected a hug but got a pat on the shoulder and a "Way to go, Mom." From Laura I expected a smart-ass remark but got a hug and a "You did fine—I expected you to bring up Juanita at some point."

"Too complicated. History, and all that. I was awful."

"Not awful. It reminded me of my first closing-argument—I mean the first I was paid for. When I got back to the table, the senior counsel said, 'Heartfelt.'"

"Did you win that case?"

"Yes, as it happens, but not because of my closing argument. C'mon, I'll spring for sodas, or do you say 'pop'? Mary, your lips look like chalk."

We'd only just commenced to sidle over when a thin but cable-sinewy logger came up, brow darkened, and said quietly, "I have a question for you."

"Okay."

"Hear you're a wood carver."

"Yes."

"So you're saying it's okay for you to carve wood and make a living but I can't cut trees?" He was kind of trembly, as if he thought the question would devastate me.

"No, I'm not saying that. I'm not out to ban logging. I just think we need to be careful. I don't think anyone should clog up a creek with stuff, whether it's mine-tailings or logging debris. But I agree—if one group's gonna be held accountable then all groups should be. Now, the real question is, can we get you something to drink? This is thirsty business."

He smiled.

"Tell me where you guys are logging," I said as we moved toward the hot-dog stand.

We got our sodas and talked for a while about where his crew was falling timber—cedars and doug-firs. Laura pulled out a cigarette for the both of them. Soon we were like old chums. His diesel-stained hands reminded me of my father's, especially the squared-off thumbs, which Gabriel had inherited from his grandfather Joaquin.

Because there was a break in the speechifying, the little crowd milled about and buzzed, then began gradually to thin out. I caught sight of a man from the Earth's Shepherds Foundation—a well-endowed, Sierra-Club-like organization, lots more powerful than its saccharine name suggests, based in the Silicon Valley, of all places. We'd gone to ESF early in our work against the dam. They'd listened so caringly, like parents to children; had commiserated and promised to stand firm with us; had offered us auxiliary-group membership—with reduced dues: gosh!

Within thirty days we'd heard they'd sponsored legislation in Sacramento that would shore up the laws and regs keeping it easy for small hydro dams to spring up all over California. Their agenda was to make sure no more nuclear-power-plants were built. None were in the works, anyway. Our subsequent letters and phone calls to them dropped like pennies in a well.

I remembered this guy—oyster-shell specs, blue oxford shirt, chinos and penny loafers. Maybe I can't hold my soda pop anymore, but with hardly a moment's thought I decided to go over there and tell him off.

However, sight of Bluestone halted my progress toward Mr. ESF. Lloyd pulled up in a squad car, stopped at the edge of the thinning crowd, the sun roaring off his windshield in a molten glare. He and Andee got out, and I was about to go to them—when Barker Updike seemed to materialize out of nowhere: Barker, the Korean-War vet we'd run into up in Tamarack on our way back from *Sheriff Arrests Wife*.

"You sly dogs," Barker shouted. "'I'd a-known Lloyd was really taking you to the slammer, I'd-a taken your picture, Mary!'"

I smiled. "Hi, Barker. How's things?"

"Good. Nice speech. I half-way agree with you. Which worries me."

I was nodding and smiling and uh-huh-ing as Barker gabbed. I really wanted to slide over to Lloyd to see how he was doing.

A nagging protective urge had situated itself in my intuition.

Then Barker stopped talking. My back was to him and to the river.

I guess I'd halfway-heard the faint sound of a jet, but now I heard-heard it as Barker shaded his eyes and lifted them up over my left shoulder. I turned to follow his gaze and—there it was, a military jet, banking, heading down-canyon. Toward us.

"'Be a sum-bitch," Barker said. "An F-6, looks like. Navy plane. Goddamn great plane. Last of the gunships. Got more kills in 'Nam than the ones carryin' rockets. Great—"

Jet-roar drowned out the rest of Barker's elegy for ghosts of military-hardware-past. I sensed everyone was looking at the plane—and all of us there, so small in the small town, sensed what each other was sensing: Something's not right: Too low, too slow.

The silver-gray beast labored. Its bank was arthritic. A dull pop in the sky, and I swear we all gasped, and I swear we all crouched like frightened cats. A lot of us sucked air to our toes when the plexiglass canopy—Sweet Jesus, the plane was so close to us now—peeled itself back, and the pilot shot straight up, then back, over the canyon like a vision from the Rapture, but I doubt if any one of us saw the chute open 'cause the roaring, whining, smoking heap caught a last richochet of sunlight and headed straight for us. Was on us.

The kids at the hot-dog stand scattered, and Barker Updike clutched my shoulders and tried to push me toward the table—to get under it, I guess—but reflexively I resisted, looking for Lloyd, reaching for Gabe and Laura—but Lloyd was lost from sight now because of bodies running, diving under vehicles, staggering.

I looked again for Laura and Gabe, who I thought had been right beside me. They weren't there. Now Barker yelled in my ear goddamnit, Mary, get down; and I swear (we all swear, to this day) the shadow of the jet passed over us/I know for sure the shadow glided across every cowering, panicked soul/the noise of the thing was a blast shaking our bones/Barker on top of me now, his body loosely arched over my head/I didn't have time or sense enough to squeeze my eyes shut/Remember getting a glimpse under Barker's armpit at the plane as it somehow, some way, stayed up/Stayed up, stayed just up/above houses/

Slammed into the hillside/God the noise, God the noise/The ground shook/it really did shudder.

The whole hillside above Claytonville seemed to take in a monstrously huge breath/Seemed to suck sense and fear not just air out of the canyon out of us/Stole one interval of time and held it/And held it/Then set it afire/The hillside exploded.

Whole huge pine trees flamed like torches/I don't know how he did it/I don't know how Lloyd did it/He made it from the car through a thicket of bodies/Stunned tangled-up bodies/Jumped up on the flatbed/Got to the mike/His voice—eery over the speakers:

Stay where you are, everybody. Stay still. Two firetrucks will be coming down this street—he pointed—soon, so don't go in the street. Don't try to drive anywhere, please. If—I say IF—we need to get people out of town, we'll evacuate through the east side. It will be orderly. Stay calm—that's the main thing. Don't run.

Now we could hear the fire up there; now the town's fire siren, situated on a derrick near the post office, began its long build-up to full-blown wail. It wailed and faded, wailed and faded for the next half-hour. It worked against the one thing on our minds: getting our wits together as the forest went up.

I'd never before been part of an event, and probably won't be again, in which two so-different versions of Time seemed to operate both at once. It just depends on which version I look through, like a lens, when I remember all that happened.

Barker Updike looked over my shoulder into the sun—the crash, the fire. It all seemed either to move immensely slow, like an ice-flo crawling away from the North Pole, or to race, like the fire-on-the-hill itself: image overtaking image, action overtaking action, all in an incendiary rush.

Slow: I see faces of firemen on the truck. Grim, they seem to float. The grim faces float through town. I see the faces.... Near Bluestone's car (the town-siren is wailing), I lift my hand to brush my hair off my brow, and the gesture...the gesture...seems to take forever, I feel the collective will of the crowd, the will to do something now—run, shout, fight the fire—but Bluestone holds back the will with his will, his focus, his relentless intent. I see his dusty boots, anchored to the bedrock beneath the town. I see flames, huge flames, mad-drunk with tree-sap and wood-fiber; sometimes they move so slowly, so gracefully, like dancers; strange physics of fire....

Fast: the hill above town ablaze, instantly a serious fire, murderous force—bewildering, completely itself; the red volunteer-fire-department engines, quaint, even pitiful, steamed down main street (gears grinding), up the hill, disappearing right and up, along a backroad, volunteer firemen trotting after trucks, Mike Cussler on Lloyd's orders following in a patrol car, his mission—paradoxically but sensibly—to tell the townsmen to slow down up there, to not attack the fire without a clear plan—and escape routes. Just try to keep it off the houses.

Loggers, Greenies, bikers, tourists, and all the rest congregated at Bluestone's patrol car, where he drew a big makeshift map on a piece of butcher's paper somebody had produced. His deliberateness, the crowd's traumatized silence: both were eery in contrast to the noise and tangle of people around the storefronts. We heard the fire eating trees and brush like a massive animal.

Bluestone... identified and dispatched three men with "heavy equipment" (bull-dozer, loader, *etc.*) to a ridge-road above town accessible by looping around the other end of Claytonville; gave them a two-fold task: stay alive but try to cut the ridge road even wider. Everybody broke off into little commando units then, with minimal fuss—Andee Munro went up to close the west end of town to incoming traffic, Ed Porter went to close the east end to incomers but keep open the right lane, a couple groups made their way to houses just below the ridge to help people soak their yards and rooves and gather belongings and dogs and cats, others (with Sybil in charge) set up a place to tend to firefighters who'd be coming off the hill exhausted and smoke-choked if not more seriously injured, and still others (Gabe and Rupert and I among them) grabbed shovels and pick-axes and made our way up to the fire. The wall of heat rose collossaly.

Novelist G.S. Fromm and the D.A. never showed their faces or bowed their backs. Tom Crimpton, in his big boat of an old Chevy Impala station wagon, went around gathering up stray, scared, spooked dogs and cats.

Bluestone called the Forest Service office in Plumas County and told them to send a helicopter with a canister-on-a-cable (to transfer water from the river and dump it on the fire) and crop-duster planes loaded with fire-retardant. When they began to quiz him, as a Bureaucracy must, he repeated his request and hung up, cursing. But the helicopter and planes showed up eventually and made sure the fire was knocked down, and a Forest Service crew came, too, to work the perimeter of the fire, keep it off the houses.

And the day and its daylight seemed then to evaporate, and the fire-break worked, and houses were saved, and we were mopping up little fires into the night, our faces painted with ash and sweat, our bodies moving like shadows of primitive people against the flames and weird fire-and-smoke-shadows, and we took breaks and came off the hill and got water and food but had inexhaustible manic reservoirs of adrenalin and gab, and people started playing music on the flatbed, one Greenie playing a guitar, accompanied by a logger on banjo and a biker on harmonica, folk songs and hill-billy songs and Grateful Dead songs and Johnny Cash songs coming over the cheap speakers, filtering into strange, volcanic light and night-air, the helicopter now parked and silent in the middle of town, and people finally starting to relax enough to laugh and count blessings and say over and over again to each other to no one to themselves how amazing it was no one was killed, and only a few houses damaged, and wasn't it lucky the wind didn't pick up, and Bluestone was sure right about the fire break, and God, what if the wind had picked up? and then I was dancing with Gabriel and Rupert was up on the flatbed singing a Bo Diddley (and if that diamond rrrang don't shy-yine) song and Laura was drinking Jack Daniels from the bottle with a biker and Carstairs Peat had his sleeves rolled up, spooning beans onto paper plates and Sybil actually had to lie down, she lay right down on a pallet, Buffalo Gals tending to her exhaustion, a scene from a *seraglio*, and somehow the sound of the river seemed to rise as the fire died and the moon rose and somehow we'd come out all right and Bluestone tapped me on the shoulder and cut in and danced with me and bandaged Gabe danced, impossibly!, with black-clad Myrna Lovetti and we'd come out all right somehow and I remember the water in the shower black with ash and I remember falling onto the cool sheets and holding Bluestone and falling asleep before I knew I'd (somehow) fallen (we'd come out) asleep (all right): secure.

Nineteen

A Viet Nam veteran named Reuben Merck, later described, of course, as "troubled" by newspapers, was the pilot of the F-6 "Crusader" jet that skimmed the air just above our heads on the Fourth of July and exploded on the hillside near Claytonville. Merck had attended the Air Show in Reno, intending merely to indulge in some nostalgia for his pilot's days past. But something apparently came over him, and he simply had to fly the F-6 one more time; or rather, he simply had to fly the F-6 immediately one more time.

In spite of all the alleged increased security after 9-11, Merck sneaked into a hangar, found a flight-suit and helmet, and probably seemed so comfortable in the suit that security on the tarmac paid him no attention. He removed the blocks from behind the wheels of the F-6, which had been flown in for display purposes only, but the cockpit of which had been left open. A mobile stairway-unit sat nearby. Reuben Merck drove that over, climbed up the stairs, got in the airplane, closed the cockpit, fired 'er up, and pivoted deftly away from the stairway. To the consternation, to put it mildly, of those in the control tower, he taxied and took off. Soon military jets were scrambled. They followed Merck and his F-6 over the Sierra Nevada. They made radio contact. He told them who he was and what he was—just a vet wanting one last ride in the old Crusader. They believed him, but they also had orders to shoot him down once he got past the canyon of the North Meredith and was headed toward the foothills and the Valley—over populated areas. Fortunately, the F-6 was not carrying its rockets, or they would have shot him down once he got over unpopulated mountains.

Unfortunately for Claytonville but fortunately for Mr. Merck, maybe I should say Captain Merck, the F-6 was light on fuel. Out of gas, Merck did indeed eject successfully, though he broke his left arm by hanging it up in the cockpit on the way out and broke his right ankle when he hit a pine tree on his way toward soil, in a clearing overlooking the North Meredith. Federal agents got to him first, for Sheriff Bluestone and the rest of us were busy with a conflagration.

Merck ended up in a veterans' hospital in San Francisco, where he recuperated from his physical injuries, received new medications to help control his impulses, and was interviewed by Ron Kuwara, the baritone-voiced newspaper reporter who'd been on the courthouse steps the day Carl Kelly went after me. The old Air Force veteran himself, Barker Updike, who'd gallantly thrown himself over me when Merck's jet flew over, read the account by Kuwara, and, not without admiration, deemed Reuben Merck "a crazy sonofabitch."

A wood-carver, I know a bit about the mysterious conflict between what the wood will be, is capable of being, what the carver wants it to be, and what the chisels can actually achieve. With limited success, I try to apply the carving analogy to the events that summer. How many of them had to do with my will or with the will of countless others? The will of a corporation and a construction company; the will of Lloyd Bluestone, sheriff of an obscure county, and his wife, a middle-aged woman who, in her mind, had welded together the idea of a dam and the memory of a lynched woman; the will of an ambitious district attorney, a drunken foreman, a drunken logger out of work, and a drunken novelist with writer's block; the will of honest Rupert Williams; the will of wealthy Sybil Burns, her Buffalo Gals, and the lawyer Laura Klein whom Sybil could afford to deploy; the will of Reuben Merck to fly, and of the eccentric gaggle of people, there in the middle of Claytonville, to put out a fire.

On the contrary, how much of what happened simply was to have happened? Was it in the cards that Cannon would accost Juanita, that she would stab him, that they would lynch her, and that I would end up, against all laws of averages, pregnant, married to Lloyd, a resident of Claytonville, and therefore in a position to learn the story of Juanita? And of course, "in the cards" means different things to different people. To José the phrase didn't mean luck; you play the players, not the cards.

If I hadn't chained myself to Bar Rock, with Rupert's help, how much of what happened wouldn't have happened? I asked Bluestone this, and he reminded me that the world doesn't revolve around me. But I told him I felt responsible, in a way, for everything, including the fire. He grew impatient. He said there's a difference between taking responsibility and behaving as if you design the world. The difference, he said, might be summed up in the contrast between Sybil Burns and Rupert Williams, or between the retired, Buddha-like deputy, Ed Porter, and the politically single-minded D.A., Miles Ward.

Chastened, I still had to wonder if my jail-mate Carl Kelley, who had kept calling me a cunt that sweltering afternoon, would have died if I hadn't gone up to the dam-site. Would Gary Stad Fromm have made the ultimate fool of himself in the sheriff's office?

Would my son have been shot, nearly killed? I think he wouldn't have been shot, and I think I'll forever be ashamed of myself for acting on an impulse and going up to Bar Rock that morning—and getting my son shot, eventually. What saved Gabriel? The blind physics of a pistol in a drunk's hand and the trajectory of a bullet? God?

What saved Claytonville from the fire? Quick thinking? Weather patterns? Why did no one die? One woman was burned, and one man had a heart-attack. Two firemen collapsed from the heat. A volunteer nearly cut her finger off preparing sandwiches. But no one died, not even Reuben Merck, not even Barker Updike and me, just a few yards, really, beneath the screaming, pilotless jet.

Who will finish the abandoned dam? Who will care for the river besides the river?

Judge Carstairs Peat threw out the felony charge against me. Laura Klein tried to work out a reasonable plea of guilty to a misdemeanor. The plea seemed sewn up until Miles decided to try to go around Carstairs. Miles took the felony "evidence" before the Grand Jury. Since Judge Peat was the only judge Miles would likely try cases before, this disrespect seemed like ego-assisted professional suicide, but Miles' plans for total war were strategic, not tactical: Several of his buddies started recall efforts against both Carstairs and Lloyd.

The Grand Jury refused to indict me on a Friday in September; the following Monday Peat called Miles and me into his office, got Laura on the phone in Sacramento, asked if a $250 fine for misdemeanor tres-passing were acceptable (it were), and, as Ralph Grimley, mountain editor, put it (in private, not in his weekly column), "Carstairs shoved that one up Miles' ass as far as it would go." The recall petitions didn't get enough signatures. Miles Ward resigned and went to work for a conservative think-tank in Sacramento. He is getting ready to run for something now. I forget what.

The Board of Supervisors badgered Lloyd weekly about everything from overtime to the cost of dog-food for the county bloodhounds. It was their way of getting back at me through him, I think, or just a way of venting because the dam sat up there in the river, unfinished, steel re-bar sticking up like hairs. Bar Rock remained.

The Reicher Corporation filed for bankruptcy, pulling out of the site mere weeks after the 4th of July. The fish swim around the pil-ings. The Supervisors fish for someone to finish the god-damned thing.

The environmentalists fight the Supervisors, and I send money to the environmentalists. Is anyone the wiser? No. Well, the fish, maybe. There were rumblings of the County suing Reicher and of Reicher suing the County, but neither can afford to sue the other. At Willow Creek, they're having trouble with the turbines, so the dam really isn't producing much electricity.

For Lloyd the Tamarack Jazz Society brought respite in the days between July 4th and October. Much of TJS's early-autumn agenda concerned a running debate about which interpretation of "What Is This Thing Called Love?" was best. Lloyd voted for Charles Mingus's. I have forgotten which version prevailed. I don't care.

Lloyd and I joined the volunteer crew that helped Lordes Vestery repair her house, one badly damaged by the fire.

Lordes, now 85, had been County Treasurer many moons ago, and for many moonlit terms; when she retired, it was discovered that she had kept all county funds in a checking account, no interest. Her impeccable financial naïvete represented, in one way, the ideal opposite of corrupt government even if it also displayed incompetence of a rare kind. And so it came to no one's surprise that her house was insured for a mere five thousand dollars. Hence the need for volunteers. Myrna Lovetti often cooked spaghetti and meatballs, with the eternal sauce, for us volunteers. Gary Stad Fromm sobered up and helped pound nails. When he sweated he smelled like sweet bourbon. He kept referring to the Crusader jet as a *deus ex machina*. He said if he'd written it in a novel, no one would believe him. Barker Updike asked him what *deus ex machina* meant. Gary tried to explain several times and finally said, "It means the goddamned ending of the story is goddamned unbelievable." Oh, said Barker. Then Barker disagreed. He said he read spy novels all the time that had stuff which wasn't even in the realm of possibility but he believed it—because it was a novel. G.S. Fromm looked completely deflated. Not only had he allowed himself to get into a literary discussion with Barker Updike, but Barker didn't seem to want to defer to the award-winning novelist's expertise.

"I defer," said Gary, "to your assessment of the novel as a form, Barker."

"Thank you!" said Barker.

And back to work we all went, hoping someone would send down a machine to sort out all of Claytonville's troubles.

In September Gabriel, who'd required no cosmetic surgery, announced he was going to take a break from college to play winter baseball in Mexico. We protested. He listened—and did what he damned well pleased. Our baby boy, conceived on that sultry afternoon at Willow Creek, had grown up with—I was about to say "a vengeance," but no: He'd just grown up.

It's been Bluestone's policy for years to visit—as plain-clothed citizen, not badged sheriff—each of Claytonville's two bars once a year. He encourages his deputies to follow the same policy, which springs from the idea that one or two well-timed, plain-clothed visits to the watering holes is good for community relations.

Bluestone paid a visit to Red's in September—one of those brisk nights when the sky's a riot of stars and every bar in the county, including Red's, contains just a handful of customers, for the tourists all leave after Labor Day.

Carstairs Peat showed up that night. Because of the historical record, this gave Bluestone pause—until he realized that Carstairs was drinking only club-soda, and that he was "with friend." With a special friend.

The man's name (Larry Walker) was as ordinary as Carstairs' was odd. This minor contrast proved to signal a larger pattern. Walker was wry, subtle, self-contained, and graceful—as over against the forced, obvious, impulsive, awkward attributes of Hizzoner.

"Happiest I've ever seen Carstairs," Bluestone reported when he came home that night. "He introduced me to Larry, and I sipped my Wild Turkey at their table. Larry was having vodka martinis"—which (Lloyd did not need to add) at Red's consisted of much chilled vodka poured into a dusty martini glass, over which the word "vermouth" was mumbled.

"Are you about to tell me what I think you're about to tell me?" I asked Lloyd when he'd returned from Red's.

"I guess," Bluestone said, sleepy from the Wild Turkey and the walk home. "I wasn't there but five minutes when I realized they were in love. I mean, in love like any old married couple in Claytonville."

"You mean, like you and me."

He ignored that. "Larry teased Carstairs—but without, y'know, wounding him. Carstairs kind of showed off for Larry—talking about hunting and fishing and weird trials we've had up here."

"And?"

"And it was clear Carstairs was kind of displaying Larry to the home-town crowd. I mean, he bought two rounds for the whole bar. Introduced Larry to anybody who came within ten feet of the table."

"Introduced him as...?"

"'My very good friend, Larry Walker.' Larry'd blush a little. Then at one point Larry looks at me and says, 'Well, Lloyd, aren't you at least glad that Car didn't bring the wedding album?'"

"What did you say?!" I asked Lloyd.

"You know me. Literal. I said, 'You really got one?' Larry howled. Cartairs turned red, then white, then something like yellow."

"He calls him 'Car'?"

"Yeah, anyway—'Car' says he's retiring after the first of the year, and Larry's unloading his landscape business, and they're gonna live in Monterey—when they're not traveling."

"How'd people in the bar react?"

"Well, you know, Larry was more at home there after an hour than Carstairs has been after thirty years. Everybody was themselves— Danny Del Ray ripped a big fart, for example."

"—Wait. Is Carstairs selling the house?"

"No. They're gonna turn it into a B&B and have somebody local manage it but keep the third floor just for themselves when they visit."

"Aren't you happy for Carstairs?"

"I'm happy he's happy, if that's what you mean."

Our mothers, Betty Kjellstrom and Eileen Herrera, returned from their Alaskan cruise to tales of the 4th of July that would end all 4th of Julys, *pax* Juanita. My mother asked me, wasn't I a little old to be protesting like a Hippie? Betty said she was proud of me. They both said it was just as well that Axel and Joaquin had passed on to the other side. They both wept when they heard how lucky Gabriel was to be alive. I wept, again, too.

About to retire, Old Boy Carstairs had a word with the State Attorney General, who had a word with the Governor, who appointed Laura Klein to fill out the remainder of Carstairs' term as Superior Court Judge. Laura Klein in Tamarack County. Sheesh. Her poor Aunt New Edna Jersey—how she must worry about her niece. How long urbane

Laura can stand Claytonville is anybody's guess, but everybody's guess is two years at the outside. There's a betting pool based on months.

Mavis Everson, the court reporter, runs the B&B now housed in Carstairs' behemoth Victorian; her husband does the handy-work; the kids got their braces. Myrna Lovetti cooks an Italian dinner one night a week at the cafe. G. S. Fromm's novel shrank to one page, which he printed in a famous magazine as a serious joke. His son tried to live with him for a while, starting a rock band in Claytonville called "The Mucous Membrains [sic]" but the band and the bonding with Dad lasted just three months. G.S. is trying to stick to "beer only," but of course it's not working, if by "it" he means dealing with his alcoholism. No word about Wade Landers, who is in prison. Lloyd wrote a letter to the judge in Landers' trial and suggested that Landers be sent to a medium-security state prison, as opposed to a hell-hole. The judge agreed, but Lloyd and I deliberately forgot what prison it is; we want to put Wade Landers in the past. We've kept in touch with Rupert Williams. I sent him a wood carving for Christmas.

Lloyd and I–quietly–have made arrangements with the Claytonville Cemetery Society (Myrna Lovetti, Chair) to build a little monument for Juanita. Lloyd will do the stone-work and help me inset a small teakwood carving encased in copper.

Twenty

Once a year my husband Lloyd Bluestone, sheriff of my heart's county, hikes up to this grove of oaks. The ritual's at least twenty years old.

He goes up when fall rains first rinse canyons of the northern Sierra Nevada, sluicing the watershed, perpetuating a mighty forest of stately conifers and determined oaks.

This year it happens on a Thursday, mid-October. This time, the first ever, Lloyd invited me along.

My leg-muscles have cooled, stiffened. I'm tired from the hike—down to the river and across it on a rickety walking bridge, just cables and boards—up the difficult mountain to oaks. It is afternoon.

Lloyd isn't tired but sits anyway, still as a boulder, a broad-shouldered man with a brown face and black hair, brown eyes that aren't fearful but rarely seem anything other than wary.

Together we sit under a blue tarp he's tied to oaks.

The grove sits on a strange shelf consisting of some five acres that jut out between two ravines. "A geological anomaly," Lloyd calls it. Once he made a Lloydly slip and said "anemone."

Whatever it is, it is what it is a mile above sea level in terrain Humphrey Bogart and the Donner Party keep dying in each time you see the famous movie, read the macabre account.

Lloyd's always said of the grove, "It shouldn't be there."

The idea is this: Ancient glaciers, eternal erosion, simple gravity, or all three should have wiped that flat protrusion off the ridge like a smudge. Sheer mountains like the Sierra don't go in much for such ornamentation as a shelf between sheer ravines. Also, oaks don't normally grow up high where manzanita brush and big conifers dominate.

Because the hushed grove and what underlies it have persisted, Lloyd goes there to watch his woods fill up with storm.

Which isn't here yet. But it's a mean-looking afternoon—the sort of day when mountains make you quiet, make you remember some of how incidental you are. The air is dark. Under the tarp, we have a Thermos of coffee, carrot sticks, bread, coats, hats, gloves. I want the storm to hurry. He doesn't. I'm grateful when he speaks. "Are you ready to die yet?" he asks.

"No, I don't think so. How about you?"

"Not quite." He shifts to the other haunch, lets his lungs take a long draw on chill air. It is after 4:00 p.m. already. I'm not panicky or anything—I've lived in the mountains for twenty years—but I don't like being up on a ridge this late in the afternoon. I'm thinking tea at the kitchen table, followed by a hot dinner. I'm thinking I've seen rainstorms before and don't need to be out in one to prove again I'm a nature girl. I'm thinking I'm too old for this nonsense. We are, Lloyd and I, middle-aged after all.

The canyon down there to the west looks black when usually it holds the last light of day. The reversed image disturbs me. It's too much like a tunnel—a tornado-tube set on its side—than the canyon I know. I pull the coat closer around me.

Lloyd continues. "But I feel myself getting closer. To being ready to die. It's so strange to see how few things I've done."

I start to speak.

"No," he says. "Don't reassure me. What I mean is, it's really strange to see how small and simple a life is—any one life, not necessarily mine."

"All lives."

"Right. Strange to admit that. This storm right here that's coming up the canyon is bigger than my life. Do you believe that?"

"No, but I'll keep an open mind. I don't think I'll ever be ready. To die." I'm opening the Thermos, wishing the storm would get with it and give the County Sheriff his climatological fix. Coffee massages alpine air with dark aroma. I continue: "I can see myself on a respirator, loaded up with drugs, fighting, gasping, clutching bedsheets, thinking of one more thing I 'must' do, never just rolling over and letting go, relaxing into the arms of death." What I'm saying surprises me.

Lloyd looks at me. He looks away again, down-canyon.

"I see what you mean," he says, saying it as if he doesn't see.

Through trees I catch a glimpse of our small Sierra Nevada town, Claytonville; by small I mean a handful of corrugated-iron roofs thrown like spare coins onto a bedroom bureau. The vantage point makes the town look sad and embarrassed, an image I could accept with ease if it didn't also reflect on my life and Lloyd's, which have taken place there. Maybe people coming in for a landing in New York or Frankfurt feel differently. I wouldn't know. I've lived in Claytonville, California. Before that, I lived in Sacramento.

For Lloyd, hiking up here is to take a bath, washing off grubbi-ness of daily life; for me, it puts my life in relief that is too stark, as if I can't marshal enough "me"—enough spirit, memory, even physical strength—to keep the daily faith. These mountains sometimes scare the hell out of me. Sometimes I think they've taken the better part of my life already. They don't scare Lloyd; and he loves them.

It begins by tick-tacking off papery umber-and-orange oak leaves, stain-ing gray-brown oak-trunks with dark blotches, like flung paint. I look at Lloyd and want to say, "Can we go now?" but he's not looking back at me. He sits up and looks hard. I sip coffee and listen to raindrops hit the tarp. I don't know why I want to cry, why I am perturbed by an urge to weep that comes up through my ribcage. Ever since the summer, I've been emotionally unpredictable, especially to myself. I'm glad when Lloyd distracts me.

"Watch," he says.

"What?" My voice cracks. He doesn't seem to notice.

He points, says, "Clouds, the low clouds."

Below ridge-level on the opposite side of the canyon, small, low, white clouds run at the storm's front edge. Their speed's not quite believable.

From the town, the highway, or the river, no one will see them; the angle's wrong. There's an excellent chance Lloyd and I are the only humans to witness their sprint up-canyon. Some clouds move so fast they start tumbling: pups whose back legs overtake them. Others dis-solve. Some remain sleek and quick. These power through the canyon and disappear into gray mass of other clouds where canyon melds with upper range. I've lived here a long time, but this is a fresh, startling image of weather on the move.

Now rain comes hard, slants in. Hard wind drives water into trees, under our tarp. The ridge opposite us, across the canyon, is over-whelmed in rain and cloud; it disappears. Claytonville disappears. I breathe harder, scrunch into my parka and try to center myself under the tarp. Lloyd won't budge. His nostrils flare, taking in wet air. Odor of wet air washes over us.

He acts like he's in a cathedral. His Holiness, Lloyd Bluestone, Pope of Western Twigs. Rain comes now in a big wave. The tarp isn't working; rain's coming in under it and soaking my butt.

"Lloyd, get me out of here," I say, but the storm swallows my words. "Lloyd!"

He turns, as if he's been expecting me to complain.

"Find me some cover," I say. "I don't wanna get pneumonia—" Before I finish, he's pulled my hood up as if I were a child, then pulled his hood up, and he's up and taking down the tarp. I throw things in the pack and arise and follow him through oaks, off the flat-top, down into a creek-canyon that'll wall off the storm. He finds a well worn deer-trail right away and follows it. As usual there's something unhurried but efficient about the way he moves; he's been taking care of himself his whole life.

We situate ourselves in the ravine, protected by a wall of blue rock and by a monstrous, overhanging ponderosa pine. This isn't a lightning storm, so we're safe under a tree. Lloyd rigs the tarp with big sticks so it functions as a porch roof. I assist. Away from the tarp he builds a fire; he thought to bring pieces of sapwood.

Hunkered under the tarp, I watch him feed fire larger pieces of pine. Smoke joins gray air.

I let my eyes drift across the creek. Through blur of smoke and rain—rain pounding the creek—my eyes search rocks and manzanita on the far bank; cold and fatigue and the sound of the storm hypnotize me. The image therefore seems to leap right out of Earth.

A bear.

I'd like to cry out—who wouldn't?—but sound gets stuck in my throat and comes out like a slow-motion squeak. Lloyd doesn't hear me.

The bear's lying down near the creek beneath a high bank of clay and manzanita. Its cinnamon-brown fur is soaked; it's lying on its side. Its forearms and clawed paws are massive. The bear's so startlingly big and out of place I actually widen my eyes and blink—it's like the damned thing fell out of the woods. And then I think: Yes, why not, a fitting way to end a hexed summer: a bear falls out of the forest and eats us, leaving us on back pages of American newspapers, an inch of filler in the *Cleveland Plain Dealer*. BEAR KILLS CALIFORNIA COUPLE.

I say "Lloyd" probably three times in ever-louder whispers—until I'm not whispering. He turns from the fire. I point. He looks. Straightens up. Stares.

Slowly he crouches again, picks up his pack, slides back to join me under the tarp. He removes a pistol from the pack.

He whispers, "This won't do much good if he charges, of course."

We sit and watch the bear through a veil of rain. It's one of those moments when you really don't know who you are, when your whole life seems so odd, so unlike everyone else's—not special, just strange, atomized—that you have trouble believing it's a life in any coherent way.

That feeling passes. I'm just cold and afraid.

"He's sick," Lloyd says.

"He?"

"She, he. She looks real bad—see?"

I look hard and see how moth-eaten the fur is—how, for a bear, she looks frail when she should be larding up for the Big Nap.

"No bear would lie next to the creek like that in a storm. She's real bad. She must have crawled to water. You don't see that pale cinnamon color much."

Sometimes the bear stirs, moves a heavy paw. We watch her for thirty minutes. Lloyd stokes the fire. The waiting agitates me no end.

Lloyd decides to cross the creek. I protest, but it's no use. He takes his pistol and wades across. I get out from under the tarp; the rain's letting up. I wonder what in hell I'll do if the damned bear mauls my husband. Ludicrously, I look around for a rock to throw.

Taking one step every few seconds, Lloyd approaches the bear. She waggles her head. I want her to be a her. He stops. She picks up her head again, tries to sit up. A charge of adrenaline hits my heart. Lloyd is still.

He gets closer, looks hard at her. He raises the pistol and shoots her in the head. Twice. The gunshots are more terrible for being less sharp than TV shots; they seem matter-of-fact. A dull pup-pup.

Lloyd stands and looks at her and waits. Looking like a cousin of bear, he ambles and shuffles back across the creek. We stand beside the fire. His face is gray and slack.

"She was real sick. Real old, when I got up to her. Hardly breathing. Couldn't quite make it into one more winter. She was a she, too."

I smile. Lloyd smiles. We stop smiling.

"Goddamnit," he says, with honest-to-God bitterness. I know what he's thinking. He comes up here to watch his storm, show it to me from the box seats, and this year even the sedate private ritual won't go right. He has to shoot a bear he doesn't want to shoot.

Darkness insinuates itself into the main canyon. Lloyd and I in the side-ravine do what we are obliged to do. We yank and haul the bear's carcass off the bank, into the creek, across the creek, up, and out. It is hard work.

Her wet fur stinks wildly. Odors and oils of a whole bear life mix with rainwater. Her gray teats are withered and sad, mortified. I slip and fall and drop her once; my face brushes her rank, reddish-brown fur. This causes a weird convergence of wildness, revulsion, and intimacy. We get the body twenty yards from the creek where decaying flesh won't foul the water. Lloyd produces a hatchet and chops pine limbs. We cover her over: Her old, sad, open-mouthed, narrow-nosed face stares into a darkening sky, which drips water into her mouth, onto the pink tongue and brown, knobby, ivory teeth. Her black nose is nicked with scars. Her small eyes are ringed in black, weary fur. I can't look at that face without believing she was a big brainy thing. A pained thing that died alone.

We cover the face last. Within twenty-four hours big-jawed coyotes, sharks of the woods, will undo our work and set upon her meat, with ants and maggots coming at her from down below, followed by relentless rot. It's just a gesture, the placing of branches.

At 5,000 feet, I'm working hard at breathing. A sweet fatigue overcomes my arms and shoulders. I tell Lloyd, Shouldn't we be heading down the hill before dark? I'm the sheriff's wife, who's always heard the sheriff rail against tourists who get lost wearing only sandals and shorts and stumble off a cliff in pitch dark.

No, he says, the trail's easy.

We go back and stoke the fire and eat our rations and get warm and dry.

There's this problem of oddity I grapple with—of being nearly extinct, beyond the reach of the culture's radar. Of being, let's face it, a hick. I know in theory I have a right to speak, but what good does talking about me, a dam, and Juanita do? Does telling matter?

For the stories projected on the walls of this our Grand Digital-Canyon, America, are so big and loud that to tell what's happened to me, to Lloyd, and to me-and-Lloyd seems like murmuring next to a crashing waterfall or mumbling a child's rhyme at a rock-concert.

On this evening of the first Fall storm and the killing of a cinnamon bear that fell out of the forest, my life seems only my own. That's good news and bad: It's a satisfying task to wonder how many other women in America—in the world—just helped their husbands cover the carcass of a bear with pine boughs, smell of freshly-bled sap mixing in nostrils with odor of old bear. It's an amusing way to accept my small, singular life.

I hold my husband's head in my hands and kiss him in dim firelight, long and deep. Cool air and presence of woods seem to come in through pores, demand awareness, tug me away from the center of the kiss. In a way I'm kissing my own life, kissing it hello and goodbye and go-with-God at the same time. When you greet the once-ness of your own life, you press your mouth against the mouth of death.

We get up, pack up. We trace deer trails back. I need to get the hell home and take a hot bath and drink hot cocoa, no tea, and sleep and sleep and hope for dreams in which cinnamon-colored girl-bears dance and sing.

From this October perch, I'm able finally to look back on the summer that has passed, when I tried to fight a dam but didn't know how, when I broke the law and fooled myself but still managed, in my own haphazard way, to honor Juanita.

And so, yes, it is October, the dark evening of the day we hiked up the mountain to watch the first substantial storm of the Fall-and-Winter. We stand on the little walking-bridge that's stretched across the North Meredith not far up-canyon from Claytonville. He is leaning on one of the cables. I'm standing. So we're about at the same level. I've said a silent prayer to the water below on behalf of poor Carl Kelly, my jail-mate and the only person in our sphere of influence to die that summer.

Lloyd and I have been talking about the bear Lloyd had to shoot. It has made us morose. We look down into the waters of the river, dark now because the October evening has darkened and the moon is still down.

I turn to the old subject—no, not my obsession with Juanita, but our marriage.

"It's a true fact," I say. "We wouldn't have gotten married, probably wouldn't have even seen each other after that summer, if you hadn't knocked me up, up there in Willow Canyon."

"And as I always remind you," Lloyd says, "we knocked us up."

"And as I always mention, who delivered the baby out of her womb and between her legs?" No response.

I move closer to him, shoulder to shoulder, the thin bridge moving underneath us as I move, the sound of the river filling the air around us, water rushing over boulders and gravel. Bluestone has great shoulders.

I make a pronouncement. "And yet here we are still, married and in love, in spite of it all."

"In spite of this summer and all," says Bluestone, my Lloyd, sheriff of my heart's county.

THE END

Sierra City, California
Tacoma, Washington

Colophon

This book was typset with Donald Knuth's TEX
typesetting system using Leslie Lamport's LATEX document
preparation system and Peter Wilson's memoir class.
The font is URW Garamond in 10/12pt on a 24pc measure.

CPSIA information can be obtained at www.ICGtesting.com
Printed in the USA
268052BV00003B/3/P